NIGHT FALL

NIGHTHAWK SECURITY - BOOK ONE

SUSAN SLEEMAN

1

She was dying, and it was his fault.

Sweat dripping in his eyes, Aiden peered through the billow of acrid smoke to take stock of the op. He didn't like what he saw. Smoke. Bullet-ridden walls and doors. The op with his four brothers had gone sideways. Completely.

He signaled for his youngest brother, Erik, to hand over their protectee, the woman draped over his shoulder and clinging to life.

Erik grimaced. Paused. Finally complied, shifting her onto Aiden's shoulder. The dying woman weighed heavy on his shoulders and in his heart, but he wouldn't let it slow him down. He motioned for Erik to take lead down the narrow alley, the path to freedom. Another flash-bang hit behind them. The boom rang out in the night.

Erik cringed and swiped a hand over his sweat-encrusted face. A look of determination darkened his eyes, and he lifted his assault rifle and set off, one foot in front of the other, carefully. Slowly. Just as Aiden had taught him.

And still...Erik had screwed up. Let the woman take a bullet. Now, they could find themselves in recovery mode instead of protection mode.

Aiden muttered under his breath and followed. Drake's footsteps pounded behind, taking up the rear of their team.

A wounded woman was the worst possible outcome. And it was Aiden's fault. Pure and simple. Sure, he couldn't control his brothers' every move, but Aiden was in charge of this op, and he was failing. Big time. Failing.

Stow it. Move. Save this woman now. Think and analyze later.

He lifted his rifle and moved into place, heading toward Brendan, who was kneeling, rifle up and firing, holding the alley. For now.

Step after step, Aiden inched forward. Carefully. Cautiously. The woman stirred. Moaned. Shifted.

A helo fluttered overhead, swinging low toward the end of the compound, swirling dust into clouds and sending pointed barbs of debris flying.

A sharp rifle report split the night. Brendan went down. Aiden's breath stilled.

Erik paused, another error.

"Move! Move! Move!" Aiden shouted, his mind torn between helping his brother and getting the woman to safety. But his mission was clear. Protect her at all costs. Even at the loss of a team member's life—at the loss of a brother.

Erik marched to the alley's opening, his boots thundering on the ground. He tossed a smoke grenade. A cloud of smoke rose in the open area. He scanned for hostiles.

"All clear." Erik darted into the street.

Aiden followed, sweat trickling down his face as he checked the open space. Skimming. Searching. Certain they were clear, he raced out of the alley. Dodged bullets. Crossed the pavement to the safe zone. Finally.

He knelt and gently laid the woman down on a soft bed of grass. The big red splotch on her T-shirt said the bullet had hit her right above the heart. She wouldn't have survived if this were real and not a training exercise at Blackwell Tactical's training facility.

Gage Blackwell strode to Aiden and stood over him, his eyes on his watch.

"You don't have to say anything." Aiden got to his feet. "We blew it. Took us too long to get through the course, and in real life, our protectee would be dead."

"Blew it?" He eyed Aiden, his face a mass of disappointment. "That was an absolute disaster if I ever saw one."

"My fault," Erik said. "The hostiles surprised me."

Sweat trickled down Aiden's back, and he looked at his brother as the others joined them. "We'll debrief and run this op again."

"No." Gage ran a hand over his inky black hair and narrowed equally dark eyes. "We'll run other ops, but you know what to expect on this one now, so it won't do any good to run it again."

Erik blinked a few times. "But I—"

"No," Gage said more firmly, proving he was used to being in charge. "You have to learn to react when surprised. Protective details are all about the surprise. Hostiles aren't going to tell you when or where they're coming. You need muscle memory built up so you respond without pausing. You don't learn that, people will die. You might as well close down Nighthawk Security before it even gets started."

Erik cringed, and Aiden wanted to offer comfort, but as the youngest member of the team and the one with the least experience, Erik had things to learn, and coddling him wouldn't help. Not if the brothers wanted to get their new investigative and protection agency off the ground.

"You need to think back to your academy training days," Aiden told his brother, ignoring the other Blackwell team members, who'd been acting as hostiles and were joining them. "We all ran the same basic drills in law enforcement training. You have the skills. You just need to practice them."

Erik ran a hand over his sweaty head. "Yeah. I need to put in extra work."

"I can help you with it," Blackwell team member Trey Sawyer said. "I had to prove myself to these knuckleheads when I joined the team, and I can show you how it's done."

"Hey, thanks, man."

Trey gave a firm nod, his red hair bright even in the low light of night.

"But you owe me a new shirt." Samantha Griffin tugged on the wet paint splotch on her T-shirt from where she'd taken the hit. "It's one of my favorites. I'll send you a bill."

"I'm sorry." Erik blushed.

"Hey." She socked him in the arm. "Just kidding. Figured I'd get shot at some point so wore the rattiest shirt I own."

"Okay, Nighthawk, go get cleaned up for the meeting," Gage directed. "The rest of you, take a break, and I'll text you when it's time to reconvene at Blackwell Street."

Gage and his team trained law enforcement officers all the time, and his large compound held the newest training course, which the Nighthawk team had just run. But the compound included a street with cutout buildings that looked like any main street in America, which was also used for training.

The sweaty team members disbursed in the unusually warm October night, and Aiden walked toward the main road running through Gage's compound that was hidden from the public's eyes deep in treed acreage.

"We'll do better on the next run," Aiden said.

"I sure hope so," Gage said. "Or I'm going to regret recommending you to the Young family."

Aiden's turn to cringe. They'd done a bad job, sure, but it stung having Gage question the referral to protect Harper

Young, Olympic downhill skier, who'd recently garnered a stalker. "We can do the job."

"That's what I thought when I set up the meeting with the Youngs, but now..." Gage shrugged.

"Everyone but Erik did fine. If he doesn't redeem himself in the next op, I can pull him from the detail."

"He's pretty green."

"Don't count him out just yet. He was a Portland police officer for several years and has learned a thing or two."

Gage met Aiden's gaze and held it. "Doesn't equate to our service as SEALS. Or even your experience in ATF."

Aiden swiped his hand over his face. "We both started somewhere, and others gave us a chance."

Gage chewed on the inside of his cheek. "Yeah, we carried the new guys back then, but I'm not willing to work with newbies anymore. At least not on my team. Just be sure you're not swayed by the fact that he's your brother and compromise your security protocols."

They reached the narrow road running through the compound just as a spotless black Escalade pulled to a stop in front of the large building holding the conference room.

Riley Glen, one of Gage's helo pilots, jumped out of the front and opened the back door. Blond and muscular, he stood at attention as an older woman with silvery hair sleeked back into a bun stepped out. Dressed in a black power suit and a white button-down shirt, she commanded attention. While she looked around, a pair of long legs in skinny jeans slid out of the back seat. They were attached to a tall woman with reddish-brown hair that fell in soft waves to her shoulders. She stood, taking a wide legged confident and powerful stance. He put her at nearly six feet tall with broad shoulders covered in a black knit shirt and bright pink down vest.

"I guess that's her," Aiden said more to himself than to Gage.

She turned to look around the space, and Aiden took a quick step into the shadows. When he met this woman, he wanted to make a good impression, not show up with sweat and dirt all over his face and wearing torn cargo pants from a failed training op.

He shoved his hands into his pockets. "Her pictures don't do her justice."

"She's a looker all right," Gage said.

"How many medals has she won?" Aiden asked.

"Four," Gage said. "She's the most successful American alpine skier right now."

Aiden had watched her events in preparation for this meeting. He'd expected her to be a burly, tough looking woman, and she *was* muscular, but also very feminine. Hence, the stalker.

"The mother is a powerhouse," Gage said. "Has to be as our governor."

"And the father?" Aiden watched the tall lanky man step from the Escalade. He had hair the color of his daughter's and wore jeans and a flannel shirt.

"He's kind of quiet. Lives in the wife's shadow, but he's a huge supporter of Harper's skiing." Gage met Aiden's gaze and held it. "The mother's the one you have to convince of your skills."

Aiden nodded, but, as he kept his focus pinned on Harper, he knew deep in his soul that she was the one he would have to get on board. Was he up to the task of persuading a woman who selected the very best so she could win to choose a startup agency like Nighthawk Security to keep her alive? Or would he be doomed to fail even before he began?

~

Harper twirled her ring around her finger and looked at Blackwell's conference room. The place smelled like a mixture of popcorn and sanitizing cleaner. It was smaller and less impressive than she'd expected for the famous Blackwell Tactical facility. But then, they didn't need impressive. They had a reputation as the best. Something her mother knew about. After she'd received death threats over her stance on gun control, she hired them to assist her Dignitary Protection Unit—DPU.

Too bad for Harper. Now, Blackwell wasn't available to help protect her from a stalker who was getting more and more aggressive. There were other teams out there. Sure there were. Tons of them. Her mother had already hired two teams for Harper. Two that failed big time when some of the guys hit on her. Seriously. She'd never expected that. So her mother had asked for a recommendation from Gage. He'd suggested Nighthawk Security and arranged this meeting.

Harper liked the agency name, but they were new to the protection game. Granted, all five brothers who owned the agency had law enforcement experience, and two of the brothers had also served in special ops in the military. But experience keeping women with stalkers alive? Nada as far as she could tell.

She looked at four of the brothers standing by the wall. Military rigid. All over six feet. Not talking. Eyes forward. Intense and buff. All dark-haired and resembling each other except the last one. A blond who looked out of place. Sort of a *one of these is not like the other* situation.

Which one was the leader, Aiden? Or was he the missing guy?

She'd read their names online. They went in alphabetical order by birth date. The missing Aiden was the oldest, then Brendan, Clay, Drake, and Erik. Cute idea, but did she want cute to protect her? No. She wanted rugged. Tough. Intense. They were that too. The ones she could see anyway.

Her mother leaned close, bringing with her the subtle scent of flowers from her pricey perfume. "He's late."

She meant the missing brother of course. Harper looked at the clock. "He has three minutes before he's late."

Her mother rolled her eyes.

Right. Mom's time. She frequently quoted, "To be early is to be on time. To be on time is to be late." How many times had Harper heard that? So often that she lived by it. But she didn't hold other people to the exacting standard.

The door opened, and for some reason Harper held her breath and fixed her gaze on the doorway.

Gage entered. As much as she liked the man, she was disappointed he was entering the room instead of the missing brother.

He crossed over to them and held out his hand. "Good to see you, Harper."

She shook his hand, his skin rough and callused but his nails neatly manicured. "You too. I wish you were available for my detail."

"You can count on the Nighthawk team." He quickly switched his focus to her mother.

"Olivia," he said and shook her hand.

"Your final guy has a minute to arrive or we're out of here," her mother said, and Gage didn't cringe under her characteristic straightforward manner like many people did.

"My fault," Gage said. "We had a training op, and our debrief ran long. Aiden wanted to clean up before the meeting. But he'll be here."

Ah, so the missing guy is the leader.

"How are my men working out on your detail?" Gage asked her mother.

"Excellent," she said. "Though with no attempts on my life, I'm beginning to think the threats were empty threats."

"You can never be too careful."

"You would say that. With the astronomical price I pay you for each day your men protect me, I could build you a dozen of these fancy compounds."

"You know what they say?" he asked, sounding amused at her mother's whining instead of irritated.

"Do tell." She rested a delicate hand boasting a giant ruby ring that had belonged to her mother on the table.

"You get what you pay for." Gage grinned, and Harper was struck by how handsome and fit he was for a guy who was nearly ten years older than she was. She knew from when her mother hired him that he was a former SEAL, married to a woman named Hannah a few years ago, bringing his daughter and her son together. Since then, they'd had a baby of their own.

"Then I hope that's true of Nighthawk Security too," her mother said. "Because my daughter deserves the very best when it comes to her safety."

"I'm sure you'll find it's true." Gage offered his hand to her father. "Nice to see you, Nelson."

Her dad shook, and they started a conversation about her dad's four-hundred-acre hazelnut orchard that he'd inherited from his father. But when the door opened again, Harper's attention was drawn to the missing Aiden Byrd, finally stepping across the threshold.

Tall and dark-haired like most of his brothers, he had a wide jaw and large nose. He looked freshly showered, but his jaw was covered in a five o'clock shadow. He wore a black form-fitting shirt and black cargo pants. All the brothers were built, but this guy was even bigger. Huge chest. Wide shoulders. His hands dropped to his trim waist, and his gaze searched the room. His cobalt blue eyes locked on her, and something jarred deep in the pit of her stomach. Something she couldn't name but somehow knew was dangerous.

"I'm sorry to cut it so close to the meeting time," he said, still holding her gaze. "Shall we get started?"

"You must be Aiden," her mother said. "The managing partner."

"I am." He turned to look at the men against the wall. "And these are my brothers. Brendan, Clay, Drake, and Erik."

Each of the men tipped their heads ever so slightly when Aiden said their names. They'd lined up in age order, an endearing action. She imagined they were used to doing so, and it came naturally to them.

"I'll leave you to it." Gage looked at her mother. "Let me know when you're ready to head back to Portland, and I'll make sure my pilot is at the chopper waiting."

"Thank you." Harper smiled at Gage, all the while feeling Aiden watching her.

Please don't let him be one of those guys who hits on me.

Gage exited the room, and Harper turned her focus to Aiden, who was picking up a remote control and turning on a slide presentation. She appreciated the work he'd probably put into it, and her mother would love all the details, but Harper just wanted him to quickly and concisely tell her why they were right for the job.

The first slide came up and held the Nighthawk Security logo.

"As you know," Aiden said. "We're a newer agency, and we—"

"How many protective details have you handled thus far?" her mother asked.

"None, but—"

"Then what makes you think you can protect my daughter?" Her mother lifted her chin.

"Because we're all trained in protection tactics and have the skills needed to do the job."

Her mother frowned. "Sounds like I could pick anyone out of the phone book and get that answer."

Harper waited for him to get irritated, but he kept a level expression. "I can see how you might think that, but we have something the other agencies in the phone book don't have."

Her mother pinned him with a skeptical gaze. "And what's that?"

"We're brothers." He raised his shoulders even more, looking every bit the warrior Harper believed him to be. "We've spent thirty or so years getting to know each other—our strengths and weaknesses. We know when to compensate for each other and when to let our strengths shine. We don't have to think about it. We just do. That's not something any team, not even Blackwell Tactical, can offer you."

He took a long breath, his gaze never wavering. "That innate something coupled with our training and experience makes us the team for the job."

Her mother tilted her head ever so slightly. "Your website says you have special ops experience. Elaborate on the that."

"Brendan and I both served in the military. Brendan as Army Delta Force."

"And you?" her mother challenged.

He looked hesitant to answer and took a breath first. "Navy SEAL."

Harper had read somewhere that spec ops guys hated to reveal that they were special. They kept it quiet and didn't need to brag. In fact, those who did were likely posers. Clearly, he was following that tact.

"After that, I was an ATF agent. Brendan, Multnomah

County Deputy and SWAT. Clay ICE agent. Drake, U.S. Marshal, and Erik, Portland police officer."

"Quite the variety."

"Yes, ma'am," he said, and her mother cringed. She was vain about her looks and hated being old enough to be called a *ma'am*, especially by a good-looking guy like Aiden. "Our father was a deputy, and we all wanted to follow in his law-enforcement footsteps."

"So why the change to the private sector?" she asked.

"We believe we can do more good outside the confines of law enforcement rules."

Her mother arched her eyebrow.

"Nothing illegal. Just not the tight constrictions of agency regulations."

"And what else do you have to offer?"

"As far as I can tell from the teams you previously employed, none of them had the ability to investigate the stalker's advances. We're not only quite capable of protecting Harper, but we're all licensed private investigators and can find and bring this stalker to justice." He took a long breath, his chest swelling in the tight shirt. "Not only that, but we also partner with the Veritas Center."

Harper had no idea who these other people were, but her mother sat forward. "Is that so?"

Aiden nodded. "Our sister, Sierra, is the trace evidence expert on the Veritas team. We office out of their building and share resources."

"Impressive."

Aiden beamed at the compliment.

"When can you get started?"

"I'd like two days to plan and tailor our approach to Harper's needs." He looked at Harper again, and a hint of a smile played on his face. It was off-center. Adorable in her book. But there was more there too. A buzz of attraction. Interest. In her.

Grrr. She should be able to count on him to protect her not have to deflect advances. Sure, this time was different. She'd had no feelings for the other men, but Aiden had this irresistible pull for her, which made it worse. She had no time for men in her life. Not if she wanted to maintain her slot as the top female skier in the country.

She stood and looked at her mother. "I've heard enough. Let's go."

Her mother's eyes widened, but for once, she didn't question Harper's decision and stood.

Disappointment crowned on Aiden's face, but he quickly hid his emotions.

Harper headed for the door and stopped at the head of the table near Aiden. She had a terrible urge to shake his hand. To see what it would be like to touch him, but she held back. "We'll call you with our decision within twenty-four hours."

He held her gaze. "I'd hoped you would make a decision today."

"And I'd hoped you were different than the guys on the other teams, but I can see the interest in your eyes, and that doesn't bode well for a strong working relationship."

His mouth fell open, and she ignored his confusion to walk out the door.

Outside the building, her mother grabbed her arm. "You're not being fair."

"How's that?" she asked, not that she really wanted to hear the answer.

Her mother rested her hands on her hips, the expensive silk fabric wrinkling under them. "You were giving Aiden the same vibes he was putting out there. How did you expect him to react?"

That couldn't be true. Could it? She was at a loss to answer, except to say she expected him to be neutral when it came to her. But deep inside, the buzz that had been racing between her and Aiden thrilled her, and she wanted more of the captivating feelings. Much more.

2

Aiden paced the Nighthawk office on the penthouse floor of the Veritas Center. He still couldn't believe they had the top floor. The Veritas partners had offered it to them because they wanted to keep the fifth floor available for expansion. And he'd scored the penthouse condo in the other tower too, when Emory and Blake Jenkins moved with their newborn daughter, Amelia, to a nearby house. His brothers' condos were on the second and third floors. The penthouse was his privilege for being the oldest. They were tough, competent men, but whenever something was up for grabs, they competed like high schoolers.

Aiden stopped to look out over the city. More than twenty-four hours had passed since the meeting with the Youngs, and the phone should've rung by now. He was still holding out hope for the contract. Shoot, not only hope but desperation. They needed this job. For the press they would get—perfect free advertising—but also for the money. They were only a few months away from running in the red.

And he'd blown it.

He looked out the glass wall at the communal area of the agency. Each brother had a work cubicle along the back wall, and the middle held a large table and chairs. They'd chosen an industrial look, as it didn't require them to finish out the walls and ceiling. The metal joists, beams, and ducts looked right at home with the black iron pipe legs topped with thick rough-cut tables milled from tall Oregon pines. The smell of spicy burritos that their mother had brought over for breakfast permeated the air. His gut had been tied in a knot, so he hadn't eaten them. Just the smell irritated his stomach.

He saw Brendan striding his way, a fierce look on his face. He wore the team's usual black tactical pants and shirt, something they would have to change if they got the Young detail as they would have to blend into Harper's world.

Aiden rolled his shoulders to relieve tension and worked on improving his attitude.

His brother poked his head into the office they all shared for client meetings. "Any word yet?"

Aiden shook his head.

"Odd. Harper seemed like the kind of person who would be true to her word. She should've called by now if we got the job."

Aiden agreed, but he wouldn't admit it. "Maybe something came up."

Brendan's dark eyebrow rose. "Or maybe ogling Harper was our downfall."

Aiden frowned at his brother. "You mean, *I* ogled her and blew it for all of us."

Brendan shrugged.

"I didn't know I was looking at her like that, you know. It was just..." He wasn't about to say that something stirred in his heart that he hadn't felt in a really long time, and it had shocked him enough that he hadn't been able to contain his emotions like he normally would. Control he'd learned as a

SEAL, which had served him well in the years since his last deployment with the team.

"I get it," Brendan said. "We all do. Why do you think we were all staring straight ahead like zombies in the meeting? Didn't want to give her any cause to question us."

"I don't get it, though," Aiden said. "The tabloids say she's the one who came on to her bodyguards and partied all the time and her mother fired them. So why would Harper be so upset over my interest?"

"Maybe she got tired of being on her mother's wrong side."

"Maybe," Aiden said, but he suspected there was more to it than that.

"None of it matters if they don't call."

"Exactly," Aiden said, "But if she does, I won't mess this up for us. I might find her attractive, but I can and will control it. I give you my word."

"That's all we can ask." Brendan pushed off the doorjamb. "I've been thinking about the stalker. I know you have too. Ever wonder if it's related to the person sending the governor threatening letters."

"It's possible, I suppose, but to what end? From what they've told us, the stalker has a romantic interest in Harper, and the person threatening the governor wants to kill her for her stance on gun control. I don't see any connection."

"Still, if we get the job, we need to keep it in mind."

"*If* we get the job." Aiden decided to change the subject. "You guys finished cleaning and storing equipment from the training?"

Brendan nodded. "I was glad to see Erik really stepped up in the final drills. You must be too."

Aiden nodded. "I knew he had it in him. He just needed to run a few more drills to teach him to trust his instincts."

"If we're called up to the big leagues by the Youngs, we can count on him performing." Brendan turned to leave.

"We can count on everyone," Aiden said to his brother's departing back and started pacing again. Almost frantic now. Not like he had anything else to do. Other than beat the bushes for more work.

So far, most of their jobs had come from Veritas, hunting down parents or children whose DNA matched to lost relatives. Investigating unsolved crimes. All things their seasoned investigator, Blake Jenkins, could've taken care of, but they claimed he was too busy to handle them. Aiden thought the gigs were pity driven, but whatever. The jobs had allowed them to pay the rent for the last three months.

The phone rang, and his gut cramped. He raced to the desk and saw the light blinking by the front desk receptionist's name. His heart dropped in disappointment, and he answered. "What's up, Lily?"

"There's a Harper Young here to see you."

His heart soared. "Tell her I'll be right down."

He hung up and charged out of the office and through their communal work area. He skipped the elevator and took the stairwell, arriving on the ground floor breathing a bit harder than normal.

Wouldn't do to arrive panting. She could take it the wrong way.

He took the time to inhale several deep breaths, run his hand over his hair, and school his emotions. He also couldn't let her think his excitement was over seeing her. It wasn't. At least he didn't think it was. Maybe that interest on his part was fleeting.

He headed for the glass door leading to the foyer and stopped to look out at her. She was talking to Lily, and even seeing Harper's profile sent his heart beating harder. He'd spent most of the last twenty-four hours looking for every bit of information he could find about her on the internet and had come up with a protection plan. But seeing her again? Did he really want this gig just so he could spend more time with her?

She was a fine looking woman. No doubt. Fit. Wearing jeans and a red knit top that accentuated her shape. But it was more than that. He was an outdoor enthusiast and had once been an avid skier too, so the fact that she loved winter sports appealed to him.

He shook his head and grabbed the door handle. She was right. That first meeting hadn't been a fluke. He *was* attracted to her. But he could contain it. He *had* to contain it. His brothers were counting on him, and he would never let a brother, be it blood or brother-in-arms, down.

He might no longer be an active duty SEAL, but he still lived the creed—*the ability to control my emotions and my actions, regardless of circumstance, sets me apart from other men. Uncompromising integrity is my standard. My character and honor are steadfast. My word is my bond.*

And he'd given his brothers his word. He said he could control himself, and he would. For them.

Harper felt eyes on her, and she turned to see Aiden staring at her through the glass door. She didn't know how long he'd been there, but she did know she liked having him watch her. And that brought a sigh and a deep breath to wash the feelings away.

He pushed open the door and strode toward her. His facial hair was thicker. Longer. Darker. He wore the same tactical attire as he'd worn the first time she'd seen him, but today it was olive green and accentuated his dark coloring. He stopped in front of her and planted his feet wide and his hands on his hips. Maybe a defensive posture, but his expression was maddeningly blank so she couldn't tell what he was thinking.

"I thought you were going to call." His tone was as neutral as his expression.

"I needed to talk to you in person." She met his gaze and held it. "Is there somewhere we can talk in private?"

"This way." He spun on the heel of his tactical boots.

She was a bit surprised he agreed so quickly and decisively, another thing she liked. She instructed her current bodyguards, who usually did exactly as she asked, to take a seat and followed Aiden to the same door he'd used to enter the calm lobby Nighthawk shared with Veritas. She'd expected a lab with a clinical setting but found comfy furniture, soft music playing, and a vanilla scent permeating the air. Not at all the way she believed this man would've decorated his lobby.

He'd open the door using his fingers on a keypad, held it for her, and led her to an elevator, where he used another keypad to summon the car.

"I'm impressed." She stepped into the car and lifted the badge she'd been required to get from the receptionist. "Tightly controlled security."

He punched the number six. "I wish I could take credit for it, but the Veritas Center needs to maintain top security for the evidence they process. The very reason you had to check in at the desk and get a pass from Lily. I assumed she told you that you can't go anywhere in the building without an escort."

She nodded, and the door whisked closed. She caught the hint of a woodsy scent from him. He looked at her, those smoky blue eyes penetrating and drawing her to him at the same time. She couldn't be falling for this guy—wouldn't fall for him—so she blinked a few times to break the attraction and said the first thing that came to mind. "Your sister works for them."

"She's one of the partners." His chin lifted. "And she's an amazing trace evidence expert. If a process exists, even new and not yet approved, she's researched it and can run it."

"I did some reading on the center after we met," she said. "They're top in their field, and this is a most impressive building."

He nodded. "The DNA expert, Emory Jenkins, inherited it from her grandfather. You likely noticed the two towers when you arrived. This one holds labs, and the other one, condos where most of us live."

Interesting and unexpected. "Sounds like a great arrangement."

The doors opened on the sixth floor, and they stepped into a large room with a big conference table and chairs. She caught a hint of spicy food in the air as she looked at cubicles filling the far wall where the other guys sat. A few of them looked up, but the others were on the phone and didn't notice her entrance. On a wall next to them hung various pieces of equipment, including Kevlar vests. No guns, though, and she suspected they were behind the closed door on the same wall.

"This way." He led her to an office decorated in industrial chic like the rest of the place. She liked the style. Unpretentious. Masculine. It fit with these guys and was how she'd imagined their lobby would look. She might be sexist in these thoughts, but this style gave her more confidence in their protection skills than the calming lobby.

He gestured at a leather chair in front of the desk. "Go ahead and have a seat. Can I get you something to drink? Coffee? Water?"

"I'm good." She sat in the chair and gripped the metal arms.

He took a seat in the high-backed chair behind the desk, and she was thankful for the space between them. She didn't want to repeat the moment in the elevator.

He folded his hands on the desk, and she noted his long fingers, telling herself not to notice anything else about him. "So, what did you want to talk to me about?"

She looked him in the eyes. "My mother has decided that you're the right team to take over my protection."

"That's great news." He smiled, broad and potent, his lips full and outlined by his dark beard, drawing her even more into the net he seemed to be casting over her.

She would put an end to the smile right now. "Not so fast. I'm not as sold."

As predicted, his smile evaporated, and he leaned back. "So you came here to do what? Tell me we don't have the job?"

"No. I came to talk to you about this attraction between us. You feel it. I know you do, and so do I. It doesn't bode well for my protection."

He took a long breath, his broad chest rising. He clasped his fingers together and let the air out slowly. "I would be a liar if I said I didn't know what you were talking about. But I'm not in a place for a relationship, so even if I am reacting to you, I won't do anything about it."

This was the answer she wanted, but surprisingly, it hurt. "And why are you off relationships?"

His lips narrowed into a hard line, and he snapped his chair forward. "Mostly because we're just getting our agency going. I don't have time for a wife or family. And I'm not a casual dating kind of guy."

"You said mostly."

His fingers curled into fists. "That's kind of personal."

"You want the job or not?" She shouldn't use the job to force him to tell her about why he didn't want a relationship, but she really wanted to know. Still... "Never mind. That wasn't fair."

"So, what about you?" His eyes narrowed. "You must still be considering our agency if you came here. So how would *you* insure things were kept professional?"

Irritation flared in her gut. "You're talking about the tabloid reports of the last two agencies we hired, right?"

He nodded.

She wanted to sigh but kept it in check. "First, don't believe everything you read in those smarmy papers. Second, I'm just like you. If I date, it would be in search of a long-term commitment. I don't have time for that. I'm too busy conquering the world of skiing."

He arched an eyebrow, looking intrigued, but didn't say anything.

"You're questioning the dating part. Tabloids again. Don't believe them. I haven't gone on a real date since my junior prom. And that was an arranged thing because I was too busy even then for dates, but my dad didn't want me to miss out on that experience."

"Not your mom?"

"No, she wants me to excel in my sport at all costs." Harper had to work hard not to sneer. Her mother often used Harper's success to further her political aspirations, and it grated on Harper.

His fists relaxed, and he planted his hands on the desk, a soft ray of sun highlighting the lighter brown streaks in his very dark hair with just a hint of a wave. "It sounds like we're both in a place where we can work together without a problem."

"I don't think it's that clear cut, but yeah, you've put my mind at ease. Some, at least."

He leaned forward, those eyes that she couldn't seem to

quit looking at burrowing into her. "Just some, but not enough?"

Was it enough? Should she do this? She'd reviewed other agencies' credentials, and none of them stood up to the Nighthawk team's qualifications. And Nighthawk had Gage's recommendation, which carried a lot of weight. But then, Gage hadn't been there to see Aiden's reaction to her. Would he be recommending these guys if he knew? Probably not.

She opened her mouth to tell him no. That she couldn't risk her life this way.

"Then congratulations," she said, shocked at her own words. As a rule, she didn't make decisions based on emotions. She could never have gotten to where she was in the ski world if she had. "You got the job," she added as if some alien had possessed her body.

A broad smile lit his face. "When do you want us to start?"

"Right now, if you can." She continued to look him in the eye. "My current team is in the lobby. I'll head home and dismiss these guys, then stay there until you can arrive."

She expected him to say they had to plan. To organize. But he nodded. "The team is in the office. We'll need a few hours of prep, but then we'll head over to your place."

"Here's my address." She jotted it down on a notepad lying on the desk, stood, and offered her hand.

His smile widened, and his big hand engulfed hers, the warmth traveling up her arm. She had to work hard to hide the emotions coursing through her body and quickly extracted her hand. Something that didn't escape his notice. His brows rose.

Had she done the right thing in agreeing to let this man and his brothers protect her? Or had she just made a big mistake that she would pay for with her life?

3

Aiden escorted Harper to the lobby, where she turned in her security badge, and he watched her leave with two beefy guys on her detail. He was pumped over getting the job, but his gut was unsettled. How long might it be before she fired Nighthawk too? She said she could control her feelings, but, when they shook hands, attraction sizzled between them. If she really was plagued by the same feelings he was battling, it would be hard. At least it was going to be hard for him.

Shaking his head, he passed through the lobby, raced up the stairs, and burst through the door to their office. The guys were sitting around the conference table, expectant gazes trained his way.

"We got the job," he said without fanfare.

His brothers erupted with shouts of joy and high fives. Aiden found himself grinning while he stepped to the head of the table. "She wants us to start right away. I don't know what to expect until we get to her place and can do a thorough threat assessment. I want to be ready for any one of us to spend the night. So head to the condos, change into civilian attire, and pack a bag. Be back here in thirty minutes to load equipment."

They jumped up and headed for the door. He walked out next to Brendan.

"You didn't blow it after all," Brendan said, holding the door.

"It was close, but we had a talk. Turns out my interest wasn't one-sided." Aiden headed down the hallway for the skybridge that connected the two towers on the upper level.

"Interesting."

"We agreed to keep things professional," Aiden added before his brother got the wrong idea.

"That should bring some excitement to the job." Brendan chuckled.

"Leave it to you to look for something exciting when the best outcome of this detail is no excitement at all."

"My point exactly. You know I don't do boring so well. Maybe she has skiing events in the near future. That way we can be outside where I can be on overwatch." He mimicked holding out his rifle and eyeing it the way he would do in his capacity of team sniper.

"If she has such events, I'm going to ask her to cancel them."

Brendan shook his head. "You're no fun. Especially since you donated the kidney to Dad."

"That's what you keep telling me." Aiden ignored the comment on how he'd reined in his physical activities since the surgery and crossed the glass-enclosed bridge that provided a full view of Portland's city skyline. He didn't take the time to look at it, but he often stopped on his way to his condo at night. Helped him shake off the stress of getting a new business off the ground.

"See you in a few." Brendan stepped into the stairwell.

Aiden kept going to his condo. The place was still decorated exactly as Emory had left it, minus her furnishings. He might repaint at some point, but right now the business came first, and he was conscious of every penny he spent of his salary, thinking he might have to put his own cash into the business. Meant even the cost of paint was prohibitive for him.

He grabbed an overnight bag and opened his closet door. The team had logo shirts made, but they wouldn't wear them on a protective detail. Their job was to blend in. That meant he wouldn't even wear his favorite cargo pants for fear of giving off a tactical vibe. He put on clean jeans, a navy knit shirt, and an overshirt to hide his gun, then packed a few days' worth of clean items, just in case. Though that was worst-case scenario. He shouldn't be the one to spend nights at Harper's place. The downtime would be too tempting for both of them.

He met his brothers back in the office, and they loaded guns, ammo, surveillance equipment, comms units, and vests into containers and hauled everything to their vehicles. They'd shelled out a pretty penny for two armor-plated SUVs with bulletproof glass. His belief, and what he was trying to impress on his brothers, was that, if they were going to do something, they had to do it right. Didn't mean everyone didn't complain when they had to empty their savings for the vehicles, but Aiden guaranteed that in the long run the investment would pay off. Assuming they made it to the long run.

Aiden handed her address to Clay, who was riding shotgun in his vehicle. "Enter this in GPS."

"Pretty swanky address." Clay entered it into the dashboard touchscreen. "South waterfront area. Overlooking the Willamette, I'll bet."

"I read that her mother's parents were super wealthy. When they died, everything went to the mother and Harper." Aiden got them out of the parking garage and headed for the downtown area.

"This family is kind of odd," Erik said from the backseat.

Aiden glanced in the rearview mirror at his brother. "In what way?"

"The mom lives in Salem and the dad still lives on his orchard in McMinnville."

"Are they still together in more than name?" Clay looked over the seat.

Erik shrugged. "I didn't get any kind of vibe from them at the meeting, but there's speculation in the news that they're basically separated. Still, he's campaigning with her this fall. As is Harper."

Clay leaned forward and hooked Aiden's attention. "I wonder if that's why she's here in Portland or if she makes this home."

"From what I've read, she's kind of a nomad," Aiden said and didn't specify how very much he'd read about her. "Training in the summer here at Timberline. Probably living in the condo and then on the road for other training in every corner of the world and for competitions."

"We'll get details on all of that." Erik sat back. "I, for one, am looking forward to it."

Aiden looked in the mirror. "Steer clear of any romantic involvement, little brother."

"You clearing the deck for yourself?"

Aiden gritted his teeth.

"No, doofus." Clay rolled his eyes. "He's being professional."

"We need this job, and that means we're all committed to being professional." He eyed Erik then glanced at Clay. "Is that clear to both of you?"

"Hey." Clay held up his hands. "I'm not the one you have to worry about."

"Yeah, look in the mirror," Erik muttered.

Aiden ignored his brother's barb and concentrated on

driving through Portland traffic to arrive at the eight-story condo building with walls of glass. He couldn't imagine living with such little privacy, but on the penthouse floor no one could look in. He circled the building to get a more thorough look at potential security risks and parked on the street. They got out and waited for Brendan and Drake to meet them at the door.

They stopped at the security desk and asked the broad-shouldered guard to call up to Harper's condo. While they waited, Aiden wandered the lobby, checking for possible security issues.

Brendan joined him. "Looks like two main entrances. This one and the parking garage, but there's likely a service entrance out back."

"Makes our job easier."

Brendan nodded. "And I scouted two possible overwatch areas if needed."

"Doubt it will be needed here. If we can keep Harper off her balconies."

"Follow me." The burly guard stepped out from behind the desk and led them to the elevator. He held the door to let them board and then stepped in to insert a key to give them access to the eighth floor. After the light on the button illuminated, he removed the key and backed out.

The doors slid closed.

"There's our first real vulnerability," Clay said. "Guards can be compromised without breaking a sweat."

Aiden nodded. "Hopefully, we'll find locked doors at the top, but how much you want to bet the elevator will open right into the condo?"

"That would be a losing bet," Drake said, not surprising any of them. He was the family's devil's advocate, questioning most ideas for strength and validity or asking for more details.

Aiden watched the numbers count up, and, when they hit eight, the doors opened to the condo, as predicted. They stepped into the wide open space with soaring windows, white walls, and light wood floors. The place had an airy vibe, and a hint of Harper's cinnamon perfume lingered in the air.

She was seated in a modern gray-and-chrome chair and came to her feet to cross over to them. She was barefooted and had changed into black yoga pants and a baby blue knit shirt that clung to her like a second skin. She'd braided her hair, leaving soft tendrils caressing her face. She had this whole sexy and strong looking vibe going on, a blend that he found incredibly enticing.

He swallowed hard and forced his focus to the job at hand. "Please tell me you have the ability to lock the elevator from access."

Her perfectly plucked eyebrow went up. "Well, hello to you too."

"Sorry," Aiden said. "I'm focused on determining your security risks."

"Since that's what I hired you for, I should be grateful," she said, but her tone was anything but. "I can lock the elevator from accessing this floor."

She turned to his brothers. "We've never been introduced." She held out her hand to Clay who stood nearest to her. "Harper Young."

He shook her hand. "Clay Byrd."

She went from brother to brother, each one returning her smile with an overly enthusiastic one of his own. Aiden totally understood their responses. She was charismatic and hard to ignore.

"Let's have a seat at the dining table and discuss your protection plan." She gestured at a long live-edge wood table with ten high-back plush white chairs.

They passed the seating area with a white sofa and chairs too. With all the white, Aiden couldn't imagine living here. Not himself or his brothers. They'd have pizza stains on the furniture in no time. In fact, when they were alone again, he would warn them to be extra careful while in the condo.

Harper sat at the head of the table, and Aiden carried his laptop to her end but left a chair between them. No point tempting his resolve by being too close.

"First thing we need to do is have the lock for your floor in the elevator changed, and we won't be giving keys to building security."

Harper tilted her head in a cute quizzical look. "But why? They're a reputable security company."

"People can be bought."

Her eyes narrowed. "None of the other companies we hired required this."

Aiden met and held her gaze. "We're not one of the other companies. You have to trust me on this."

His words seemed to still her into silence, and he suspected she had a hard time giving over control. Especially when her mother was the one who insisted on hiring protection for Harper. If so, she could be difficult to protect.

She placed her hands, palms down, on the table. "I'll call maintenance and have the lock changed."

"No," he said firmly. "I'll have my locksmith come out."

"I should have foreseen that," she said matter-of-factly. "You don't trust maintenance either."

He kept his focus glued to her. "When it comes to your safety, I don't trust anyone but my brothers."

"Not even my parents?" An undercurrent of misgiving ran through her question.

That wouldn't deter him. He was here to protect her, and he would do whatever he thought necessary to keep her alive and well. "Especially not your parents. They may love you and want the best for you, but they have no idea what it takes to keep you safe."

She shook her head. "You're definitely taking this to a whole new level."

"If you're uncomfortable with our work, maybe we're not the company for you," he said, but sincerely hoped she wouldn't fire them before they even got started.

"No, it's good." That skepticism still lingered in her tone. "I just need to wrap my head around the differences."

"I can understand that." He smiled, but he had to force it. "Can we move ahead, or do you want to take some time?"

"Move ahead."

He wanted to say *that's my girl*, but she wasn't his girl or his anything. Still, he liked her ability to quickly adapt. That might help in her protection. "I'll need a contact for the building's security service."

"I'll get that for you when we're done here." She jotted a note on a small notepad.

"I'll also need a roster of the building's residents so we can run background checks."

She opened her mouth as if to argue, but then nodded.

"We'll have to inform them of the stalker unless your other teams did so."

She tilted her head. "But why tell them?"

Seemed like she was going to question his every move. "One of us will be in the lobby every minute you're in the building, and they're going to ask questions."

"The others didn't—" She shook her head. "Right. I'll get a roster for you."

"If you think it might take some time to get it, I can have the cyber expert at Veritas run one."

"And I'm assuming that would fall under the extra charges in our contract."

He nodded.

"Let me see what I can do first."

Aiden found it interesting that she was pinching pennies when she lived in a place like this and was shelling out big bucks for their protection services. Maybe she hadn't inherited money. Just the property.

One thing was certain. He sure wouldn't ask about it and start a personal discussion. He planned to avoid those at all costs.

4

Harper was impressed with Aiden and his brothers. She really was. They'd asked questions that the other firms had never broached, and that was a good sign. They might be going overboard on the security details, but she already felt safer under their care.

"Before we talk about your stalker," Aiden said, that gaze still pinned to her. "There are some basic ground rules we need to cover."

"Such as?" she asked, genuinely interested in hearing how they differed from the other firms.

"First, no going out on the balconies and stay away from the windows. Next, never leave the condo without telling us and having one of us with you."

"I can do that."

"If you hear from the stalker at any time, we're the first people you tell."

"Okay."

"If we give you directives when we're out of the building, you comply without question. Any questions you do have can be answered later, but our directives are meant to keep you safe."

"Understood."

"If we're not together and I call you, I need you to answer your phone. No hesitation. Just answer, as it will be important."

This attention to detail was what she'd hired them for, but she was used to calling the shots in her life and was starting to get irritated at all the restrictions and details. Still, she would comply.

Aiden's gaze softened. "This is infringing on your freedom. I get that, but we need ground rules so we can keep you alive."

"He's never threatened my life."

"Trust me, if he can't get you to fall for him, he will."

She gasped. "But I—"

"Tell us about him," he said before she could argue her point.

She sighed. "What do you want to know?"

"Everything."

She didn't want to recount everything again. After all, she'd had to tell her story to the police, to two protective agencies, and to her parents. Another telling was almost beyond her, but she took a long breath and started. "About four months ago I started receiving letters addressed to me via Timberline Lodge where we were training. I guess he somehow found out I was in town and doing strength training there."

"Do you still have the letters?" Brendan asked.

She shook her head and was glad to be able to look away from Aiden to one of the brothers. "When I reported him to the police, I gave them to the detective."

"What's his name?" Aiden asked, drawing her attention again.

"Frank Johnson."

Aiden typed something on his computer then looked up.

"Did they process the letters and envelopes for DNA and prints?"

"Yes, but they didn't find anything to match."

"I'll need to talk to Johnson to get access to his files and the evidence." He tapped a finger on the table. "What did the letters say?"

"They started out being complimentary about my skiing. Then turned into raving about my looks and what he would like to do with me. He was very explicit." She tried not to react, but the memory of his vivid descriptions made her shudder.

Aiden gripped the edge of the table, his fingers turning white. "Were they handwritten? From a computer?"

She shook her head, more of a way to shake off the tension. "The early ones were typed, and the detective said they were created on an old fashioned typewriter. The most recent ones are handwritten."

"Did he have any leads on the typewriter?" Clay asked.

"No."

"How long did you continue to receive the letters, and what happened next?" Drake asked, looking as upset over the subject as the other brothers.

"I got these letters for about a month. Then small presents started arriving." Her stomach cramped at the mere thought of the items she'd received, and she didn't want to describe them. She took a long breath before going on. "He sent things for my hair. Sexy lingerie. Other things I'd rather not mention. Then the letters changed. Hand-written now, and I started getting objects that I loved from my childhood on the farm. These came with letters saying how well he knew me. These were handwritten letters."

Aiden gritted his teeth. "Objects like?"

"An FFA patch."

"FFA?"

"Future Farmers of America. It's an organization you can join. I once imagined myself taking over the family hazelnut orchard. My best friend, Tanner, lived on the farm next door. He wanted to be a farmer too, so we joined FFA together."

"Any other items?" Brendan asked.

"A vintage Mount Hood lapel pin."

Aiden's fingers tightened more. "He's making things personal. Trying to connect with you on a deeper level."

Interesting take. "If Detective Johnson thought the same thing, he never mentioned it."

Aiden tipped his head as if thinking about Johnson's capability. "Does he have these items too?"

She nodded. "You should know, though, during August and September, I was traveling to glaciers for training. The stalker continued to send the items to Timberline, so I didn't get them until I got back."

"Did the stalker ever try to contact you in person?" Erik asked.

"In September, he somehow got ahold of my phone number and called. He used an untraceable phone and one of those voice-altering devices. He complained that I didn't return his affection and chastised me for reporting him to the police."

"How would he know you reported him unless the police questioned him?" Erik asked.

As much as talking about this was raising her angst, she was impressed that all the brothers asked good questions. "I wondered about that too, but the press got wind of it, so I'm guessing that's the way he heard about it."

"Did he say anything else?" Aiden asked.

"He told me if I didn't go out with him that I would regret it. And warned me to take back what I'd said to the police or I would pay. I hung up on him and changed my number right away. That's also when I hired bodyguards. So maybe they scared him off." She sat back. "Or maybe he's all talk and no action."

Aiden's nostrils flared, and he breathed deep. "So he hasn't tried to contact you since September?"

"No," she said. "I left for training in the Alps right after the call. Maybe that stopped him."

Aiden pulled his shoulders back. "He's displaying a typical pattern of escalation. It would be unusual if he stopped."

"And his next step will likely become physical," Brendan said, his eyes narrowed. "Trying to meet you or even abduct you. Or, he could revert back to the earlier stages and then escalate. Not every stalker fits the typical pattern, of course, but for now we'll go on the assumption that he does."

She twisted her ring, a habit she'd had since she was little and used to ease her worry. "Then what you're saying is he'll likely try to contact me in person."

Aiden nodded, a grim expression on his face. "Which is frequently the best way to figure out his identity. Did Johnson have any suspects at all?"

"None," she said and tried not to let any of the defeat trying to take her down into her tone.

"Stalkers are often jilted boyfriends," Aiden said. "Is there someone in your past who might have been upset over a breakup?"

She took a moment to think, but she really didn't need time. The answer was simple, but she didn't want them to lay every part of her life bare for examination. With all the questions, it seemed like she was the criminal here, not the victim.

"I hope you know we're only asking these questions because we have to," Aiden said, his tone softer.

"I know. I haven't dated anyone seriously since I was a teenager. And that was my neighbor, Tanner Gidwell, who I

38

mentioned before. We grew up playing and skiing together. But we drifted apart when I started winning events and he didn't. I haven't seen him in a long time."

"Was he upset at the breakup?" Drake asked.

"Sure, we both were. But that was over ten years ago. Why would he suddenly start stalking me now?"

"You never know what triggers someone," Aiden said. "Do you know where he lives?"

"Still on the farm with his parents. He's taking over the business."

"Did Detective Johnson talk to him?"

She eyed Aiden. "Do you think he should have?"

Aiden shrugged. "Tanner would have knowledge of your past and know which items would impact you the most."

Harper had never considered him as her stalker, and, despite this conversation, her gut said it wasn't likely. "Johnson didn't talk to him that I know of."

"We'll check in with Johnson and give the evidence and his report an in-depth review. Then, if we think it's needed, we'll give this Tanner guy a call."

Having put this part of her past out there for everyone to dissect was almost as bad as receiving the items in the first place, but she had to agree to their plan. They were the professionals here, and she would have to trust them. "You think Johnson will give you the information?"

"Maybe not to me." Aiden nodded at Erik. "But Erik's former PPB, and he can accompany me. Johnson will be more likely to cooperate with him."

"PPB?"

"Portland Police Bureau."

"Oh, right." She sat back.

Aiden gave a nod as if cementing something in his mind. "I'll also need your phone. Actually, any device you use to access the internet."

"Why on earth do you need that?"

"Your stalker got your phone number once. He could have done so again, and we can't risk you being tracked this way. Nick Thorn, the Veritas cyber expert, will make sure the devices are clean and the settings correct."

"I can't be without my phone for long," she said, but even more troublesome was that they were going to see everything it contained. Personal things. Like her latest text arguments with her parents over having to leave training to join the last two weeks of her mother's campaign. Harper wanted to argue again, but she knew by Aiden's insistent look that she wouldn't be able to keep her phone without it being cleared. "How long will that take?"

"Assuming they have the time to handle it right now, a few hours."

"Okay. Just let me text my mom and dad and tell them I'll be unavailable." She thumbed in a text on her phone and then slid it across the table to him. "I also have a laptop and iPad. Should I get them now?"

"In a minute. I need a copy of your schedule for the next two weeks so we can decide what's absolutely necessary and what can be cancelled."

"Now wait a minute." She jerked forward. "If it's on my schedule, it's necessary, and I won't be cancelling anything."

"We'll see."

"I've gone along with all your rules and questions so far, but you aren't going to tell me which events I can attend. I won't let anyone control my life like that."

Aiden looked at her, his gaze level and calm. "That's why you hired us, right? To tell you how to stay safe."

She crossed her arms and focused on him, his brothers all but disappearing for her. "And to protect me in whatever I *have* scheduled, not to just cancel everything and lock me up here."

He remained infuriatingly calm. "If we do a risk assessment on the venue for your activities and find that the risk is too high, then we'll ask you to postpone."

"Ask or tell?"

He didn't answer for a moment, those full lips pursed. "Honestly, it's the same thing, right? I mean, it's ultimately your decision. We can't stop you from going anywhere."

"Sounds like you want to find me one of those safe houses and lock me up."

"Actually, that's not a good idea," he said. "If you go into hiding, your stalker will stop."

"Isn't that what we want?"

"Yes, but it will only be temporary. He'll start up again the moment you surface. And he'll likely be so frustrated that he'll escalate even faster."

She sighed. "Seriously, none of the other guys told me any of this. They just came with me where I went."

Aiden's lips pressed together in a slight grimace. "Then you're lucky the stalker didn't amp up his game."

"You think he will?"

"You're a very beautiful woman, Harper, and he wants you. Likely thinks you belong to him. So he will stop at nothing to get to you." Aiden's steely gaze locked on hers. "Nothing."

Aiden had dispatched his brothers on errands. Erik had taken Harper's electronics to Nick at Veritas and was waiting for Nick to review them so he could return the items to Harper as fast as possible. Drake, the brother who could convince anyone of anything, was meeting with the building manager to convince him that their locksmith was capable of changing the lock. Clay was completing a recon of the neighborhood, and Brendan was assigned to lobby duty.

Leaving Aiden alone with Harper. Not an auspicious beginning, but he wanted to be the one to review Harper's schedule. And his blood was still simmering over the explicit things the stalker had sent to her. Terrible, horrible, embarrassing things. It all made Aiden's skin crawl.

She didn't deserve to have items sent to her that upset her so much—no woman did. If only Aiden could get his hands on that guy and pay him back. But now he had to stick by her side. This creep could try to get near her. Aiden couldn't let that happen.

How he was going to deal with this need to stay by Harper's side later tonight when it was time to go home, he had no idea, but maybe he'd have cooled down by then and could leave.

He took out his highlighters and ran his finger across the column for this week. She had a charity event in Salem and two appearances with her mother's campaign.

He looked up to find her watching him, her hands cupped around the lemon tea she'd brewed and was scenting the air.

"Don't tell me," she said drolly. "You're going to strike everything off."

"I'm not that mercenary." He smiled, but she didn't respond. "We'll have to evaluate these venues in person, then make a decision."

"How do you determine that?" She pushed back and tucked her long legs up on the chair.

"Exits. Public access. Windows. Manageable crowd size. An area our team can cover and see every inch of the room you're in. Nothing outside at all."

She rested her chin on a knee and looked overwhelmed. "Don't get me wrong. I'm glad for your thoroughness.

Appreciate it even. But not only do I feel like my whole life is being exposed to you, but that you're going to be there every second of every day."

"I promise to let you sleep alone." He chuckled.

She smiled along with him, but it didn't seem genuine. He and his brothers had likely scared her with all the questions and demands, as she stared ahead, her eyes blank.

He wanted to erase it, but he had a job to do, and he would do it to the best of his abilities. Which meant making sure she was on alert. "I know Blackwell Tactical has already vetted the venues that involve your mother, but I still want to do my own recon."

She gave a nod and a tight smile, which he took to mean she was pleased he was being thorough, but he couldn't be sure.

"Once we visit the venues and know where you'll be going for the rest of the week, I'll schedule our team assignments so you'll know who to expect on your immediate detail."

"You won't be here all the time? I mean, it felt like you were planning to move in." She laughed, but it seemed forced.

"Sorry if I gave that impression. We'll rotate schedules. Depending on the venue, we might all be on the detail at times. Can I get the addresses for each of these events?"

She grabbed her mug and sipped. "I could if I had my phone, but I can give you the names of the places. We can look them up."

"Okay. Shoot."

"The first one is the Radisson Red Hotel in downtown."

"Inside or outside?"

"I'm not sure. We'll have to ask my mom."

"If it's outside, we can rule it out before even evaluating the space," he said and waited for her to argue.

"I can't see how we can rule it out if Blackwell hasn't cancelled it for her. But if you do, you'll have to be the one to tell my mother."

"It can't be that hard."

"You met her, right?" Harper shook her head. "Once she gets something in her mind, she doesn't let it go until she makes it happen. Like becoming governor. At first I thought she was crazy, but after I gave it some thought, I knew she would accomplish her goal. And she did."

"I have to admit to not being up on politics. I don't know her political background."

"She had none. Like, zero other than as a college student and intern. She met my dad on a campaign and married him. Then put her all into the orchard and making me a ski champion. But when Granddad died and left her a fortune, she decided it was time to quit letting his money sit in the bank gaining interest and use it for good. To her, that meant entering politics."

Aiden couldn't fathom making a decision like that. At least he couldn't fathom his mother doing it. She'd always been a stay-at-home mom and hadn't wanted to do anything else. "And what did your father think about it?"

She frowned. "He'll never leave the orchard, so he's coping the best that he can while still letting her live her dream."

Just like Aiden suspected. They were basically separated. "Do they see each other very often?"

"Now that she's campaigning for reelection, yes. But otherwise, not a lot."

"That must be hard on you," he said, and, at the narrowing of her eyes, he wished he hadn't moved them into her personal world.

"It is," she admitted but seemed reluctant to say it. "But I'm usually too busy to get involved in their drama."

He wanted to know more. Much more, but it was irrelevant to her protection, so he moved on. "And the other venues?"

"The Grand Hotel in Salem and the Hilton in downtown Portland."

"If these are both inside, they'll likely be doable, but I won't commit until after we do our recon." He tapped on the end of the month where it said FIN and CAN. "Are these ski events?"

She nodded. "World Cup. I sure hope this guy is caught before then. There's no way I'll bail on any World Cup events, and you'd have to travel to Finland and Canada with the team."

"Shouldn't you be in training right now with the U.S. Alpine Ski Team?"

Her very expressive eyes widened. "I'm impressed that you know the team name. Or did you just learn it when doing research?"

"I'm a skier. I mean, was. Was an avid skier." He worked hard to keep his angst at having to give up the sport out of his tone.

She gave him a nod of approval, and he was ridiculously pleased by it.

"Anyway," she said, dropping her bare feet to the floor. "I had to come home for my mother, and I can train at Mount Hood."

Right, her training. A potentially huge problem they were going to have to deal with. "I probably should've started with asking what your typical day looks like while you're here."

"I always start the day in the gym." She raised a hand. "Before you ask, it's on the first floor of the building, and I go around four a.m. so there's no one around."

"Why so early?"

"I like to be on the slopes by sunrise. Then back up here for a shower and breakfast and on to Mount Hood for as long as daylight lasts."

"I know Timberline's not open to the public yet," he said, mentioning one of the Mount Hood's ski resorts.

"Right. Just the local race team and me."

"And I assume, since you're our local sensation, you have extra privileges."

She frowned. "I try not to take advantage of them, but yeah, they're pretty willing to accommodate my needs."

Her reaction was so different than what he'd expected based on the articles he'd read online. She was reported as not being a team player and seeking the limelight, but her comment was just the opposite. What had she said? Don't believe the tabloids? Looks like he needed to extend that to the internet as well. He knew not to believe everything he read there, but he'd seen several articles saying the same thing so...

"Hello," she said. "Where did you go?"

He opened his mouth to tell her what he'd read, but he figured it didn't matter. The important thing was that he was getting to know the woman sitting next to him, and, if he discovered she was a publicity hound, he would have to put a stop to it in order to ensure her safety.

He jotted a few notes on his legal pad and looked at her. "Did the other protection companies vet your teammates?"

"No, but you can't honestly think one of them is my stalker."

"Until proven otherwise, I will suspect anyone and everyone as being your stalker." He held her gaze to drive home the point. "How many people are at the resort when you are?"

"Ten skiers maybe. A few instructors. And then a

minimal staff." She nibbled on her lip. "All people I trust, but I know you don't."

"Exactly. Is it possible for you to delay tomorrow's training so we can check out the facility and staff first?"

"You really think this guy could show up there?" Her fingers reached for her ring, but she frowned and let it go.

"What I think is that, if your stalker is determined enough, he could appear at any time and anywhere, and you need to accept that no place is completely safe."

"Not even here?"

He knew he was scaring her, but he had to get her to think in terms of her safety, not life as usual. "Not even here."

5

Aiden was freaking Harper out. Totally. The other body-guards had played down the risk to her safety. Acted as if they had everything under control at all times. She wished Aiden would do the same thing. Though, after talking to him, she was smart enough to know he was probably more accurate on the danger than the other men.

"I'd also like to visit Detective Johnson," he said. "And I'd like you to come with me in case I have questions about the evidence or report."

She would have to look at the disgusting and sexually explicit things this man had sent her. And this time, with Aiden watching her. She would be mortified. Sure, a lot of women freely engaged in sex these days and talked about it with each other. She'd heard teammates discuss it enough on the team, but she wasn't one of those women. Her faith kept her pure, and she didn't want to go with him to the police precinct, where they would look at the obscene items together.

"Is that a problem?" he asked.

She suspected he would think she was a prude. After all, that's what they called her on the team. But she didn't care about what her teammates thought about the way she lived her faith. She did care about Aiden's opinion, though. A lot. Shocking, when she hardly knew him.

Still, she didn't run from things, and she wouldn't run from this either. "I'd rather not look at what he sent to me again. Especially not in mixed company. You'll learn soon enough that I'm kind of a prude when it comes to things like this. My faith is more important to me."

"Right. Yeah. Got it," he said but looked surprised. Maybe because of those stupid tabloid stories that painted her as a party girl. And as a girl out for herself.

When she'd first become famous, she didn't know how to handle it. She was only nineteen, and she'd let the adoration of fans go to her head. She'd acted out. Gotten into a bit of trouble and garnered negative press. Her dad finally got through to her and set her straight, but that reputation seemed to linger, no matter how much it wasn't true.

"As a Christian myself, I can totally understand your feelings," he added. "If you're uncomfortable when it comes time for me to look at the items, I'll try to do so in private."

Her heart warmed over his consideration, and she was glad to hear he was a man of faith, as that should make him more able to understand where she was coming from. "I appreciate that."

His phone chimed, and he grabbed it from the table. "It's from Drake. Locks have been changed, and he's on his way up with Erik and Clay."

"Your brothers work quickly."

"Quick but cautious and thorough."

"Right." She shook her head. "More thorough than I could've imagined."

Aiden frowned. "I have to ask. Do you have any reason to think this stalker is someone you know?"

49

"I've spent a lot of time thinking about that, but nothing seems to point to anyone I know."

"You mentioned Tanner, but what about another old boyfriend who you broke up with who might not have wanted the relationship to end?"

"I went out with Matthew Ennis for a few months, but travel pretty much ended the relationship. And, like I said before, I can't imagine someone from my past suddenly developing an interest in me again."

"I don't know," he said. "When you become famous, others want to be associated with you."

"Oh, I get that." She squeezed her eyes shut for a moment, as she'd experienced this so many times. "Trust me. It's often hard to tell if someone likes me for me or if they like what they think I can do for them. But still, if that's the case, I figure that would've happened years ago."

"You really shot to attention this past year, though, right? What with the records you broke for female skiers in the U.S."

"Yeah, but I don't think these guys would do something like that."

"Are you still in touch with them?"

"No. Tanner still lives in McMinnville, but I don't see him when I visit my dad. And Matthew moved to Colorado years ago to join the Vail Ski & Snowboard Club. We're friends on Facebook, and I run into him occasionally at competitions where we say hi, but that's about all."

"Are either of them married? Engaged, have a girlfriend?"

"Matthew's Facebook posts show he's dated a lot, but, like I said, I don't keep in touch with Tanner, so I don't know about him. And I don't think he's on Facebook."

"When you run into Matthew, do you get any vibes from him?"

"You mean romantic interest? No. He's usually hanging with the other guys and more into whatever is going down in the ski events. Nothing personal at all."

Aiden still looked skeptical. "They would both know the kinds of things from your past to send to you."

"Yeah, I suppose. But then, a lot of that stuff can be found online. I've done a bunch of interviews where they ask about my past in FFA, as the reporters all think it's unusual that I split my interests between farming and skiing."

"It's not real prevalent in the online articles, though." He locked gazes, as he'd done often since they'd met. "At least I didn't run across it in my research, and I read a lot about you."

Wow. He'd taken the time to read about her. Her neck warmed and the heat rose up her face. Why in the world was she blushing over something as simple as researching her? He was just doing his job. Not like he was looking for information on her to further his interests in her. Quite the opposite. He didn't want to be interested in her, and she'd best remember that. She'd only spent part of a day with him, and it seemed as if she'd known him for years. She had a sense of comfort, but her senses were tingling at the same time. Both emotions that could get her to think about a relationship and she had no need for that in her life at the moment.

The elevator dinged, and she turned her attention to the doors. The three brothers, laughing and joking, stepped into the condo. She liked seeing them together when they weren't focused on her. Her family had always been serious. Tremendous stress came with their family income being dependent on the orchard and the products they sold. That had changed when her mother had inherited a huge amount of money from her father. Her parents were Christians, but they worried every year. Would the weather cooperate? Would they have a good harvest? Or would there be a drought, which was happening more frequently? Would they be struck by pests or disease? The list went on and on.

Being dependent on so many factors out of their control made life hard, and she learned from watching her parents that trusting God wasn't enough. That was why she'd decided not to follow in her dad's footsteps and manage the business. She'd disappointed him, but she didn't want to live her life in fear of financial ruin.

Funny—and not in a ha-ha kind of way—that now that she looked back at it, she'd chosen a career that had immeasurable uncontrollable factors. Weather. Slope conditions. Injuries. Mental attitude. All this when she wanted to be able to control most of the factors surrounding her life.

But now, she'd come to rely on God when stressed. Or at least she tried to. She often failed. Like with this stalker. And she still didn't know what she wanted to do when her ski career ended, which would likely be in the next five years. The pressure to figure that out was haunting her.

The brothers' laughter stilled, and they crossed over to the table. They all dropped into chairs, but not in alphabetical order this time. How often they must've been teased about the naming, but she found it endearing and looked forward to meeting the parents who'd decided on their names. *No. Wait.* She wouldn't be meeting the parents. That was just crazy thinking.

"Can I get anyone a drink?" she offered. "Water. Coffee. Tea."

They all shook their heads, but it seemed more from professionalism than disinterest. At least the other guys she'd worked with weren't allowed to accept food and drinks, and they'd followed that rule. Interesting that two of them chose to break the fraternization rule instead.

"Your phone should be done in a few hours," Erik said. "Nick will text when his team finishes, and I'll go pick it up for you."

She smiled her thanks.

Aiden looked at Erik. "Will you get Nick to do a background check on Tanner Gidwell and Matthew Ennis? They're Harper's former boyfriends. The usual kind of stuff. Social media. Finances. Internet mentions."

"Sure thing." Erik got out his phone and started tapping the screen.

Aiden shifted his attention to Clay. "Tell me about the recon."

"As we suspected. Two main entrances into the building. Garage and front entrance, and a service entrance in the back. A first floor back door leads into the garage."

"We use it to access our cars," Harper offered.

"The rest of the block is rounded out with high-rise buildings," Clay said. "One with a rooftop garden. That could present some risk if a sniper was involved, which I don't foresee in this situation."

Harper clutched her chest. "I should hope not."

Aiden switched his focus to her. "But we have to—"

"Consider every possibility," she finished for him and smiled.

"Guess I've made that point clear." He returned her smile with a beaming one of his own.

Wow. Just wow. His whole face came alive. Bright. Alluring. If she'd been attracted to him before, this smile drew her in like a sunny morning with fresh pristine powder on the slope, and she wanted to linger there for as long as the sunshine lasted.

Clay cleared his throat, and Aiden's smile evaporated.

"I'll draw a neighborhood map and point out the vulnerabilities," Clay continued. "I suggest we use the garage for all ingress and egress for now. Too great of exposure on the street."

"I want to head over to PPB to talk to Johnson," Aiden said. "Erik, give the guy a call and see if he's available to meet with us."

"Roger that." Erik got up and took out his phone as he strode across the room. As the youngest and the one who looked nothing like the rest, she suspected the brothers often picked on him.

Aiden turned his attention to his other brothers. "Harper will come with us so she can answer any questions we might have on the evidence. Means everyone will be needed for safe transport. Then I'll work up a schedule from there."

Aiden paused. "Erik will go with Brendan in the decoy vehicle. Drake and Clay, you're with us."

His brothers nodded and didn't ask any questions. Harper couldn't believe it had only been a few hours since she felt relatively safe in leaving her condo. But, now that she'd spent time with Aiden, she knew the real risks and was afraid to get in that elevator and leave the building.

Aiden left Brendan and Clay behind with the vehicles that still had the new car smell and whisked Harper into the Portland Police Central Precinct only a few miles from Harper's condo. But it'd been a tense few miles, and Aiden was thankful they were off the street and in the building. Especially since they couldn't carry in the building and had to lock their weapons in the car.

They stepped into an impressive entryway with curved stone staircases on both sides of the space leading to the second floor. But Erik led them straight ahead through glass doors, where he stopped at the desk to request Detective Johnson.

The short, pudgy guy soon exited the elevator, and Erik introduced everyone.

"Good to see you again, Ms. Young," Johnson said to Harper.

"Thank you for agreeing to talk with us."

"Glad to help out law enforcement officers even *if* they've left the force." Johnson looked at Aiden and Erik, drilling them with a penetrating gaze, belying his words.

The last line was said as a jab. Not surprising. Leaving to pursue private employment was often seen as a betrayal to the brotherhood. Aiden got that. He'd once have had the same opinion, but his views had obviously evolved.

"Follow me." Johnson led them to an elevator, and they rode to the detective's floor. He took them past a reception desk with thick bulletproof windows to a door on the side, and Johnson used his keycard to open it.

They trailed him into a wide-open area running the width of the building with a sea of cubicles, chest-high dividers giving privacy. The scent of burnt coffee and a low buzz of conversation filled the room. He wound his way past the busy homicide and vice detectives, many of them with phones pressed to their ears, to a small conference room. On the table sat two evidence boxes and a binder.

"Have a seat," he said and dropped into a chair nearest the boxes.

Aiden waited for Harper to choose a chair. After she settled next to Johnson, Aiden took one across from her so he could watch her expressions. Erik sat next to Aiden.

Johnson leaned his chair back, the metal leg emitting a high pitched squeak. "Where do you want to start?"

"I'd like you to take me through your investigation,"

Aiden said. "Your leads. Where you struck out. That sort of thing."

Johnson snapped his chair forward and shoved the binder toward Aiden. "My casebook has all the details."

Aiden forced down his irritation. "I'm sure your book is very thorough, but reports don't contain every investigative detail, so I want to hear it from you, if you have the time."

Johnson frowned. "Time, what's that? This is just one of a huge caseload." He glanced at Harper. "And don't mind me saying so, but your mother has put a lot of pressure on us to find this alleged stalker, but we have nothing to go on."

Harper frowned. "Sounds like something Mom would do."

"What about prints and DNA on the letters and gifts?" Aiden asked, hoping to get this conversation moving forward.

"We ran everything, sure. Got a few good latents and DNA, but no database matches."

"And suspects?"

"None. I mean there's really not much we *do* have." He tapped a box. "These items arrived by mail. No return address. All with Portland postmarks. The old-fashioned typewriter was our only real lead, but not much of one. The guy could've owned the typewriter for years, but we went to pawn shops, antique stores, thrift stores, even went online to auction sites to look for locals who recently purchased a manual typewriter. Turned up zilch."

He reached into the box and drew out a document. "We also had the typewritten documents examined, and we know that the same typewriter created all of them." He tapped his finger on one of the words. "See here. The A is misaligned. It's true in all of the letters. So when we locate a suspect, and if he's in possession of a typewriter, we can match it to his machine. Until then..." He shrugged.

"Who examined the pages?" Aiden asked, making sure not to sound in the least bit questioning of anyone's skills.

Johnson crossed his arms. "Expert at the state forensic lab."

Aiden was trying hard not to cause the guy to get defensive so he kept his tone level. "Would you be open to having the trace evidence expert at the Veritas Center take a look at them?"

He scowled. "Pretty pricey, isn't it?"

"The expert's my sister."

Johnson watched Aiden for a long moment, his brow arched. "I'll have to get my lieutenant to approve it."

"I'd also like them to check everything sent to Harper for prints and DNA. And I'd like a copy of your casebook."

He sat back and crossed his arms. "Not sure what you think you'll find that we didn't."

"Probably nothing, but I like to be thorough," Aiden said, though honestly, he was hoping Sierra would pull out a miracle.

"Like I said, I'll have to check with my lieutenant."

"If it would help, I could have my mother call him." Harper's suggestion sounded innocent enough, but she had to know having her mother call his supervisor would put Johnson on edge.

Johnson slowly unfolded his arms and clamped his hands on the edge of the table. "That won't be necessary."

"I wouldn't mind," she added.

"Let me get his approval right now." He grabbed his phone and stepped out the door but continued to watch them through the glass wall.

He wasn't being nosy. He'd left them alone with evidence, and he needed to keep an eye on them to maintain the chain of custody.

Erik smiled at Harper. "Nice work in getting him moving. If only we had a governor-mother to help us out."

She frowned. "It was kind of a low blow though, wasn't it?"

"Policing is filled with politics," Erik said. "Johnson will get over it."

She looked at Aiden. "Is politics like this part of the reason you all wanted to go out on your own?"

He nodded and opened his mouth to further explain, but Johnson came back. "You're cleared. I'll have an evidence clerk deliver everything to the Veritas Center by the end of day. And once our assistant finishes copying the casebook, I'll messenger it to you at whatever address you wish."

"Our offices are in the Veritas Center," Aiden said.

He arched an eyebrow. "Then I'll make sure the book is delivered there."

"Thank you so much." Harper flashed a dazzling smile.

Johnson stared at her and relaxed his shoulders.

Aiden understood wanting to stare at her, and he wouldn't mind being on the receiving end of that smile.

"I'll make sure my mother knows how helpful you've been," she added.

Johnson jerked his gaze free and looked at Aiden. "If that's all—"

"Actually, I'd like to ask a few additional questions," Aiden said. "And take a look at this evidence before you send it to Veritas."

"Won't your sister let you do that?"

His snide tone didn't sit well with Aiden. "She has to follow the same chain of custody rules you do and won't be authorized to show it to me."

Johnson waved a hand over the boxes. "Have at it."

Aiden glanced at Harper before he stood. He didn't want

to offend her by taking out the sexual objects that embarrassed her.

"Go ahead," she said, but he saw her twirling her ring around her finger, something he'd come to know she did when nervous or worried. "I'm okay."

He lifted the lid from the nearest box and found bags of items. He started through them, keeping the bag sheltered in the box so Harper wouldn't be embarrassed, but tilting it so Erik could see. Aiden could easily see why she was uncomfortable. Sex toys, lingerie, and pornographic pictures filled the bags. He moved on to the second box, already opened by the detective, and found the more personal items that she'd described. He lifted out a bendable rubber doll in bright colors.

She looked at it and frowned. "Betty Spaghetty. One of my favorites. Got her for my eighth birthday. More memories I'll have to work hard not to let him ruin for me."

Aiden wished he could somehow restore the memories, but hopefully putting the stalker behind bars would do the trick. "Do you ever remember talking about her in interviews?"

She shrugged. "I could have, I suppose, but I don't think so."

"Which makes it even more likely that whoever sent this knows you from the past."

"Or they could just know about popular toys during my childhood years and guessed."

"That's true enough."

Aiden finished reviewing the items and looked at Johnson. "You said you didn't have any suspects. What about Tanner Gidwell and Matthew Ennis? Did you interview them?"

"The old boyfriends? Yeah, we chatted." Johnson waved a hand. "No red flags there."

Aiden wouldn't rule these guys out until he personally interviewed them. But with Johnson having talked to them, they wouldn't be top priorities if other leads presented themselves. "Thank you for your cooperation and for agreeing to send this information to Veritas. We'll get out of your hair now."

"I have a question before you go." Johnson opened a laptop on the table and turned it to face Harper. He tapped the screen. "Do you know this man?"

She leaned closer to the picture taken at one of her ski events, and Aiden did the same. Johnson was pointing at a stocky man in the crowd. His head was shaved and his wide jaw was covered in dark whiskers. His dark eyes were focused, penetrating. Not the sort of look you'd expect from a casual spectator.

Harper looked up. "No. Should I?"

"Not necessarily."

"Why are you interested in him?" Aiden asked.

"This morning, I finished going through the news media's uncut footage from your last World Cup events. This man was in the crowd at each event."

"Are you able to run facial recognition?" Aiden asked.

"We can't use it at PPB, but I have a request in with the FBI."

"We might be overreacting here," Erik said. "This guy might just like skiing, be scouting skiers, or—"

"Or." Harper gripped her hands together on the table and stared at the screen. "Or he could be my stalker."

6

Harper slid into the backseat of Aiden's car, and he climbed in next to her. Her phone, now holding the three still shots of her suspected stalker transferred from Johnson, seemed to be burning a hole in her pocket. Still, she wanted to look at the creep. To memorize his face in case she ran into him.

"Where to?" Drake asked from behind the wheel while Clay opened their gun safe and handed out weapons.

Harper knew they and her previous bodyguards carried, but they'd concealed them. Seeing them handle the guns raised her concerns about her safety even more.

"Veritas." Aiden explained about the video while Drake got them headed in that direction. "I need Nick to run facial recognition on a suspect."

"Can't we just email or text him the pictures?" Drake asked.

"We could, but I want to be there to plead our case for making it a top priority if he's too booked with other things."

Harper clicked on her seatbelt. "If Johnson couldn't run facial recognition, how can Nick?"

"From what Sierra's told me, he has immediate access to

facial recognition software," Aiden said. "Plus, he can probably run it against the county databases too."

"I don't get why PPB doesn't do facial recognition."

Aiden shifted to face her, adjusting his seatbelt as he moved. "The city is pretty strict on people's privacy rights, and city officials think it violates those rights. In fact, they're considering banning its use in the city altogether."

She shook her head. "I understand banning it for local businesses who collect images and use them, but a police department is a whole other story for me."

"We all agree with you," Clay said from the front seat.

She looked at him, then back at Aiden. "I suppose this falls under the rules thing for you, too, and another reason why you left law enforcement."

"It does." Aiden gave her a tight smile and turned his attention back to the road.

He and his brothers continued to scan the roads, their bodies in hyper-alert status. She might be in danger, but Aiden said that, with the Veritas Center being an unplanned stop, it was unlikely that her stalker knew where to find her. And Drake announced that he was making several false turns to determine they weren't being followed.

Despite Aiden impressing on her the danger she might be in, these men gave her more confidence in her safety than her prior bodyguards. When she'd learned Blackwell Tactical wasn't available, she should've asked Gage for another agency, not let her mother go with the list of agencies from her research. But Harper had been focused on training and had let her mother do her thing. Then, trouble ensued. Trouble Harper was going to avoid with the tempting man sitting next to her.

She scooted away from him. That gained her a raised eyebrow, but too bad. No point in placing undue stress on either of them.

Rain started spitting from gray skies as they pulled into the Veritas Center parking lot. The sun—what little of it she could see—was dropping toward the horizon, outlining the building in shadows. She'd been impressed with the size of the buildings the first time she'd come to the Veritas Center. Now that she knew the second tower held condos, she realized the business wasn't quite as big as she'd first believed, but it was still impressive.

Drake pulled to a stop in front of the center and left the SUV running.

She started to get out, but Aiden held out his hand. "Let Clay get the door unlocked first so we can go straight in."

Clay slipped from the vehicle and pressed his fingers against the reader. When he had the door open, he gave a clipped nod. As Aiden escorted her inside, she was struck by the fact that Clay and all the brothers were fine looking men, but she had zero romantic interest in any of them. Just Aiden.

It was odd how she reacted this way. It was almost as if the attraction was so intense that God was using it to get her attention. Telling her to let go of her unwillingness to get involved and give this guy a chance. Or it could have nothing to do with God at all. She didn't know. And hadn't asked. Maybe she should.

The fall wind whisked across the lot, and she put her head down and followed Aiden to the front desk, where a stout man with buzzed salt-and-pepper hair stood looking at her.

"Pete, this is—"

"No need to tell me. I'd recognize Harper Young anywhere." He shoved out his hand. "Pete Vincent. Wife and I follow skiing. You've got the goods for sure. So impressive."

She shook his sandpapery hand. "Thank you, Mr. Vincent."

"Pete. Just Pete." He smiled broadly and held out an iPad. "Fill out the form, and I'll get your badge ready."

She tapped her information into the screen and felt Aiden's eyes on her. Then Pete's too. She was used to her celebrity status, but at times, being the center of attention was still uncomfortable. Not that Aiden had shown any inkling that he was one of the many people who admired her skills.

"I assume Nick is still working," Aiden said to Pete.

"Yeah. He'll be here for hours. Night owl, that guy is."

She finished the form and took the badge dangling from a lanyard. "Thank you, Pete, and nice to meet you."

He nodded vigorously. "My wife will be so jealous when she hears I met you."

"Maybe we can arrange a time for me to meet her and talk skiing."

"That would be awesome." Another big smile brightened his face, and she instantly liked him. He seemed tough enough to be the security guard but had a warm heart. A perfect balance.

Aiden frowned. "Once we have your stalker behind bars."

Pete's smile disappeared, and his forehead knotted. "You have a stalker?"

She waved a hand and tried to act as if it was no big deal. "These guys will protect me and find him."

"Yeah." Pete's eyes narrowed. "Yeah. You're working with the best."

Aiden pointed at the door. "We should get moving."

"May God go with you," Pete said as they departed.

Drake had parked the car and was waiting for them with the other brothers by the inside door. In the elevator, Aiden tapped both the third and sixth floor, and Drake looked at Erik. "Did you get the PPB detective to cooperate?"

"Of course," Erik said and smirked.

Clay lifted his eyebrows. "You or Aiden?"

"Aiden might've said more, but I just needed to be there." He lifted his shoulders. "You know. The enforcer."

Brendan snorted.

"What?" Erik challenged. "You don't think I can be an enforcer."

"In your dreams, yeah," Brendan said.

The brothers laughed, and Erik sputtered.

Harper loved seeing them spar, but she felt out of place. Must be what their sister felt when they were all together. Harper couldn't imagine growing up with five brothers. An only child, she couldn't imagine having any siblings. Though she had very much wanted them. It would be interesting to be part of such a big family.

"They can be a lot to get used to." Aiden eyed his brothers. "We need to work harder at being professional when with clients."

"No, it's fine. I'm an only child, so it's a bit overwhelming, but I don't mind. I like seeing how you all know each other so well. Just like you said in your presentation."

"Not much of a presentation." Drake raised a dark eyebrow. "Your mother hijacked it from the very beginning."

"She's like that sometimes," Harper said, not intending to defend her mother, just explain. "Quick and to the point."

Aiden looked at her. "You didn't seem to inherit that from her."

He really was starting to get to know her in such a short time. "I'm more like my dad in that regard. My desire to achieve goals, though—that's from her."

"Allowed you to become an Olympic champion," Clay stated.

Harper thought about her growing up years. "Yeah, that along with her pushing me."

"Was she a helicopter mom?" Aiden asked.

Harper gave a nervous chuckle, as she didn't like the way her mother drove her to succeed in skiing. Harper was glad to be a medal winner, but sometimes she wasn't sure the cost was worth the achievement.

The elevator dinged on the third floor, and the doors opened.

"This is our floor," Aiden said.

The guys split apart to let her exit first.

Aiden stepped out beside her and looked back at his brothers. "We'll come up to meet you when we're done with Nick."

He received affirmative nods, and, before the door was closing, the brothers were back to joking about Erik being the enforcer.

"I really don't mind your brothers joking around," she said when the doors closed. "Please don't be hard on them because of me."

"Thanks, but it's something we need to work on for the future, and there's no time like the present to start." He pointed down the long hallway. "We'll check Nick's main lab first. If he's not there, he'll be in his private lab, where he works on top-security items."

Aiden took off down the hall, his strides long. Even at her height, she had to hurry to keep up with him. He got the first door open and glanced inside. Through the cracked opening she could see a large room with computers on tables lined up against the walls.

"Nick here?" he asked.

"Other lab," the male at the table in the middle of the room answered without looking up.

"This way," Aiden said, and they went to the next door, which Aiden opened and held for her. The room was chilly and hummed with computer equipment.

"Hey, man," Aiden said to the guy sitting at the table, who she assumed was Nick.

He wore jeans and a T-shirt with a slogan she couldn't read from this angle. His hair was brown, and he had a close-cut beard with eyes a matching color. He glanced at her and arched an eyebrow.

She stepped forward, hand outstretched. "Harper Young."

"The skier." He clasped her hand, his skin cold. "I heard Nighthawk was providing your protection and investigating the stalker."

At first she was surprised at him knowing about her, but then she remembered that he'd reviewed her electronics.

"You look concerned." He extracted his hand and waved. "Don't worry. Any information we hear is confidential, and we'd never share it with others."

"Thank you."

He leaned back and looked up at Aiden. "If you're here to follow up on those background checks, my team is still working on them."

Aiden shook his head. "We have a few photos of a suspect and need them run through facial recognition. You can do that, right?"

"Sure thing."

"Can you do it now?"

He glanced at his watch and pulled out the chair next to him. "Yeah, sure. Have a seat and text or email me the photos."

Harper sat. "Be sure to bill this and the time you all spent on my electronics to my account."

Nick cast a questioning look at Aiden.

"Actually, bill it to us, and then we'll pass it along." Aiden looked a bit embarrassed by discussing billing issues. "Harper has the photos."

Nick slid his business card down the table to her. "Here's my number."

She got her phone from her purse and started tapping the screen. When she'd sent the three photos, she looked up. "Sent."

Nick snapped his chair forward, and his fingers flew over his keyboard. "Got them. Now to search."

His focus was pinned to the screen, and Harper wasn't quite sure what to say or do. She didn't think she should distract him with chitchat, but the silence was awkward, so she turned to Aiden.

"Do you really think Sierra will be able to locate something that the PPB criminalists missed?"

Aiden shrugged. "She's my sister. Makes me prejudiced about her skills. I don't know many of the details of her job, so maybe I think she can do more than she can."

"Nah," Nick said without looking at them. "She's amazing at what she does. Just like all of us. We're tops in our fields."

"And modest too," Aiden said.

"Yeah, that too." Nick laughed.

She and Aiden laughed with him, and the tension in the room evaporated.

Aiden looked at her. "I'm sorry this creep has sent you such explicit things. You don't deserve any of this."

"Thanks," she said, but tears threatened at his sincere kindness, so she looked away until the threat passed. "I'll rest a lot easier once he's behind bars."

"I won't rest until that happens." His eyes were dark and serious and filled with a wash of emotions she couldn't read. "I promise."

His promise settled in, clear to her bones, and her heart started racing with her own emotions. Despite Nick sitting a few feet away, and the reason for being there, Aiden's complete focus was on her, and she warmed under his gaze. She lifted a hand to reach out and touch his arm. To let him know she appreciated his care.

"Bingo!" Nick pumped his fist in the air, and she dropped her hand. "We have a match."

Harper swiveled to look at him, easing out a long breath to stop her racing heart. "Who is he?"

Nick looked up. "Jeffry Gurly. Sound familiar?"

"Not to me," she said.

"I can do a background search on him and get the info to you," Nick offered.

"Can you do it now?" Aiden asked.

Nick glanced at his watch. "I'm having dinner with Piper in a few, but I can set an algorithm to scrape the internet for data before I meet her. Then after we eat, I can forward the details to you."

Aiden looked at Harper. "Newlyweds. He and Piper just got back from their honeymoon in Japan."

"Congratulations," Harper said. "Japan's an interesting choice of honeymoon location."

"Hello...technology." He grinned. "We're both into it."

"Piper's an FBI agent on the local cyber squad," Aiden said.

"Ah, that explains it." Harper smiled at Nick.

"We should grab something to eat too," Aiden said.

"Sounds good," she said, but she wasn't in the least bit hungry right now.

Aiden stood. "Call me when you have anything."

"Expect to hear from me tonight." Nick turned back to his computer.

"Thank you for making it a priority," Harper said.

"If the Byrds need our help, we're gonna be there for them."

Aiden motioned at the door, and they stepped into the

hallway. After that unspoken but emotion-filled exchange in the lab, she didn't know what to say. Did she acknowledge it or wait for him to say something? Or did she let it go?

She looked at him. His focus was pointed straight ahead, and she couldn't get a read on his thoughts. *Fine.* She'd keep things professional. After all, that was what she wanted. "It's great how helpful Nick is."

Aiden's head bobbed more forcefully than needed, as if he had to release his emotions too. "The whole team is like that. Blackwell Tactical too. We trained with them for two weeks to get our team rhythm in sync."

"You were doing that the day we met," she said, because she couldn't think of anything else to say except talk about Gurly. Until she had more information on the man, she didn't want to speculate on why he'd chosen to stalk her, if indeed he even was her stalker.

Aiden nodded and got the elevator doors open. "They've been working the protection business for over six years and have developed tricks and techniques that we can use. We'll continue to train with them on a regular basis. Hopefully, someday we can teach them a thing or two."

They boarded the car and rode in silence to the sixth floor, that unease back between them, but she bit her tongue so she didn't say anything to make it worse. Aiden's brothers were sitting in their cubicles but stood. She watched them cross the room and imagined them in an action-adventure movie striding her way in slow motion. Protectors. Intent on keeping her safe. Giving their life if needed. It was a humbling feeling to know they would do that for her.

Brendan arrived first, looking at her, his gaze probing, and then facing Aiden. "Any luck."

Aiden nodded. "Guy's name is Jeffry Gurly."

Clay planted his feet wide apart. "We know anything about him?"

"Nick's running background on him now."

"So what's the plan?" Drake asked.

"We'll grab something to eat and take it back to Harper's place, then, after we get details from Nick, we'll make a plan." Aiden looked at her. "If that works for you."

Harper nodded, but now knowing they'd soon have information that could confirm Gurly might be her stalker, she didn't think she could eat a thing.

7

Pizza had been the easiest food type to pick up, and the tangy sausage and pepperoni filled the air with a tempting spicy aroma, but Aiden couldn't eat another bite. Not when the acidic tomato sauce burned in his stomach as he waited for Nick's call on Gurly. It seemed nearly impossible that they might have a suspect this soon, but Aiden had worked enough investigations to know some of them fell into place right away. Very few. But some.

Drake set down his pizza and looked at Harper. "How old were you when you started skiing?"

Harper picked at the pepperoni on her slice that she'd hardly touched. "Six. My dad was a skier, and he took me." A fond smile warmed her face. "I was hooked right then on the bunny slope."

"Most of us still have bunny slope skills." Clay chuckled.

Brendan sat back and looked offended. "Speak for yourself."

"I said most of us." Clay rolled his eyes.

"I know. Just wanted to make sure Harper knew I wasn't one of the bunnies." Brendan grinned.

Erik swallowed a bite and lifted his shoulders. "I'm a

bunny-sloper and proud of it."

Drake smirked. "Yeah, but you still need training wheels on your bike."

Erik socked his brother in the arm. "Not true, but someone has to be the careful one in the group."

Brendan eyed Aiden. "Aiden's taking up that charge just fine lately, so you can let go."

"Give it a rest, bro," Erik said. "He needs to be more careful, and you know it."

"Why's that?" Harper asked.

"Nothing," Aiden said, giving his brothers the stink eye to shut them up.

They suddenly got very interested in their pizza, and they polished off several of them. But not Harper. She kept picking at her piece. After seeing the disgusting letters and suggestive items the stalker sent to her, he couldn't even begin to imagine how she must feel. Vulnerable was the word that came to mind. No woman should feel that way, and he desperately wanted to make her feel safe.

His phone rang, and he saw a video call from Nick. Aiden grabbed his iPad and answered. "Got you on my iPad, and the whole team and Harper are here."

Nick frowned, and Aiden's gut clenched around his pizza.

"I wish I was calling with good news," Nick said. "But you're not going to like this."

Harper curled her fingers and laid her fists on her knees. "Go ahead and tell us."

"Gurly has a record for multiple counts of rape."

Harper gasped.

"I know it sounds bad, and it is." Nick let out a noisy breath. "He was a ski instructor in Vail. Had sex with two of his underage students. He was arrested and sentenced to twenty years. Served only ten."

"Half his sentence?" Harper gaped at the screen, her fingers reaching for her ring.

"Unfortunately, it's typical of rape crimes," Aiden said.

That raw vulnerability lingered in Harper's eyes again, cutting right to Aiden's core.

"He's been out for two years now," Nick said. "And he has to stay away from minors, so he couldn't go back to his coaching job."

"Not like anyone would hire him anyway." Harper's posture was stiff and unyielding.

Aiden met her gaze. "Sounds like he's into underage girls, and that's not you. Might not be our guy after all."

"Or these girls were just who were available for him to manipulate," Brendan said. "Young girls are more impressionable."

"Could be." Aiden looked at Nick. "What's Gurly been doing since he got out?"

"It looks like he's still following skiing. I checked his financials and found credit card charges proving he did attend the events we have the photos from and others. Appears as if he's a transient worker who quits his jobs to leave town and then picks up something else wherever he goes. Last known work was as a day laborer for produce farms in Colorado."

Harper's eyes narrowed. "The letters are all postmarked Portland. Did he move here?"

"I have a local address for him," Nick said. "A motel room. I'm including that in my report, but he's not there."

"How do you know?" Aiden asked.

"Because he has an arrest warrant out for another rape charge in Colorado, and the detective there has local police looking for him here, but locals say there's no sign of him living at the motel."

"Another charge." Harper clutched her chest. "Tell us about it."

"The victim was an underage skier he groomed at several of the events he attended. He wrote letters to her and gave her suggestive gifts."

Harper bit her lip. "Like he's doing with me."

"Except he didn't hide his identity with this girl. When her parents found the letters, they brought charges, and he fled. They tracked him to Portland, but he hasn't been seen since."

"I'd love to get my hands on one of the letters to see if it was typed on the same typewriter as the machine used for the ones sent to me," Harper said.

"First thing in the morning," Aiden said, "I'll call the Colorado detective who caught this investigation. I'll do my best to get copies of his report too."

Drake shifted in his chair. "I've got contacts who would run this through ViCAP. If there are any similar crimes that haven't been solved, maybe we can find him that way."

"ViCAP?" Harper asked.

"Violent Criminal Apprehension Program," Drake said. "It's an FBI-managed database where officers enter details for unsolved crimes so other officers can search it looking for similar crimes."

"Please do that," she said to Drake. "Sounds like a wonderful idea." She smiled at him.

Drake preened under her compliment. Aiden had to admit to a hint of jealousy at not receiving such a compliment, but he wasn't here for compliments. He was here to do his job.

"If Johnson knows about the alert on Gurly," Brendan said. "I wonder why he didn't consider it could be connected to Harper's stalker."

"He might not have paid attention to the alert," Erik said. "I saw that happen enough times at PPB. Detectives had enough on their plates, and they figured patrol handled the alerts."

"Still, if the guy was good at his job, he would've looked at it," Aiden said. "I'm not saying he would've made the connection to these photos, but still..."

"Gurly's record means his prints and DNA are in finger-print databases," Aiden said. "So, if Johnson didn't get a match for any of the prints and DNA, then Gurly's either not the guy who sent the items or he wore gloves."

"It could all make sense once we see Johnson's case-book," Drake said.

Aiden nodded. "Do Gurly's credit card or banking records give us any idea of where he might be?"

"No," Nick said. "He drained his checking account, and his last charge was for a hotel in Colorado nearly sixty days ago. He had a good chunk of money in his account back then, so he must be using that or working jobs for cash only."

"So how do we go about finding him?" Harper asked.

"We should start by getting footage for the rest of your ski events this year," Aiden said. "Look for the guy and see if he's in any of the shots."

"And if he is?"

"Then we try to track him from there."

"I can get the footage for you," Nick offered. "Might take me a day or so, but I can do it."

"Then please do," Harper said.

"You got it." Nick gave a firm nod. "And I'll email Gurly's background report to you the minute we end the call."

"What about Tanner and Matthew?" Harper asked. "Did you find anything concerning on them?"

"Concerning, no. Interesting, maybe. Tanner has no internet presence at all. Like zilch. His finances are in bad shape. Looks like he took a job at a local produce processing plant recently and has been helping keep the family business afloat after a bad harvest. No evidence of dating at all, but then, with no internet presence, that's not odd but could mean he's still into Harper."

"And Matthew?" she asked, looking uneasy. She probably didn't like her dating past out there for everyone to analyze. Aiden could understand that for sure.

"He's just the opposite," Nick said. "A social media hound, so we can track his movements that way. He was in most every location you were, Harper, all year."

"Not surprising. He's on the U.S. men's team now, and the men's events are scheduled on the same weekends."

"Makes sense, then. He's not the kind of guy to stay with one woman for long. Could be something there. Or not. But the biggest thing is that he's not in the area. Training in Vermont. So if the stalker makes an appearance, it's not likely him, but he could still send things through the mail."

"You're sure about Vermont?" Aiden asked.

"Positive," Nick said. "That could change, but the guy was photographed on the slopes today."

"Thanks, Nick," Aiden said. "I owe you."

"And I'll hold you to that." Nick grinned, and the call went dead.

Aiden closed the iPad and sat back. "I'll need to contact Johnson and tell him about Gurly."

Harper narrowed her eyes. "What do you think he'll do about Gurly?"

"If Gurly's truly in the wind, there's not much Johnson can do other than put out an alert on him." Aiden looked at his brothers. "We need a plan. I'll only need two people for Harper's detail tonight. Someone for lobby duty and someone to stay with Harper."

"You all could stay with me if it's easier," she said. "I have four bedrooms."

Aiden met her gaze. "The person who stays with you won't be sleeping."

"Oh, right."

"I'll take lobby duty," Erik said. "Figure, as the youngest, you'd give it to me anyway."

"I can do the condo," Brendan offered.

Aiden jotted it on his notepad. "In the morning, we'll need to do recon on upcoming venues, which includes the Radisson Red Hotel and Timberline ski area."

Clay looked at Aiden. "No doubt you'll volunteer for Timberline."

"No doubt," Aiden replied and left it at that. "But I'll also be on the other venues."

"Then you'll need to head home and get some sleep," Drake said.

Aiden didn't want to leave Harper, but, if he had to let her out of his sight, it would be here with two of his brothers on her detail. He sure wouldn't leave the venues to his brothers to scout. Not when he needed to be sure every possible risk was vetted and the places were safe enough for her to visit.

"I'd appreciate it if I could get on the slopes as early as possible," Harper said. "Which I can't see happening if you have to personally check out the hotel venues."

Her comment was justified, but Aiden didn't like it. "Tell you what. I'll only do the Radisson tomorrow and manage the others as we get closer to the dates. That will get me out to Mount Hood faster to clear it, and you can be on the slopes by lunchtime."

"It's far better to be on the slopes when it's colder and the snow's harder, but I can make it work for one day. Thank you." She smiled at him, a genuine one that lit her face. One that he'd hoped would be directed his way since he met her.

He was helpless to look away but swallowed hard and forced his gaze to his brothers. "Drake and Clay, you'll take second shift. You can decide between you who has lobby detail."

His brothers nodded.

"Want company on the recon?" Brendan asked.

"Sure, but you need to get some shuteye after that so you can take the next shift here."

"Will do."

"Okay." Aiden clapped his hands and stood. "We have a plan until the recon is done, and then we'll regroup."

His brothers got up and grabbed their things, except for Brendan, who would be staying the night in the condo.

"Aiden," Harper said. "Can I talk to you a minute?"

"Sure."

She stepped to the other side of the room, and he followed.

"I meant what I said about the bedrooms," she said. "I would appreciate it if you would stay."

He'd be lying if he said he wouldn't mind that, but it wasn't a good idea. "Why's that?"

"You're obviously in charge, and if you're here, I can be involved in any decisions that come up."

"I can just be sure to loop you in."

She wrapped her arms around her waist as if needing to protect herself. "Is there a reason you don't want to stay?"

"You know the reason."

"We're both adults. We can control our emotions."

He blew out a breath and considered her comment. She might be confident in her ability to keep him at arm's length, but he was already starting to fall for her, and staying with her would surely accelerate that. He opened his mouth to tell her no.

"It would also make me feel safer," she said before he

could respond.

And there he had it. His desire to make her feel safe trumped any risk of falling in love with this woman.

"Okay, sure. I'll stay," he said, and, even as he spoke the words, he knew it was a mistake. One he hoped he wouldn't regret.

~

Harper joined Aiden at her dining table. He sat across from her looking at his computer, and Brendan had gone to sit in a chair he'd moved next to the elevator doors.

"We should review this tonight in case we need Nick to do additional research." Aiden slid Nick's report on Jeffry Gurly across the table.

She wasn't surprised he was acting all professional with her, but the atmosphere in the room was tense. Still, she dug up the skills she used to concentrate on the slopes and tuned him out to start flipping through the ten-page report.

The first sections listed Gurly's affiliation with a small ski club in Colorado. He'd coached the team for five years before the allegations of sexual assault were brought against him. He denied them at first, saying that he didn't touch the girls. Later when evidence was collected, he admitted he'd had sex with them but claimed it was consensual.

Of course, due to their ages—thirteen and fifteen—it didn't matter if it was consensual or not. He'd broken the law and had to pay for it. Those poor girls. Harper couldn't even imagine their pain. She opened the internet and looked up their names in a search engine to see if they'd continued to compete after this terrible tragedy or if they hung up their skis. Harper had no idea what she might've done in their shoes. Thankfully, she'd only had good experiences with her coaches.

She found links for the first girl, Gretchen Dickerson, who was still on the circuit, but Facebook was the only link for the other girl, Eliza Rashard. Harper opened Eliza's page and found nothing about skiing. Based on the photos, the girl had turned to a very dark and goth kind of look and attitude.

Harper sat back and looked at Aiden. "Do you think it would help to call the girls Gurly attacked to find out if he's tried to contact them?"

He tapped the table with his long index finger. "It could, except it might bring up bad memories for the girls."

"They'd be in their mid-twenties now, so I would think they could handle it." But he was right. The last thing she wanted was to cause the girls extra trauma. She sat back. "Maybe we should save that for a last resort."

"I'll jot it down, and, if we strike out on ViCAP and details from the detective handling Gurly's current rape charge, we can consider it." He noted the item on the legal pad that had fast filled with pages of notes. She didn't know what all he'd written down, but it must have been important.

She went back to her screen and decided to read down Eliza's Facebook page for any mention of Gurly. Harper spent an hour scrolling back in time. She was shocked that Eliza had left her posts open to the public.

"Someone should warn Eliza to secure her Facebook page," Harper said. "She's just asking for predators, which seems odd after what she's gone through."

"Not all females react to a rape in the same way," Aiden said. "She could be blaming herself and acting out as a result."

"That's so sad, if that's what she's doing." At the idea, tears pricked at Harper's eyes. Just having a stalker left her nearly breathless. She couldn't imagine what it must feel like to be in Eliza's shoes. "And she gave up her skiing career too. Or the trauma ended it."

"Either way, she lost out on that dream."

"What about you?"

Aiden flashed his gaze to Harper. "What about me?"

"You said you were once a skier. Did you ever dream of participating in the alpine skiing race circuit?"

"Dreams, sure, but I wasn't fast enough, and I wanted other things more."

"Things like?"

He leaned back, looking comfortable with the discussion now. "I wanted to follow in my dad's footsteps. To serve in the military, then go into law enforcement."

"And are you glad that's what you did?"

"Absolutely." He draped an arm over the back of the nearby chair. "Being a SEAL taught me so many things that I still apply to my life."

"Such as?"

"I guess the biggest things are integrity, how to face adversity, and the importance of loyalty. All things in the SEAL creed."

"I've never heard of that."

"Probably because none of the guys mention it." He leaned forward. "Like now. We just make light of it. But you deserve a sincere answer. The thing is, in the creed, we agree not to talk about our work or seek recognition for it. I love that about the teams when humility doesn't tend to come easy to most of the guys on SEAL teams."

"Guys like you, you mean?"

He flashed a quick grin. "I was typical in the day. An adrenaline junkie. Someone who always believed he was right. A tough guy."

"But not now?"

"No, not now," he said, sounding sad or sorry about it.

82

"How about you? Still glad to be a skier after all these years?"

"Mentally, yes, but my body is another story." She shook her head. "World Cup ski racers fight around five g-forces per turn. That's about nine hundred pounds of pressure per turn. With up to ninety turns in a race, that's a lot of wear and tear on your body."

He gave a disbelieving shake of his head. "I read somewhere that Olympic champ Bode Miller has been clocked at twelve Gs on certain turns."

She nodded. "Fighter-jet pilots experience those kinds of forces. Then there are the injuries, and it's not uncommon for racers to die in the sport."

He lifted his eyebrow. "And yet you keep doing it."

"I don't have a death wish, if that's what you're implying. I mean, if I did, I wouldn't have hired you all for protection."

"So, why do you take the risk?"

"Because I love it. Love besting my records. Love working toward being the winningest female in history."

"And once you accomplish that?"

"Then I'll retire," she said. "But that's a few years off before I have to make that decision, and I honestly don't know if I'll retire then. Not when I don't know what I want do with the rest of my life."

He sat forward. "Do you want to get married and have a family someday?"

"Yeah, sure," she said. "*After* I retire. Obviously, I couldn't ski while pregnant, and it's not fair to ask a guy to tag along with me all winter. Or to sit home and wait for me."

"If it's the right guy, I don't think you'd have to ask." He made strong eye contact. "At least, if I was crazy in love with a woman and free to be in a relationship, I hope I would find a way to make it work."

8

Aiden looked out over the city in the bright morning sunshine as he waited for Detective Walters in Denver to come on the line. Harper had gone to the gym with Drake, and Clay was on lobby duty. Erik headed home to sleep, and Brendan was dozing on the couch, waiting for Aiden to finish his call so they could check out Harper's upcoming venues.

"Walters." The booming voice came through the call.

Aiden introduced himself, shared his law enforcement experience to form a connection, and explained their situation. "This is strictly confidential. We don't want to encourage the news media to jump on the story."

"Understood," Walters said. "What do you need from me?"

"I was hoping to ask you a few questions about the investigation."

"Not something I'm free to talk about. We're not releasing any of the information to the public at this point."

"Could you provide your case file for our review?"

A long pause. "As former law enforcement, you know I can't do that."

"Sure you can. You just need your supervisor's permission, and maybe to redact the girl's name."

"And why would I do that?"

Aiden swallowed down his frustration so he wouldn't come across as demanding. "Because we both want this creep behind bars, and you don't have anyone local working the investigation for you, so it's dried up. Even if it turns out Gurly isn't our stalker, I'm glad to keep you apprised of our developments, and, if we find him, we'll make sure he's taken into custody."

Silence was his answer.

"Come on," Aiden encouraged. "It's a win-win."

"I suppose." The detective blew a breath through the phone. "Let me get with my sarge and get back to you."

Aiden shared his phone number. "Time is of the essence."

"I get it." He ended the call.

Aiden shoved his phone into his pocket and tried to put himself in Walter's place. Back when Aiden was with ATF, he wouldn't have wanted to share a report with a private investigator either, but Aiden also suspected he would want to arrest this creep more than keeping things hush-hush and would get permission to share.

He shook his brother's foot to wake him. Brendan came instantly alert, reaching for his sidearm and dropping his feet to the floor.

"Time to head out." Aiden grabbed his jacket and went to the elevator.

Brendan rubbed his eyes as he joined Aiden.

Aiden searched his brother's face. "You good to go, or do you want to head home for some sleep?"

He shrugged into a leather jacket. "Let me grab a cup of coffee on the way, and I'm good."

"From the bags under your eyes, you'd better make it a large one." Aiden grinned.

Brendan rolled his eyes. "Maybe look in the mirror. You didn't sleep last night, either."

"How do you know that?"

"I heard you pacing the floor in the guest bedroom." He tapped his ear. "Nothing gets past these ears."

"Yeah, because they're so big."

Brendan jutted out his chin. "People tell me I look just like you, so you might want to reconsider that."

Aiden shook his head, though sparing with his brothers was one of his favorite pastimes. That was true of all of them and always had been. Growing up, there had been times it got out of control, and their mom used a few choice words to put them back in line, but as adults they didn't let it get to that point. At least not very often.

The doors opened at the lobby, and Aiden greeted Clay. "Everything good down here?"

"Quiet as can be." Clay made a bored face, but underneath it, Aiden saw his usual intensity while on the job.

"I'm going to check in with Drake, and then we're heading out. Call me if anything happens."

Clay gave a firm nod. "You could just call Drake. No need to visit."

Aiden ignored the comment and started for the gym. Clay was right. Aiden could just call. But he also wanted to say good-bye to Harper. Purely for professional reasons. After she'd asked him to stay last night, he realized she'd come to depend on him, and he wanted her to know where he was at all times in case she needed him.

He unlocked the door. Drake spun, his hand shooting to his sidearm. When he spotted Aiden, he lowered his hand. Aiden glanced into the room where Harper worked an elliptical machine. She wore shorts and a tight top that left her middle bare. The woman was solid muscle, and her skin glistened with perspiration.

"What's up?" Drake asked.

"We're heading out. Just wanted to let you know."

"There's this thing. I'm not sure if you've heard about it. It's called a cell phone." Drake smirked.

"I'm just being thorough." Aiden walked over to Harper. "You need anything before we go check out the venues?"

She shook her head, her ponytail swinging. Up close, he could see the definitions in her muscles and was even more impressed. He and his brothers were fit. Very fit by today's standards, but Harper had taken it to the Olympic champion level that she competed in. She deserved a medal just for her determination.

"I know you want to hit the slopes," he said. "I'll be back as soon as I can."

"Thanks," she said, her breath coming hard. "FYI, I asked for a list of the building tenants, and the guard said he'd have it for me by the time I get done here."

"Great." Aiden forced himself to turn away and start toward Brendan and Drake.

"FYI," Drake said. "I had my friend check ViCAP for similar crimes. Found nothing."

"Thanks for trying. Call me if anything comes up." Aiden held Drake's gaze until he nodded and then departed with Brendan.

"That woman is seriously built," Brendan said as they stepped outside. "She must have some fitness routine."

"Yeah," was all Aiden said, as he didn't want to encourage the conversation. He needed to erase the sight of her toned body from his mind so he could concentrate on his work. Of course, his brother had commented on it. Not in a sexual way, but in a way of showing respect for her hard work. All the brothers knew what it took to reach her level of fitness.

They stopped in a small shop outside the building, and the smell of freshly brewed coffee almost enticed Aiden to get a cup, but he was jazzed enough as it was. While Brendan grabbed his coffee, Aiden made a better study of the street than he'd taken yesterday. The Radisson Red Hotel was located in downtown. Far enough away to drive. Even if it wasn't, if Aiden approved the venue, he would drive Harper for security reasons. Meant he needed to scout out the drive too.

Brendan joined him with a large cup of coffee and blew on the rim. "The smell alone brought me back to life."

"Good, 'cause you're driving." Aiden clicked open the SUV door with the remote, tossed his keys to Brendan, and climbed in. He did question for just a moment if it was a good idea to give a sleepy driver the keys, but Aiden knew his brother could do his job.

They passed retail stores, the outskirts of Pioneer Court-house Square—a popular destination for locals and tourists —and an urban residential area with old but well maintained buildings.

"I don't like this," Aiden said. "Too many places to hide on the route."

"We could take the freeway for part of the trip, but we'd still end up on city streets."

"I'll plan an alternative route that no one would expect us to take. We can run it on the way home." No longer needing to watch the streets, Aiden got out his phone and mapped out the route, but he did look up when they came close to the hotel boasting a vivid red entrance. Brendan pulled into the parking lot, but, depending on the hotel layout, Aiden might take Harper in through the front door or even another door that the manager could give them access to.

Harper's mother had arranged for Felix Waterside, the events manager, to meet Aiden in the lobby, and he tapped his foot as he waited for them. He wore a black suit, white shirt, and red tie, and his shock white hair stood out like a beacon. Aiden almost chuckled at the fact that the guy's hair was color coordinated to the hotel, which was decorated in gray and red, fitting with the Radisson Red theme. The man strode confidently through the hotel, his chin raised in a haughty angle, and took them to the room where the governor would be holding her meeting.

Aiden stepped into the room and made a full circle. "Room capacity?"

"Two hundred max. Which is what we're expecting. Governor Young had to limit her group to very select patrons." He preened as if somehow the fact that these people were select reflected on him.

"Two exits only," Aiden said more to himself than asking.

Waterside gave a sharp nod. "The back is reserved for staff only unless there's an emergency. And I've personally selected the staff for the evening. Of course, they've all undergone background checks."

"I'd like a list of their names and addresses," Aiden said.

"I'm afraid I—"

Aiden eyed the man. "I'm sure you've already given this information to the governor's advance team, and you wouldn't want me to have to bother her for it, would you?"

Waterside gave a quick sniff as if finding something distasteful. "I'll print a copy and get it to you before you leave."

Aiden went to the windows and looked out. He noted several locations where a sniper could hunker down.

Brendan stepped up behind him. "Plenty of sniper hides out there."

Aiden glanced up to see automatic blinds on the window. "I'd like to have the blinds closed at all times. I'm guessing the governor's advance team requested that as well."

"They did."

Aiden turned. "Show us the staff corridor."

"Follow me." Waterside spun, his shiny dress shoes grinding on the tile.

Brendan made a comical face, mimicking Waterside's snooty behavior, and Aiden had to work hard not to snort. Trying not to cut-up when on the job was one of the many joys and challenges with working with brothers.

He gave Brendan's shoulder a light punch as he passed, and Brendan chuckled lightly. If Waterside heard it, he didn't turn but unlocked the door and entered the hallway. It led straight ahead to an area dedicated to pitchers, glasses, and a large ice maker humming next to an even larger refrigerator. They passed through the area to a big kitchen bustling with staff and smelling like fish.

Aiden turned to Waterside. "You may have handpicked the waitstaff for the meeting, but anyone could come in through the kitchen."

"The staff for the event will be dressed in black tie, so they will stand out, and the governor's advance team has already submitted a proposal to block off the kitchen from others. Plus, they will have staff at the entrance, and we are providing our staff with unique name tags that have never been used before so no one else could have one in their possession."

The governor's team had been thorough, but before Aiden approved Harper's attendance at the event, he wanted to talk with Coop, one of Blackwell Tactical's operators who was heading up the governor's private detail. She still had her six-person Dignitary Protection Unit staffed by the Oregon State Police, so she was well covered. As a result, Harper would have additional protection at the venue too, though they would all be focused on the governor.

"Take pictures, Brendan." Aiden flipped open his notepad and sketched the layout of the areas, and his brother snapped photo after photo. They worked their way back to the main room, both actively recording the layout.

Aiden shoved his notepad in his jacket pocket. "I'd like to see the entrance the governor's using for the event."

Waterside arched an eyebrow that looked as if it had been plucked to precision. "Ms. Young won't be coming with her mother?"

Aiden shook his head but didn't explain having them arrive together put them in jeopardy by both foes.

Waterside's clipped steps took them down an employee-only service corridor that led to a loading dock. This entrance was protected and perfect. Aiden wished he'd been on the job earlier so he could have snagged it for Harper, but now the Blackwell team or the governor's staff wouldn't even consider giving it up for Harper. Aiden could arrange for Harper to arrive earlier, but having her on site longer than needed was just as dangerous as using a different entrance. Maybe the governor would agree to arrive later, but he doubted that she would go for it, and, in any event, Blackwell wouldn't move their vehicles, as they needed them on standby for an emergency getaway.

"Which entrance did the governor's team designate as their secondary arrival area?" Aiden asked.

"They didn't." Waterside frowned, making his narrow face look even longer. "They said it's this spot or not at all."

Aiden wasn't surprised, as this location was as good as it

got. "If they *had* asked for a secondary place, what would you have recommended?"

"The parking garage. In fact, I took them there, but they still asked for the loading dock."

"Do you have an employee entrance from the parking garage?"

Waterside nodded. "Top floor access."

"Take me there now."

Waterside's lip curled as if he didn't like being told what to do, but he quickly raced through another corridor to an elevator that led to the top floor.

Aiden followed him out in the garage and was happy to see they could pull right up to the elevator for Harper to disembark. The location limited her exposure. "If we use this entrance, we'll be parking our vehicles in front of the elevator and leaving them there for the duration of the event."

"That's fine," Waterside said. "Now, if there's nothing else—"

"Those names and addresses," Aiden said.

Waterside frowned as if he'd thought Aiden might forget.

"We'll take a walk down the parking ramps and meet you back in the lobby," Aiden said.

Waterside didn't respond but spun on his heel and hurried into the elevator.

"Guy's something," Brendan said as they walked down the ramp.

"Let's just hope he comes through for us on the night of the event." Aiden focused on the ramps, noting a stairwell on each floor along with elevator access for guests. "We'll need to clear the stairwell that night."

"This is going to put us kind of thin," Brendan said.

Aiden nodded. "We'll have to time everything just right."

"Exactly."

They reached the first level and entered the lobby via the guest entrance. The large space smelled like orange cleaner and was humming with guests. Definitely the last resort for Harper's entrance to the event.

Waterside approached a concierge desk, his shiny shoes gleaming in the light, where he shooed the guy sitting there away from his computer and took over. Aiden bet Waterside spit-shined those shoes every morning before work. Having a military background, Aiden appreciated organization and attention to every detail. He just didn't appreciate the I'm-better-than-you attitude that came along with Waterside's demeanor when, a moment later, he flapped out his hand with the list.

Aiden grabbed it before the guy changed his mind. "Thank you for your time. I'll be in touch if I have additional requests after I meet with the governor's team."

Waterside gave a sharp nod and took off toward the back of the room.

Aiden headed for the door but memorized every area of the lobby so he knew where they could take cover if they came under attack and had to use this entrance.

"We need a fallback plan," Brendan said, his gaze searching the large space too.

"I'll draft one tonight." Aiden opened the door and took another long look around. He didn't like the nearby high-rise buildings, as they were perfect sniper hides. Even the brick apartment building across the street could pose a problem.

He turned the corner for the parking garage. Thankfully, an empty lot sat next to the garage, giving him a clear view of the area. The church with a second story could be problematic. Aiden would send a vehicle ahead of them to check the area and clear the stairwell.

He entered the garage, noting what it would take to break out of the space if needed. Brendan opened the vehicle, and Aiden climbed in.

"Looks like this is doable," Brendan said.

"Yeah, I don't see a reason yet why she shouldn't come to the fundraiser." *Except that I'd rather lock her up until this stalker is caught.*

Aiden gave Brendan directions to follow his alternate route back to Harper's condo. It struck him then. They both worked in fields where their jobs had life-or-death consequences. Her profession was a little different, as she chose to barrel down those hills at speeds that could kill her. His career was a choice too, he guessed, but he did it to protect and help others. Not just because he loved the job but because he felt called to it, and, until his kidney donation, no one in his life had objected to the danger.

But what if, once the business was successful, he decided to settle down? What if the woman he fell in love with asked him to step away from the job because of the kidney or just because she couldn't handle the risk? Or what if he fell for someone like Harper? Would he be able to watch her race down a slope where she could break her neck and die? He sure couldn't ask her to stop skiing and still put his life on the line for others.

He shoved a hand into his hair. He wasn't one for double standards, but he could honestly say it would be too hard for him to watch the woman he loved do something so risky.

Then you best not fall in love with Harper. She isn't retiring anytime soon.

"Mount Hood?" Brendan asked.

Aiden almost said yes, but shook his head. "Let's take a look at Gurly's place on the way. Never know what we might find."

9

The seedy motel was pretty much what Aiden expected. The low-slung building looked forlorn in the hazy sunshine. Single story. Doors with chipping paint opening onto a crumbling parking lot. The red neon vacancy sign blinking and announcing hourly rates.

Brendan parked on the far side of the lot. Aiden focused on Room 4. No light shone through the curtains. What he thought he would find, yet he was disappointed.

"Want to kick the door down?" Brendan asked. "Looks like it might fall in with a strong breath."

"I do."

"But...?"

"But I've followed the rules for so long that I don't know if I can break them."

"Then there's only one option." Brendan opened his door. "I go charm a key from the woman working the front desk."

Aiden slid out of the vehicle, the smell of coming rain lingering in the air and dark clouds butting up against each other in the distance. He dug in his pocket and caught up to Brendan. "How much cash do you have?"

Brendan glanced at Aiden. "A couple hundred. Why?"

"We might need to bribe her."

Brendan displayed a wide grin. "You're underestimating my charms, bro."

"You must be more tired than I thought. Erik's the charmer of the family. You?" Aiden paused and raised an eyebrow. "You're our sniper and you know it. Direct and to the point. Even with women."

"But I—"

"Have a better chance of bribing her than anything. We both still have law enforcement written all over us, and she'll pick up on that."

Brendan frowned. "You could be right."

"So start with a hundred bucks, and we'll see how it goes from there. I think four should be our max."

"Agreed." Brendan opened the glass-walled lobby door, and a strong musty smell drifted out. A woman Aiden put in her fifties with stringy blond hair, heavy makeup, and a faded red hoodie sat behind bulletproof glass—a ready indicator of the motel's clientele.

She curled her arms tight against her body. "Whatever it is, we didn't do it or know anything about it."

"When's the last time you saw Jeffry Gurly, the guy staying in Room 4?" Brendan asked, ignoring her comment.

She tilted her head then shook it. "Don't share that kind of information with cops or anyone else."

"We're not cops."

She snorted. "You must think I'm an idiot."

"No, ma'am," Brendan said, his tone soothing. "We were once law enforcement but have moved into the private sector."

"Hah!" she said. "You still have the cop stink on you."

"Guess I need to head home and take a shower then,"

Brendan joked, but the woman didn't even crack a smile. "Do you remember the last time you saw Gurly?"

"Been weeks."

"His stuff still in the room?"

"He's paid up until the end of the month. He don't come back by then, I'll clean it out."

Brendan smiled, a flirty one that he used with women. "I'd like to get the key to his room."

She unfolded her arms and leaned forward to plant her hands on the worn Formica countertop. "Like I'm going to give it to you just because you're a pretty boy trying his best to be charming."

Aiden slapped a hundred-dollar bill in the metal tray at the bottom of the window. "Will this buy us a key?"

"Not hardly."

"Seems like it should," Aiden said.

"Listen. These are brass keys, not your fancy hotel plastic numbers," she said but her focus was on the money. "You don't bring it back, I have to pay to have another one made."

Brendan reached into his pocket, likely for another bill. Aiden grabbed his hand to stop him and stepped forward.

"I guess we'll be on our way." Aiden reached for the bill.

The woman shot out a hand and snatched up the money. "This will do."

Aiden resisted smiling over his success.

She sat back. "Was a pleasure doing business with you."

"The key," Brendan demanded. Gone was his good mood, replaced by the fierce warrior Aiden knew his brother to be.

"Like I said, we don't hand out other people's keys."

Anger curled in Aiden's gut, and he wanted to release it in a verbal tirade on this woman, but he swallowed it down and put a deadly confidence in his tone. "You may be behind a wall of impermeable glass, but that door next to it is flimsy enough to come down with one well-placed boot." Aiden locked gazes with her. "And I just so happen to be wearing my door-kicking boots today."

"Fine." She scowled and grabbed the key from a pegboard behind her. "But you best be returning it."

She dropped the key into the metal tray, the clinking sound reverberating through the air. Aiden grabbed it before she changed her mind. "We'll be back in a few."

He strode out the door, glad to have the musty and stale feeling washed away by the wind kicking in from the east.

Brendan caught up. "How'd you know she'd go for the hundred?"

"Her eyes never left the money. She was almost salivating."

"Nah, it wasn't that obvious or I would've seen it too."

"Guess you're just not as observant as I am." Aiden knocked on Room 4's door, just in case Gurly was inside.

As Aiden waited for an answer, he dug latex gloves from his pocket. He handed a pair to Brendan and slid his fingers into a glove, tugging and snapping the latex as he got his long fingers inside without tearing the latex.

"Ready?" he asked Brendan.

He nodded and pulled back his jacket to rest his hand on his sidearm. Aiden shoved in the key and opened the door. The musty odor mixed with rotten food hit Aiden hard, and he cringed before flipping on a lamp with a yellowed and stained shade that stood in the corner of the forlorn room.

The bedspread had once been vivid blue-and-pink floral but was now a washed-out and snagged version. Two flat pillows sat near a thick oak headboard, also holding scars of years of guest abuse.

Aiden pointed at an opened sandwich wrapper with

moldy bread sitting on the small table. "Looks like he bolted in the middle of a meal. Maybe his quick departure means we'll get lucky and find something of value."

"Let's hope."

"Place really is a dump." Aiden moved over stained pale blue carpet and opened drawers on a low dresser.

Brendan went to the nightstand. "Ammo," he announced. "Two boxes, 9mm, 12-grain full metal jacket. No gun."

"Likely a handgun then."

"Likely, but not a hard-and-fast rule," Brendan said and, as the ballistics expert on the team, he would know better than Aiden. "The 124 works better in a handgun, but 9mm is a common submachine gun caliber as well as a popular carbine caliber. Still, if I was firing one of those, I'd be using a higher grain round."

A ball of dread formed in Aiden's stomach. "I don't like the fact that he's carrying, whatever the model. Makes our job more difficult, and we should start wearing vests. Including Harper."

Brendan closed the drawer. "You think she'll agree to that?"

"I'll convince her. We also need to keep eyes on this place, twenty-four/seven, in case Gurly shows."

Brendan looked up, his hand on the next drawer knob. "We don't have the manpower for that."

"Agreed. Normally I'd suggest we give Blackwell a call, but all of Gage's operators are on the governor's protection detail."

Brendan pressed his lips together and released the drawer knob. "What about Blake? Maybe Grady too? Think they could do it?"

"They both have the skills to protect themselves if Gurly showed up with a gun, so it doesn't hurt to ask."

Aiden dialed Blake, who answered in one ring. "I hate to impose, but we need two people to sit on a motel where our suspect has a room but hasn't been seen in some time. We have reason to believe he's armed, and we were hoping you and Grady could do it. We'll pay the going rate, of course."

"I can probably rearrange my schedule for a few days," he said without hesitation. "Let me check in with Grady to see if he has anything urgent that he can't hand off to his team."

As the Veritas Center's weapons expert, Grady performed ballistic tests and analyzed bullets for the center's law enforcement cases and also provided knowledge on a vast array of weapons. Blake organized and led all law enforcement investigations for the agency. Both were busy guys, and getting their help was a long shot.

But Aiden wanted someone he could trust not to panic and react appropriately if Gurly showed up. With Blake's law enforcement background and Grady's army service, they could handle it.

"Let me know, and I'll text you the address," Aiden said.

"Will do." Blake ended the call.

Aiden looked at Brendan. "He'll try to make it work."

"We can't ask for more." Brendan stared ahead, looking pensive. "They've really bent over backwards to help us get this agency off the ground."

"We owe them a lot." Aiden's mind went to how fragile their agency remained as he squatted down in front of the bottom drawer and worked the sticky glides out. He looked at the items filling the drawer, and his mouth dropped open. "Well, look at this."

Brendan joined him and shook his head. "Similar items to the ones that were sent to Harper. Looks like the guy buys in bulk."

Aiden looked up at his brother. "Could mean he has other women or girls in his sights."

"Johnson didn't say if he interviewed other women on Harper's team. You think Gurly targeted them?"

Aiden had no idea, but... "Only one way to find out."

Brendan nodded. "Ask them."

Harper paced her living room, clasping and unclasping her hands with each step across the polished wooden floor. She'd already missed ideal snow conditions for the day, and she was antsy to get out on the slopes. Plus, Aiden had been gone far longer than he'd said he would be, and she dreaded what he was going to tell her when he arrived. She doubted he would bring good news. Maybe there was a problem at Timberline. He'd texted to say they were running late, but they were just finishing up at Timberline. If he said it was too dangerous for her to ski, she would go anyway. She only hoped he wouldn't try to forbid her from going.

The appearance at her mother's event tonight was a different matter. She could easily miss that and not care. Her mother used Harper's Olympic fame to garner money from her supporters. Most everyone loved Olympic medalists. They'd upped their contributions in the past because of Harper's appearance at fundraisers, and she didn't want to disappoint her mother, who needed the money for a final push in TV advertising. Still, Harper would listen to Aiden if he told her she couldn't attend.

Drake's phone dinged, grabbing her attention.

He looked up. "Aiden's on his way up."

"Finally." She blew out a breath.

Drake's intense blue eyes remained on her, interrogating her with a single look. She could easily see him in his former job as a deputy marshal in the fugitive apprehension division, hunting down fugitives. She didn't want to explain her unease, so she looked away. Thankfully, he didn't push.

The elevator whirred into action, and her heart sped up. She planted her feet and faced the door, preparing herself for a battle.

The doors opened, and Aiden stepped into her condo, a deep frown on his face. She'd seen him earlier in the day so knew he was wearing tactical pants, boots, and shirt. He looked confident and dangerous, just like Drake and Brendan. She wondered how his mother felt about having raised five intense guys. Harper imagined the woman putting them in their place, and she almost chuckled at the thought.

Aiden carried bags of take-out food and set them on the table. He shrugged out of his military-style jacket, and she hoped taking off his coat didn't mean he was planning to stay here and keep her at the condo.

"Did everything go okay?" She searched his face.

He nodded, but the frown remained.

"What's wrong? Is there a problem?" She held her breath.

He rested his hands on a chairback. "I need to get with Blackwell on the hotel before deciding on that, but we can work with Timberline."

She let out her breath. "Then why the frown?"

"I decided to stop by Gurly's motel room." He got out his phone, tapped it a few times, and held it out. "Found a drawer filled with these things."

She looked at the picture, and her heart sank. "He must be sending items to other women."

Aiden showed the picture to Drake, who'd joined them at the table. "Or girls."

"That's horrible," Harper said.

Drake met Harper's gaze. "Do you think he might be stalking your teammates?"

She clasped her hands and sighed. "They all know about what's going on with me. If it was happening to them too, I think they would've said something."

"They could be hiding it for some reason." Aiden's frown morphed into a scowl.

"He's right," Drake said. "Sometimes women blame themselves in situations like this and are embarrassed to talk about it."

Her eyes widened. "These are all really strong and determined women. I don't think they'd hide it."

"If Johnson hasn't talked to them, we'll need to give them a call."

She hated having to involve her teammates in this mess, but knew he was right. "They're training in Vermont all day, and they'll have an early curfew. If we need to call, we'll have to take that into account."

Aiden nodded.

"So are we good to go to Timberline?" Drake asked.

"We are. I already reviewed the layout and plans with Brendan and Clay in the lobby. I called Erik back to duty. It'll take all of us to make this work."

Drake pointed at the table. "But it looks like we're having lunch before we go."

Aiden nodded. "We can review the plans while we eat."

Drake's phone chimed again, and he looked at the screen. "Erik and Brendan are on their way up."

"After night duty and no sleep, they're going to be exhausted."

He looked at Harper. "If it's okay, they can catch some sleep in your spare rooms when we get back from Timberline."

"Of course."

He smiled, but it was strained. "I grabbed a variety of sandwiches. I hope that's okay."

"Sure. Thanks." She smiled at him. "I'll get some plates, and there're drinks in the small fridge at the end of the island. Help yourself. Oh, and the list of tenants is on the table."

"Perfect. I'll get it to Nick to do background checks on everyone."

The elevator whirred in the distance, and she went to the kitchen and took down handcrafted stoneware plates her granddad had loved to use. Memories of the gentle man with a big heart and strong Christian values nearly brought tears to her eyes. He'd been a huge supporter and encourager as she grew up, and she missed him so much. She'd kept many of his things in the condo, only redoing her bedroom and the main living space. The memories of seeing his things were hard some days, but other days they brought a smile to her face. Today, she would enjoy seeing the plates used again.

She distributed dishes around the table, and Erik and Brendan joined them, both looking alert and ready for action.

She smiled at them. "Drinks are in the small fridge."

Aiden handed out sandwiches, and they all sat.

"What about Clay?" she asked. "Won't he want to eat?"

"We still need him at the door, so I gave him a sandwich on the way up." Aiden pulled out a chair for her. "One of the reasons I chose sandwiches. Easy to eat while on duty."

She smiled her thanks for his assistance and sat, wishing he wasn't turning out to be such a fabulous guy, making it far harder to ignore him.

"Let me get this report texted to Nick along with the list of servers for the event tonight." Aiden sat across from Harper and, between bites, snapped pictures of the tenant list and then sent a text. His phone dinged right away. "Nick will get his staff on it."

He set down his phone and looked at his brothers. "Before we review today's plans, you should know we also found ammo in the motel room. We've got to assume Gurly is carrying."

Harper's bite of the delicious turkey-and-avocado sandwich turned to a lump in her mouth, and she had to work hard to swallow it down. "He's armed?"

Aiden nodded. "Which means we'll want you to wear a Kevlar vest anytime you're out of the condo."

A vest. She couldn't even imagine it. "It will mess with my skiing."

"I can't make you wear it, but I really can't recommend you don't."

"But if it's a handgun, wouldn't he have to be close to me?"

"An average person with reasonable experience should be able to hit a man-sized target at about fifty yards, but reality is closer to half that. Still, that's well within the range to take you out on the slopes."

She could see herself whooshing down the slope and Gurly popping out with a gun. Firing. Taking her down. She'd be helpless. Totally helpless. There weren't many places to hide on the Palmer Snowfield. Still, it would be possible for him to find a spot, and she did want to be safe. "How about we start with it on my first run? If it's too problematic, we can talk about it."

"Okay," he said, frowning at her response. He took out his notepad and displayed a map of Timberline. "The manager said you'd be skiing on Palmer Snowfield."

She swallowed her bite of sandwich piled high with sprouts. "It's at the top of the resort and the most challenging slope."

"And the most difficult to reach. We'll station ourselves at the chairlifts to monitor the skiers." Aiden set down his bottle of water and tapped the map at the Magic Mile lift. "We have to take this lift to get to the Palmer Express lift. Drake, you have the bottom of this lift. Erik, the top. Brendan, go ahead of us and take a stand up here." He moved his finger north of the Palmer Express chairlift.

"A stand?" Harper asked. "As in a sniper kind of thing?"

"Exactly. Brendan served as a sniper when he was a Marine Raider and for the Multnomah County's SWAT team, so he's very good at hitting his targets."

She looked at Brendan. She didn't know what made a good sniper other than a trained marksman, but he seemed intense, which she suspected was also a trait good snipers possessed.

Aiden tapped the map on Palmer. "Clay will station himself at the bottom of the Palmer lift. Since the resort isn't open to the public, very few skiers other than the Timberline ski team and Harper will be allowed into the resort."

"No other training going on?" Erik asked.

Harper cocked her head. "Timberline's a summer training partner with the U.S. Ski and Snowboard team, but that program has ended, and most skiers are training where the conditions are more like the next World Cup competition in Finland. We need manmade snow."

Aiden tapped the map again then looked at her. "What I'm more concerned about is getting you from the parking area to the slopes. You're probably used to changing into your ski gear at the lodge, but can you dress out in your bedroom to eliminate one stop?"

"Of course," she said but knew it would be awkward if she ran into her neighbors while wearing a speed suit. "With the early snow this year, you'll all want skis to get to these areas."

Aiden set down his water bottle. "I've already arranged rentals for all of us."

"Time to put my bunny-hill expertise to use." Erik chuckled. "But not everyone is as lame as I am. Aiden has mad skills."

She looked at Aiden. "You going to join me on a run down Palmer?"

"No," he said, but there was a hint of longing in his eyes. "I'll be manning a drone at the top of the hill."

Harper was shocked. "Timberline gave approval for that?"

Aiden nodded. "We can only operate it during your runs, but yeah, they agreed."

Brendan snorted. "After some fancy talking from my big brother. And he got them to close down the Palmer Snowfield to everyone but you."

"Impressive," she said.

Aiden looked at her. "I hope the drone doesn't distract you."

She waved a hand. "After competing for so many years with spectators, cameras, and helicopters, I can tune it all out."

She folded up the wrapper on the second half of her sandwich. She needed to eat, but not too much before skiing. "I'll get ready while you finish your meals."

Feeling their eyes on her, she put her sandwich in the refrigerator. She was used to scrutiny and public appearances, but this felt more intimate. For some reason she couldn't fathom, she really wanted the Byrd bothers to like her. Maybe more, she wanted them to respect her. And if she were truthful, she especially wanted that from Aiden.

10

Brendan entered the Wy'East Day Lodge with his rifle in a case, and Clay followed to clear the place before Aiden allowed Harper to go inside. He watched her get out of the vehicle and haul out her equipment bag. He tried hard not to stare at her, but she looked so amazing in her white race suit with blue and red stripes winding over her body. He'd seen first-hand her level of fitness in the gym, but the suit accentuated the power in her legs.

Stop it. Your job isn't to admire her. It's to protect her.

He got out a small Kevlar vest and handed it to her. She looked at it as if it were a snake but lifted it over her head and fastened the Velcro while everyone else slipped one on. She grabbed a bright blue ski jacket and shrugged into it. He suspected she would discard the jacket for her ski run, but he hoped she would keep the vest on all afternoon.

"Let us know if you want us to carry anything." He hung a pair of binoculars around his neck, slid on his sunglasses, and a put on a hat that covered his comms device that the team would use to communicate.

"I'm used to schlepping all of this." She hung her bag

from one shoulder, put her skis over the other, and held her poles in her left hand.

He didn't like not helping her. If his mother were here, she would call him out for not insisting. But he'd offered, and Harper had said no. Their relationship was already tenuous so he wouldn't push it.

He didn't need a helmet or goggles, not with the little bit of skiing he would be doing. He grabbed the backpack holding the drone and maneuvered his arm into the straps.

"We're clear inside." Clay's voice came over the comms unit.

"Roger that," Aiden said and looked at Harper. "We're good to go."

He and his remaining brothers circled Harper, leaving room for the skis, and they crossed the parking lot.

The four of them probably looked odd from a distance, but that was the least of Aiden's worries. He kept his gaze trained on the area glistening in the sun and hitting the slick snow, blinding in spots. He blinked rapidly to clear his vision and kept his vigil all the way to the lodge.

They checked in and grabbed their rental equipment in the modern-looking lodge with sharp angles and gray stone. In a nearby locker area, Harper put on her helmet, goggles, and boots, and then stowed her bag and everyone's shoes in a locker she'd rented for the season.

She took a long drink from her metal water bottle then stowed it, too, and set another one aside to take with her. "Electrolyte drink."

He figured she wanted the second one for when they came back here at the end of the day. He took a deep breath and prepared himself to go back into the open. The moment they stepped out, a big St. Bernard came bounding toward them.

A bright smile lit Harper's face, and she patted her thighs. "Come here, girl. Come on."

The giant white, black, and tan dog with soft fluffy fur passed everyone and lunged at Harper. She grabbed the dog up in a tussle of love. One big swipe of the dog's tongue and Harper started laughing like a little girl.

Aiden had read that the resort started a tradition in 1950 of having St. Bernard mascots at the lodge and maintained it ever since. Currently, Heidi and Bruno fit the bill. The dogs actually belonged to one of the managers—likely the woman smiling fondly at them—and she took them home at night.

"Come, Heidi," the woman called out. "Enough loving for now. Harper has work to do."

The dog lumbered back to her owner. Harper waved at the woman, who returned the wave then turned back toward Timberline Lodge.

The building always reminded him of a true Alpine ski lodge with peaks and rough-cut wood siding. He'd skied up here countless times, but only stayed at the lodge as a kid with his family. He still remembered the animals carved into newel posts on the inside stairway and the miraculous view of Mount Hood's summit. His dad had told him that the lodge had been cast as the Overlook Hotel in *The Shining*, but he'd never watched the movie.

On this bright sunshiny day, Aiden couldn't imagine it being anything but a cozy ski lodge. Even with the potential danger surrounding Harper.

He motioned for her to move, and they all started across icy and slippery hard-packed snow. Aiden had to keep an eye out for Harper's safety, so he couldn't concentrate on his skis as much as he'd like. Since he hadn't skied for a while, he lacked his usual confidence.

Please. Please. Please. Don't let me face-plant.

Her simple delight from the dog remained on her face. "I always wanted a dog, but my mom never let us have one. It's one of the first things I'll do when I retire and stop traveling so much."

Aiden hadn't considered what such intensive travel might do to her life, but he knew from his SEAL days how being gone from home so frequently ruined most relationships. The whole long distance thing just didn't work. At least not in his experience. It failed every time.

"How often are you gone?" he asked.

"We train and compete for about a hundred and fifty days a year. Most of that time's spent on the road somewhere."

Yeah, a relationship trying to survive under those terms would be rough. "And when you're not on the road?"

"I sometimes stay with my dad if he needs help with the orchard. If not, I'm at the condo."

"And what do you do with this downtime?"

"Mostly train to keep in shape. That's pretty much a full-time job, which thankfully, due to my endorsements, I don't need to have like a lot of skiers do. Especially women, who are paid less than men."

"That's unfortunate."

They fell silent and made their way to the chairlift. Aiden carefully maneuvered over the glazed snow. It made perfect snow for ski racing, but past experience told Aiden that it would be too fast on the steeper slopes for his rusty skills, and the ruts would be like sliding over corrugated metal. He much preferred the softer powder.

They left Drake at the bottom of the lift and skied into the lift barn. Aiden and Clay sandwiched Harper between them on the chair, but Aiden didn't pay her any attention. He had to keep scanning the slope for any danger. The sun frequently reflected off the snow, making him squint just to have a clear view. A strong breeze blew over them, and he had to admit to feeling weightless on the ride, the ground whisking below them.

Near the top of the Magic Mile lift, Aiden stowed his binoculars to prepare for disembarking. Wouldn't do to fall flat on his face in front of his protectee. That wouldn't inspire any confidence in her, and he wanted her to feel safe when she was with him, not need to rescue him from a ski disaster. He saw the sign posted on the tall tower running the cable to keep his ski tips up, and he lifted them to prepare to unload.

Their chair entered the small barn structure, and, thankfully, he managed to get off the chair and glide down the small slope next to Harper and Clay. Erik disembarked from the seat behind them and slid down the small incline, snow-plowing to a stop, and almost toppling over.

His face flushed red, and he held up a hand and looked at Aiden. "Don't say a word. This was your sport, not mine."

Aiden had to bite his tongue not to offer a smart-aleck comeback.

"You really didn't have to tell us." Clay smirked. "It's pretty obvious you're not a skier."

Erik looked like he wanted to punch Clay, but he stabbed his poles into the ground instead.

Aiden met Harper's gaze. "Erik will stay here, and I'll ride up to Palmer with you."

"Then let's go." She led him and Clay to the Palmer chairlift.

Aiden looked at Clay. "Let me know if you even have a suspicion of a problem."

Clay nodded, planted one of his poles in the snow, and freed his hand to lift his binoculars and scan the area.

Aiden and Harper got on the Palmer lift. Aiden pulled down the safety bar, and they were off, winging their way over the treetops and climbing up the majestic mountain to an elevation of nearly nine thousand feet. The wind was sharper, biting into his face, the temps in the low thirties. He wanted to simply enjoy God's panorama surrounding them, but he raised his binoculars and scanned the area. With zero skiers on the intermediate slopes below them, any movement caught his eye.

He paid particular attention to the out-of-bounds area, looking for the glint of a rifle or scope, where someone could hide and set up a sniper shot. Not that they'd had any indications that Gurly could handle his weapon and was a good enough shot to take one from a distance, but Aiden didn't have proof that Gurly was their man, and he couldn't be too cautious.

He successfully offloaded again after going through the Palmer tunnel and took note of how to get back on it to head down. He doubted many skiers did that, unless they chickened out once they reached the top and got a firsthand view of the steep incline.

He came to a stop in an out-of-the-way area and planted his poles. It would be great to race down the slope with Harper. No way that would happen. She was going all out for speed, and he couldn't keep up with her. Far better for him to stay put and take charge of everyone. "I'll be following you with the drone. Give me a second to get it launched and check in with Brendan, okay?"

She nodded, but absently. Something had changed in her. She was focused. Intense. Breathing deeply. The competitor in her had come out to play. Man, that was as appealing as everything else he'd learned about her.

He dragged his gaze from her face and pressed his mic. "Report, Brendan."

"We're clear. No hostiles in sight."

"Roger that." Aiden launched his drone, the motor

humming as it climbed high enough to see the entire width of the groomed area.

Harper looked at him, and he nodded. She planted her poles. Faced the slope. Sucked in a huge breath. Took off. Her rapid breathing came over the comms unit. The others had push-to-talk enabled, but, since she didn't have a free hand available, her mic was hot all the time.

He moved his attention to the drone controls and zoomed it ahead of her to find and warn her of any dangers. As much as he and the team were giving their best, they were out in the open, and he couldn't protect her from all dangers.

His heart lodged in his throat. He forced himself not to watch her graceful shushing skills but to pay attention for that glint of a gun. For a skier coming out of nowhere to join her on the empty slope. Thankfully, she whisked her way to the bottom of the slope and over to Clay.

"Clay, report."

"All good here," he said.

"I'm heading back up," Harper said between heavy breathing that puffed through the comms.

He moved the drone to the chairlift. He couldn't see inside the barn, but only the operator was inside. Still, with limited time Aiden had only been able to do a basic background on this guy.

She glided into the barn. He knew she would be stopping in the wait area until the closest chair passed by then would be sliding into the loading area, but it seemed like forever while she was out of his view, and he didn't like it.

"Anything off in the barn?" Aiden asked.

"We're clear," Clay said.

Aiden held his breath until her chair rolled out and he could see her again as the lift climbed up Palmer. She arrived next to him, and he waited for her to remove her vest, but she kept it on and poled to the slope.

As the day wore on, he lost track of how many times they followed this procedure. She had to be exhausted, but each time she'd come up and comment on what she did wrong and how she was going to fix it. Finally, she called it quits, and Aiden joined her, Clay, and Erik at the Magic Mile lift. They all rode down to Drake and headed for the locker area located in the back of the small store.

Aiden darted a glance at Drake. "Anything to report?"

Drake shook his head. "I'll scope out the lot for departure."

"I'll go with him and take mid-position," Erik offered.

Aiden nodded, glad to have his brothers taking the initative to think ahead and volunteer for duties. They all turned in their skis, Erik looking relieved. At the locker, Harper grabbed her water bottle and unscrewed the cap, but her focus was on his brothers as they walked away. She started to lift the bottle to her mouth.

He shot out a hand. "Stop."

She fired him a look. "What's wrong?"

He pointed at the top of the bottle. "White powder. I didn't see that before. Did you put something in your water?"

"An electrolyte tablet, but not powder." She held the bottle out like it might bite her.

He met her gaze. "Could be poison. We need to get it to Maya to analyze."

She reached for her ring, but her finger was bare, and she dropped her hands to her side. "Who would do this? I mean, my stalker wouldn't want to poison me, right?"

"Not unless he's figured out you will never be together, and he's moved on to revenge." Aiden glanced around.

The only person in the immediate area was the same rental guy they'd talked to when they'd arrived. Not someone Aiden had time to vet thoroughly and could be a suspect.

Aiden returned his focus to Harper. "Hopefully, whoever tampered with your bottle left prints, and we'll soon know who wants to poison you."

11

In the ski resort's small store, Aiden cornered the thin resort worker whose name tag identified him as Iggy. He brushed a hand over his bleached blond hair that matched the color of his goatee. As the only worker on duty, the guy was likely the only one with access to the locker keys, so either someone had another key, or Iggy put the powder inside Harper's bottle.

"I didn't do it." Iggy's tanned face lost color, and he looked like he might hurl. "Must've happened on my break."

The passioned response left Aiden believing the guy, but that wouldn't stop him from asking additional questions to form a clear picture of what had happened while he and his brothers were on the slopes with Harper. "Who replaced you for the break?"

Iggy's gaze darted around the area as if looking for help, but there was no one in the store to help him. Aiden had dispatched Erik and Drake to the parking area to look for anyone out of place, and Clay and Brendan stood watch over Harper, where she sat on one of the benches near the ski boot sales area.

"No one replaces me," Iggy finally answered. "Not in the off-season. I just put up a sign and close the gate."

Now that changed things. Aiden glanced at the heavy security gate. "Did you lock it?"

"Um...well..." Iggy tapped his chin. "I think so."

"But you're not sure."

"No." He twisted his fingers together. "I mean, I was on the phone with my girlfriend. She was yelling at me for leaving the apartment a mess, so I was distracted, you know?"

"How long were you gone?"

"Fifteen minutes." A sheepish look covered his face. "Maybe longer. Don't tell my boss. Please. I need this job."

Aiden honestly wished he could help the kid out, but he couldn't. "I have to close down the area for forensics and your boss will want details."

"Aw, man. I..." He shrugged.

"I'll make sure he knows you were straightforward with me."

"Like that'll help."

Aiden wasn't going to waste any more time on this. "Were you still on the phone when you came back?"

"No."

"Did you need a key to get in?"

"I used the key, but I don't know if the lock turned or not. I'm just not sure. You know how it goes. Your brain is mush from your woman nagging at you, and then you do something that you've done so many times you just don't pay attention to it."

Aiden didn't know if his brain was ever mush from a woman, but, if it could be, Harper would be the woman behind it. "I don't see any security cameras in the area. Are there any?"

"Not that I know of." Iggy looked around. "I suppose the boss coulda hidden some that we don't know about."

Aiden didn't think that was likely, but he'd only briefly talked to the manager, Stan Rosen, in their morning visit and didn't know what the guy might actually have done regarding cameras. "Would you call Stan down here?"

"Sure. Okay." Iggy picked up the phone and cradled it by his mouth "Hey, man. There's someone down here who needs to talk to you. Guy named Aiden Byrd."

He leaned back to listen, making a sour face before pocketing his phone. "He'll be right down."

"Thank you," Aiden said. "And you should know, a detective is on the way to investigate. He'll be taking your statement, so you might want to do your best to remember what actually happened with the lock."

Iggy swallowed hard, the large Adam's apple in his neck bobbing. "Am I in trouble?"

"That will be up to the detective to decide." Aiden turned to look at Harper. Man, the fear in her eyes made his gut clench. His fault. All his fault. He'd put her in a position where someone could have gotten to her. Sure, he'd done his best, but his best wasn't good enough today. Maybe he should've posted one of his brothers in this area. Nah. That would've left Harper vulnerable to attack on the slope. Far more dangerous for Harper out there.

He wanted to order her not to come back here again tomorrow, but he couldn't do that. What he *could* do was make sure they didn't use the lockers again and figure out if there was something else he'd missed and not let it become a problem tomorrow.

He might be disappointed in what happened, but he wouldn't let it get him down. He couldn't let it get him down. He called up a portion of the creed.

I will never quit. I persevere and thrive on adversity. My Nation expects me to be physically harder and mentally stronger than my enemies. If knocked down, I will get back up, every time. I will draw on every remaining ounce of strength to protect my teammates and to accomplish our mission. I am never out of the fight.

He not only had teammates who needed him to have their back, but today he was protecting an innocent woman who needed him to be his best. And he would be. For her. For them. For his own expectations of himself.

He heard footsteps and turned to find Stan stepping down the hall. He wore athletic pants and a long-sleeved T-shirt with a ski company logo on the chest. He'd pulled his dull brown hair into a ponytail, accentuating his long, narrow face.

He held out his hand. "How can I help you?"

Aiden shook hands and explained the situation.

Stan shot a look at Harper. "I'm so sorry this happened. What can I do?"

"Do you have security cameras?" Aiden asked.

Stan shook his head. "We've never needed them."

Aiden curled his fingers. "A detective is on the way, and I expect everyone to cooperate with his investigation."

"Of course."

"That means I need this area cordoned off so our forensic team can process the area."

"Sure thing. I'll stay right here, and you can let me know what else I can do." He looked at Harper again. "Harper's very important to us, and we want to do whatever we can to help."

"Thank you," Aiden stepped away to call Sierra in to process the scene.

He'd appreciated his big sister all his life. For the most part anyway. But today? Today he appreciated her just a

120

little bit more and hoped she would find evidence to lead them to the stalker.

Harper could hardly handle seeing her beloved ski resort overrun by deputies and forensic staff, all due to her. Thankfully, Aiden had called the Veritas forensic staff in right away, and they'd already gotten a good start. She glanced up at him as he left a message for Detective Johnson about the incident. Aiden was so upset over her nearly drinking what could be poison, and she wished she could alleviate his concern, but nothing she'd said had helped him.

He turned to gaze across the room and Harper followed it to see his sister, Sierra, start toward them. She was wrangling her thick, dishwater-blond hair into a ponytail, and Harper admired her perfectly cut bangs. Her white Tyvek suit hung on her slender frame. She looked nothing like Aiden, but resembled Erik in so many ways that it was easy for Harper to tell Sierra was a Byrd.

She lifted a gloved hand in greeting. "You must be Harper."

"I am. Thank you for coming." Harper smiled at Sierra.

"Glad to." Her honey-brown eyes narrowed. "It must be awful having a stalker."

Aiden had already filled Sierra in on the investigation, and Harper had nothing to add so she nodded and left it at that. Plus, she was close to tears and didn't want to lose it here. Not only because of all the professionals around her, but she could tell that Aiden was blaming himself for this incident, and she didn't want him to feel worse. She could melt down later in private.

Sierra shifted her focus to the locker, and determination

crowned on her face. "There's a jacket in the locker. Was it there when the suspect tampered with your bottle?"

"Yes," Harper said. "I put it in there when we first arrived and left it while I skied."

"Hold on. I'll be right back." Sierra jetted out the lodge's main door to the parking lot.

Harper looked at Aiden. "What do you think she's doing?"

He shrugged. "I can't even guess. I probably should know more about the tests she runs or what she uses to collect evidence."

Harper cast him a surprised look. "I would've thought, being in law enforcement for so many years, you would know quite a bit about forensics."

"Forensics, yes. Her actual job and how she gets her results, no. When I was with ATF, we rarely hung around crime scenes long enough to see the processes forensic techs used. Just got the reports afterwards."

Sierra returned carrying a backpack-sized device. It was white with what looked like an IV bag on the front, and a handheld wand with a brush at the end was mounted on the side.

"What in the world is that thing?" Aiden asked before Harper could.

"It's a wet vac system that will collect microscopic traces of evidence that can't be gathered any other way." Sierra's eyes sparkled with excitement as she talked. "Works on fabrics when nothing else will. So even if the suspect wore gloves, he might've brushed against your jacket and left skin cells behind. If so, I can collect DNA for Emory to process."

"Wow." Aiden seemed impressed with his sister. "I tell everyone you're the best at what you do, but I've never seen you in action."

"Then be prepared to be amazed." Sierra laughed and

crossed over to the locker, the legs of her Tyvek suit whispering together.

"She seems like a lot of fun," Harper said.

"She is, but she can also be a bit overbearing when it comes to meddling in everyone's personal lives." Aiden frowned. "She means well, but the nurturer in her can't see any of us unhappy, and she wants to fix it. Since she got married, she wants all of us to find someone too."

"It's fun getting to know your family," Harper said, thinking about what it would be like long-term to be part of this group. Would she fit in or stick out? "I'd love to meet your parents. They must be something."

He gave her an incredulous look.

"No, oh no." She grabbed his arm. "I didn't mean I wanted you to take me home to meet them. I was just speaking figuratively."

"Right." His gaze cleared. "They are amazing. The best parents you could hope for. Mom devoted herself to raising us. Still fusses over us. And Dad, well, he was gone a lot for the job, but, when he was home, he gave time to each of us. Quality time. You know? Made sure each of us believed we were the most special kid to him."

"Sounds wonderful."

"Your parents seem great too."

"Mostly. You might not believe this, but Mom stayed at home to raise me too. Of course, she spent a lot of time helping Dad succeed with the orchard by starting to sell hazelnut products, but she still had plenty of time to devote to my skiing. Too much time, I think." She wrinkled her nose. "But I know it was because she loves me."

Brendan and Erik marched into the room and straight for Aiden, catching Harper's attention. Their expressions raised her concern, and she prepared herself for more bad news.

"What's up?" Aiden asked.

Brendan shoved his hands into his pants' pockets. "We talked to two guys on the ski team. They were loading their car in the parking lot when a guy wearing a ski mask barreled into them from behind. Knocked one of the guys down before peeling out of the lot in a Jeep."

"Did they get plates?"

"No, but one of them took a video on his cell phone of the guy." Erik got out his phone, held it out for Harper and Aiden, and started the video playing.

As the skiers had described, the guy bolted away, quickly got into a red Jeep, and took off.

"No clear view of the plates," Aiden said. "And no way to ID the guy. Even if he'd looked at the camera, the mask would prevent getting an ID."

"Look closer at the driver's window," Erik said. "As he takes off, he removes the mask. I can try to enhance it. If I can't get a clear shot of this guy's profile, maybe Nick can."

12

Harper had never been in a forensic lab before and wasn't surprised by the strong chemical odor or the cleanliness and organization of Maya's toxicology and controlled substances lab. Several long stainless steel tables sat in the middle of the room, and the walls were ringed with cabinets and a variety of machines that Harper couldn't begin to identify.

The one person in the lab sat in front of a machine about the size of a microwave, and she swiveled to look at them. She had shoulder-length blond hair, and she fixed striking blue eyes on them, a question in her raised eyebrow.

"Maya," Aiden said. "This is Nighthawk's client, Harper Young."

Maya stood and snapped off latex gloves to offer her hand. "Nice to meet you, and congratulations on all your successes in skiing." Her tone gushed with admiration.

Harper was sometimes embarrassed when accomplished people like Maya—a scientist holding a doctorate and who really made a difference in the world—made a fuss over her skiing. "Real congratulations goes to you for this amazing lab. Aiden told me you're the founder."

"Thank you." She beamed a bright smile at Harper. "It's a labor of love."

"Can we end the mutual admiration party and get down to work?" Aiden held up the water bottle that he'd put in an evidence bag.

Maya looked up at him. "I take it you need my help."

"Yeah." Aiden took a long breath. "Sorry for being cranky, but Harper has a stalker, and it looks as if he tried to poison her."

Maya shot a look at Harper. "I'm sorry to hear that."

Harper waved a hand to play down the horror, but she was terrified enough that she planned to cancel her ski practice until the guy was caught. She would settle for working out in the gym, where the Nighthawk team had more control in keeping her safe.

Aiden handed the bag to Maya. "There's white powder on the bottle's lip."

Maya held the bag up to the light. "There sure is."

"Can you test it and tell us what it is?" Harper asked, not liking how desperate she sounded when all she wanted was to be in control of her emotions.

Maya tilted her head, evaluating Harper as she did. "I can run it through the mass spectrometer, but it will only identify the substance if it's in our database of known chemicals."

"Can you do it right now?" Aiden asked.

Maya glanced back at the machine where she'd been seated. "I have a process running on the mass spectrometer at the moment. It should complete in about fifteen minutes. I can start it then."

"Thanks," Aiden said, sounding relieved. "Can you take

the samples now so we can get the bottle to Sierra for prints and DNA?"

"Sure." Maya moved to a lab table, sliding her hands into fresh latex gloves. She covered the table with white paper, grabbed a fresh swab, and swiped the bottle in various areas.

Her movements were efficient and seemed like second nature to her as she capped the tubes and labeled them, but none of this was second nature to Harper. Everything that had happened since they opened the locker brought back the horror of discovering someone had tampered with her water—maybe tried to poison her. The stalking was escalating to a level Harper never imagined it could reach.

She couldn't be more thankful to have Aiden by her side. All the Byrds, actually. And now the Veritas staff too. Harper owed them all so much.

"I'm assuming you're going to turn the evidence over to law enforcement," Maya said as she bagged the bottle again.

Aiden nodded.

"I'll enter it into our evidence database then." She handed the bag back to Aiden. "Tell Sierra I've done so. That way she'll know I created the record, and she can add her remarks and findings to it."

"Will do." Aiden smiled at her.

"We should mention that I put an electrolyte tablet in with the water," Harper said.

Maya arched a perfectly plucked eyebrow. "Do you have one of the tablets with you?"

"I sure do." Harper reached into her jacket pocket and withdrew the portable tube holding her tablets and gave one to Maya.

Maya bagged the tablet. "It was nice to meet you, Harper. I hope Aiden succeeds in finding this stalker soon."

"We will." Aiden set his jaw.

Harper smiled at Maya. "Thank you for your help."

Aiden strode to the door like a man on a mission, and Harper followed.

In the hallway, his phone chimed, and he dug it out of his pocket. "Erik can't improve the photo of the man in the parking lot enough to get an ID. He sent it to Nick to work on."

"I'm really starting to get discouraged." She sighed. "We need something to break in our favor."

"Hey, don't get down." He stowed his phone. "I know it's hard, but keeping a positive outlook will make things easier."

"How do you do it?" she asked as they headed down the hallway. "Stay positive, I mean."

"I learned to think that way as a SEAL. If one guy on the team got down, it brought everyone down, so we worked hard not to let that happen."

"From everything you've said, it sounds like an amazing experience."

"Yeah. Sure. But we faced some hard things that will always stick with us, and no amount of determination to stay upbeat about it worked. And that's where my faith came in—knowing God had whatever we were facing in His hands, and it would all work out the way it should."

"I get that, but sometimes it's easier to say it than live it." She'd always considered herself a strong person, but hearing about his experiences, she wished she possessed his strength. Maybe she could learn to do better by watching him.

He stopped by the stairwell. "Mind taking a few flights of stairs?"

"Not at all."

"Not sore from the workout, I take it."

"It takes a lot more than that to make me sore these days."

He stepped into the stairwell. "I'm impressed with all the training you do. I work out almost every day, but you take it to another level. How do you stay motivated for such intense workouts?"

"I've always been very competitive and learned at a young age that you only win if you work hard. So, right now, it's about taking over the female record as winning the most events." She pushed past him. "Race you."

She grinned then took off, taking the steps two at a time. With his longer legs, he soon passed her by. At the top of the two flights of stairs, he breathed deeply and looked back at her.

"You may have won in distance," she said, "but look who's sucking air and who isn't."

He shook his head and laughed.

"To be fair, I run step drills for hours in training."

"Hours? You must really love the sport." He pulled open the door on the fourth floor.

"I do, but lately it's seemed more like a job than anything. I've had to fight through that to keep going. Keep reminding myself of the wins."

He held up his hand and peered into the hallway. "You mentioned retiring and not knowing what you want to do. Any thoughts at all?"

"My dad wants me to take over the orchard, but I've really become a city girl, and life on the farm isn't as fun as it used to be. I've tossed around the idea of developing a line of ski wear. Maybe start my own company even."

He motioned for her to proceed. "Do you have any experience in running a business?"

"I've watched my dad do it for years, but no. Not really. Maybe I need to go to college. Get a business degree."

"Or hire someone to run it for you." He stepped back. "I only ask because I didn't have a bit of experience before we started Nighthawk. As the oldest, they voted me in as the managing partner. All the operational details are falling on me, and I'm clueless. Other than I can see where we're hemorrhaging money instead of making it. We need to increase our client base, and I don't have a lot of ideas how to do that when this business is often built on referrals and that takes time."

She went into the long hallway that looked like the one they'd just left, but it had different labels outside lab doors. "If I hear of anyone who needs your services, I'll be glad to refer you."

He tapped the keypad outside the trace evidence lab. "You'll probably want to wait until after we wrap things up to see how we do."

"I have confidence in you and know you can do it."

"I appreciate that." He held the lab door open. "Now, we have to live up to it."

"You will." She squeezed his arm as she passed, surprising him and herself at the physical contact. She shouldn't have touched him, but it felt right and automatic.

She looked at the lab designed very much like Maya's space, but with different equipment. Three females were working at lab tables, and all three looked up when they walked in. Sierra stood behind a long stainless steel table and wore a white lab coat. The boxes of items from Detective Johnson sat on the table.

Aiden stepped over to her, and Harper trailed him.

He nodded at the boxes. "I see you got Johnson's packages."

"I was just going to get started on them," she said.

"You'll find typewritten letters in the box. Johnson had them evaluated, and they determined there was a wonky A on the typewriter. Can you confirm that when you evaluate them and check for anything else that might help identify this typewriter?"

"Sure thing."

"Can I ask you to take care of this first?" Aiden handed the bag to Sierra. "This's Harper's bottle from the locker. Maya opened a report on the computer so you can add your findings there."

"Please," she replied, a twinkle of mischief in her eyes.

"Please," he responded in a teasing tone.

"I love working with my brothers." Sierra rolled her eyes.

"No offense," Harper said, glancing between them. "But I've spent some time with them now. How did you survive growing up with this herd of testosterone?"

Sierra laughed. "They can be a handful, but I can tell you that you couldn't be in better hands."

Harper's mind went to having Aiden's hands on her, holding her, maybe kissing her, and she looked at him. He was watching her with a keen eye, and a rush of heat went up her neck and over her face. She glanced at Sierra to find her staring back. Sierra shifted her gaze to Aiden. Her eyes widened, and she opened her mouth as if she planned to say something.

"About those prints," Aiden said before his sister could speak.

Harper wanted to shout a word of praise for putting the focus back on the job at hand.

"Fine," Sierra said but looked at Harper. "There's more here. I know it, and you and I need to talk later."

Harper didn't know how to respond. She really didn't want to talk to Sierra about her brothers. Especially not Aiden. Harper might give away her developing feelings for Aiden, and Harper suspected, after what Aiden had said about Sierra meddling in his life, that she would run with it.

Sierra looked at her brother. "I'm assuming you'll want DNA done too."

He nodded.

"Okay, good." She disposed of her gloves in a biohazard bin, put on clean ones, and took the bottle to a table she covered in the same white paper as Maya had used. She got out swabs and ran them over the bottle then capped them in their original containers and labeled them.

She got a fresh swab and looked up at Harper. "We'll need to take a sample from you for elimination purposes. Open your mouth, and I'll scrape your cheeks."

Feeling like a criminal, Harper complied, and Sierra ran the swab through her mouth, then labeled the container and looked at Aiden. "You want me to have someone run these samples over to Emory, or do you want to do it?"

"I can do it on the way out," he said.

"Sounds good." She took the bottle and sat in front of a machine that had a hood above and metal grate on the bottom, a fan humming below the grate. She got out brushes and a vial of black powder. She loaded the brush with powder and swirled it over the bottle, holding it over the fan that sucked away the extra powder.

"Several nice latents on here, but they're all the same." She glanced over her shoulder at Harper. "I'll need to take your prints next to see if these match yours, which I'm suspecting they will."

With wide tape, she removed the prints from the bottle and placed the tape on small cards. "Let me get the lid going with the cyanoacrylate, and then I'll take your prints."

"Cyanoacrylate?" Harper asked, stumbling on the word.

"Basically, Super Glue." Sierra went to a tall machine with a glass front. "You put a nonporous item that's difficult to dust for prints—like the top of your bottle that has the ridges on it—inside an airtight chamber like this one and add the cyanoacrylate and water. The fumes fix the print on the item and make it visible."

"Interesting," Harper said and meant it. "I always liked science."

"Not me." Aiden feigned a shudder.

Sierra smiled fondly at her brother. "Nah, you just liked shooting guns and most every sport."

"Most," he admitted.

Sierra glanced up. "And girls. At least you used to like them. But I haven't seen you with one for a long time."

Aiden fired her a testy look.

Sierra shrugged. "I'm just saying."

"Well, don't." Aiden folded muscular arms over his broad chest and aimed a warning at his sister.

Harper would drop it if he cast the same look at her, but Sierra just shrugged and went back to work. Harper was now eager to talk to Sierra—not about this thing with Aiden. Definitely not that. Harper hoped she'd learn more about this man who had captured her interest, but that wouldn't be a good idea on so many levels.

Sierra placed the bottle top inside the machine, dropped some glue and water in, and closed the door. She set the timer and turned to Harper. "Now for your prints. Follow me."

They crossed the room, and Harper was prepared for black fingers from an ink pad, but after taking off her gloves, Sierra went to a computer down the way and tapped on a black cube with blue light. "We'll start with your thumbs. Press them firmly against the screen."

Right. With all the technology Harper had seen in this building, she should've expected an electronic scanner. No old-school methods here.

They worked through her fingers a pair at a time until all ten prints were recorded on Sierra's computer.

"Okay, you're good to go." Sierra smiled.

"How long before we know on the prints?" Aiden asked.

Sierra spun in her chair. "The cyanoacrylate takes about ten minutes, so we have five minutes or so left."

"Could we wait?" Harper asked, not sure if Aiden or Sierra would be the one to answer.

"Sure." Sierra flashed an excited smile up at Harper. "It'll give me time to have that chat with you."

13

"Or we can take the DNA swabs down to Emory and come back," Aiden said to his sister, giving her a pointed look.

"You could go, and I could talk with Harper." She gave him an innocent smile that he knew was far from it.

She'd obviously picked up on his interest in Harper and was going to pursue it. Her recent marriage to Reed Rice, a stellar FBI agent, made her determined to marry off every brother. They'd heard about it plenty of times already. More than a single man could endure. But they put up with it. How could they not when they loved her, often spoiled her, and wanted to see her happy?

Still, he didn't want her messing with a work client. "I'm sure Harper would like to meet Emory and see her lab."

"Sure," Harper said, though he couldn't tell if she really meant it.

"We'll be back in a few." He grabbed the swabs and headed for the door, listening to be sure he heard Harper's boot heels click across the floor behind him.

"Your sister really doesn't look like most of you guys," Harper said in the hallway.

He headed down the hall toward the DNA lab, thinking

for a second before answering. He didn't think he should share that Sierra had a different dad. She'd recently just discovered that, and it was her story to tell.

"She takes after our mom," he said, feeling like he was almost lying by withholding the whole story. "So does Erik."

"Yeah, I can see that resemblance," Harper said. "She continues to amaze me with her knowledge."

"Tops in her field." Aiden wasn't surprised that he sounded like a proud brother. He was proud of her. Very. And proud of all of his siblings. He was incredibly blessed to have been raised by two Christian parents who taught them values and respect for others. Gave them a good foundation for when they rebelled in high school and college, which most of them did. But thankfully, they'd all found their way back to center.

He pressed his fingers on the print reader outside the DNA lab. The place was bustling with Emory and three of her techs. Not surprising. Processing DNA was the bread-and-butter income for Veritas.

He looked at Emory with fresh eyes as Harper would be doing. Emory had shoulder-length honey-red hair and large brown eyes behind black glasses that fixed on them when they walked in. She wore a lab coat, covering the pooch she still carried from her recent pregnancy.

She smiled at them, a sincere welcome-to-my-world smile, and Aiden introduced Harper.

"The skier." Emory stared at Harper. "You're amazing on the slopes. Don't you get scared going so fast?"

Harper looked as if she'd heard this question a million times before. "Raises my adrenaline for sure."

Emory shook her head in disbelief. "I could never do it. Good on you for being brave enough to handle it."

Aiden didn't want to spend more time here than it took Sierra to fume the fingerprints, so he moved closer to explain about the stalker without the rest of her staff over-hearing.

Emory looked at Harper. "Oh, wow, I'm sorry about that."

A tight smile claimed Harper's mouth. "That's something that scares me for sure."

"I can totally understand." Emory looked at Aiden. "I assume those are DNA swabs for me."

"They are." He handed them to her. "From Harper's water bottle. Sierra will likely be bringing you more samples from the things the stalker sent to Harper."

Emory gave a firm nod. "I'll make them a priority along with these."

Harper's eyes suddenly glistened with tears, surprising Aiden. She'd seemed so calm and even in a joking mood as she'd raced him up the stairs.

"I'm sorry about getting emotional on you." She fanned her face. "But you all are so wonderful to put everything aside and help me like this."

Emory waved a hand. "Of course. Aiden and his brothers are like family, and we'll go to the ends of the earth for family."

Aiden's heart swelled at her attitude. Emory wasn't just spouting words. They did whatever they could to help Nighthawk not only survive, but thrive. Sure, they thought of them as family, but the Veritas team lived their faith, helping others all the time. He looked forward to the time that Nighthawk was successful enough to do the same thing.

"We'll let you get to it," he said. "And thanks from us too."

The door opened, and Emory's husband, Blake, entered, carrying their fussing baby. Amelia was about three months old with pudgy cheeks and a cute button nose. Right now, that was all usurped by red watery eyes and a face screwed up in displeasure.

Blake glanced between them and spoke loudly. "Hope I'm not interrupting, but someone thinks it's dinner time."

Emory eagerly took her daughter. "Aw, don't cry, precious. Are you hungry?" She cradled the baby against her chest. "Excuse me. This little one takes top priority."

She cooed sweet words as she went to a door at the back of the room. When she closed the door behind her, silence reined in the lab again.

Aiden introduced Harper to Blake. "Blake's a former sheriff in Cold Harbor and is now the investigator here at Veritas."

He shook hands with Harper. "Glad I ran into you two. Grady and I can babysit the motel room. Just text the address, and we'll get on it as soon as we can."

Aiden shared the details they had on Gurly. "He has a warrant out for his arrest, so if he shows, call me and 911."

"Will do." Blake shifted his focus to Harper. "And I'm sorry to hear about your stalker."

"Thank you," she said, her eyes narrowed as if thinking about the guy brought her pain.

Aiden offered his hand to Blake. "Thanks, man. We owe you."

He shook forcefully and grinned. "And you know I'll call it in."

Aiden returned the smile with an exaggerated grimace. "Do you by any chance know a Detective Johnson at PPB?"

"I know *of* him. Seems like a capable detective."

"He's working Harper's investigation, and he said he'd send over a copy of his casebook today, but I haven't seen it."

"Let me know if he doesn't follow through, and I'll check in with a lieutenant I know over there."

"Thanks, man." Aiden led the way out of the lab and found Nick stepping out of the stairwell.

He held out a flash drive. "Brendan told me you were down here. This is the raw video footage for this year's ski competitions."

"Perfect." Aiden took the drive and pocketed it.

"The enhanced photo Erik texted me is on there as well. Too grainy to make out an ID"—he focused on Harper—"but maybe he'll look familiar to you."

"That was quick," Aiden said.

"Yeah, well, I know it's important to you." He got a boyish grin on his face. "Don't tell my other clients that I keep bumping their jobs for you."

"Thank you," Harper said. "I'm so blessed by all your help."

"It's what we're here for. And the team is just finishing up the tenant backgrounds too. Nothing out of the ordinary so far, but I'll send them to you as soon as they're done. And let me know if you have any questions about the items on the drive." Nick jetted back into the stairwell.

"He seemed like he was in a hurry," Harper said.

"Busy guy, as are all the partners here."

"And yet they stopped everything to help me. I don't know how to thank them."

"I feel the same way, but they honestly don't want thanks. They're glad to do it." Aiden opened the trace evidence lab door, releasing a strong chemical smell. He didn't know how his sister worked in the smell all day. Actually, he didn't know how she worked in a lab at all. Sure, she got out to go to crime scenes, but he needed more of a variety in his day, and their new agency really provided that for him.

Sierra looked up from the fingerprint station, Harper's water bottle still in her hand. "Oh, good. You're back. Just finished. Most of the prints on the bottle match yours, Harper, but I got one partial from the top that didn't."

"Is it enough to run through AFIS for a match?" Aiden asked, hoping the prints would be in the FBI's Automated Fingerprint System.

"Sorry, no, but it's enough for comparison to any complete prints you can provide." Sierra set down the bottle. "If I had Gurly's actual prints, I could manually compare them."

Aiden was baffled. "His prints are in AFIS. Can't you get them from the database to compare against?"

"No," Sierra said. "Law enforcement can input specific names in the database, but we're limited to querying the database with prints we've recovered from a crime scene."

A pang of disappointment hit Aiden. "What about Reed? Can you ask him to check the database?"

She turned a frown in Aiden's direction. "We might be married, but you know I can't do that. He'd lose his job at the FBI. I would never have asked one of you when you were in law enforcement, either."

"I know, but..." He shoved a hand into his hair. "Then I need to get Gurly's prints from Johnson or Walters or have them give you probable cause to do so."

"If Gurly has a record, Johnson can look them up," Sierra said.

"He doesn't even know we've identified Gurly. I'll call him, but instead of waiting around for an answer we could go back to Gurly's motel room and recover his prints."

Sierra frowned. "That's not a good idea. It's one thing to search the room, but what if Gurly *is* Harper's stalker and there's evidence in that room that could be used to convict him? If we unlawfully enter and take samples, it will nullify any samples taken when the room is processed by the police."

Aiden crossed his arms. "Not if they don't know."

"It's impossible to take fingerprints and not leave powder behind." Sierra narrowed her eyes. "You know I'm right, Aiden. You need to let your brain take over here, not your heart."

She *was* right. He was letting his interest and the strong desire to protect Harper usurp his common sense. That was a recipe for disaster and one that could get her killed.

He relaxed his arms and planted his hands on his waist. "Then I best find a way to get Johnson or Walter's to turn over Gurly's prints."

"Maybe reading Johnson's case file will give you the ammunition you need," Harper said.

"If Johnson has identified Gurly since we talked to him and thinks his prior arrests are related, he could have Gurly's prints in his casebook." Aiden worked hard not to frown and raise Harper's unease. "If he doesn't have it delivered soon, Blake said he would go above his head to a lieutenant he knows."

"Then you better hope he gets it sent over soon," Sierra said. "I've worked with enough detectives that I know pressuring him to get the file might backfire on you."

"I can call the Denver detective first thing in the morning," Aiden said. "I need to follow up on his case file anyway. And based on the charges against Gurly, he should be able to get a search warrant for the motel room and have Johnson serve it. Then all I need to do is convince him to let us in on any evidence they find."

On the drive to Harper's condo, she'd sat in the backseat running through everything they'd learned today. When they'd arrived at her place, Brendan and Erik went to the guest rooms to take a quick nap. Clay stood guard in the lobby, and Drake took a seat in a chair next to the elevator.

Aiden hadn't said a word the whole time. His lips were pressed tight, and his shoulders slumped. Clearly he was disappointed in not having Gurly's prints to compare to the partial from the bottle and was likely wishing he still had the same access to records as a law enforcement officer. But the minute he got back to her place, he dialed Coop. For over an hour now, they'd been coordinating her mother's fundraiser, Aiden making diagrams on a notepad as they spoke.

The fundraiser. Talk about something Harper didn't care if she attended. But if Aiden deemed it safe, she would go for her mother's sake. Or maybe she just didn't want to tell her mother she wouldn't be going. Her mother didn't respond well to the word no. She would just pick up the phone and badger Harper until she gave in.

Harper stifled a sigh. She was a strong woman. At least she tried to be, but when it came to her mother, she reverted to thinking like a child. She didn't like doing it and tried not to. But did you ever outgrow feeling like a child with your parents? Maybe some people did, but her mother still tried her best to rule Harper's life.

Aiden ended his call and she opened her mouth to talk to him but he made another call. She glanced at the clock above the fireplace. Only four o'clock. Not time to get ready for tonight yet.

"Johnson." Aiden's annoyed voice broke through her thoughts. "Did you get my message? I need to talk to you. I don't have your casebook on my desk, and I have information on the man in the photo and other details on the investigation that you need to hear about. Call me back ASAP."

He started to shove his phone into his pocket but it dinged, and he looked at the screen as he came to sit next to her on the sofa. "We're good to go with Coop at Blackwell and your mom's staff. I also got a text from Nick, and he cleared the waiters for tonight so we can attend. All I need to know is the dress code."

"Black tie."

"Figures," Drake said, and Aiden made a face as if he wanted to groan.

She looked at each of them. "I take it you all don't like that."

"Don't mind dressing up, but..." Drake ran a finger around the collar of his shirt. "Not in a penguin suit."

"It'll only be for a few hours," Aiden said. "Just pretend it's your dress uniform from the army."

"Yeah, that was equally uncomfortable." Brendan grinned. It was lopsided, and he had a slight dimple in his right cheek.

Harper could easily see women falling for him. *If* they could get used to his straightforward personality. But seeing all of his brothers in tuxes? Just seeing Aiden in a tux? Oh, yeah. She could easily imagine how fine he would look, and her heart fired in response.

"We brought the appropriate clothes just in case, so no worries," Aiden said. "We won't stick out."

Harper doubted that. The handsome Byrd brothers in tuxes would most definitely stick out. At least to the women attending the event.

Aiden's phone rang. "It's Maya."

He answered. "I'm assuming you're calling about results. I'm putting you on speaker so Harper can hear."

"I do have results," Maya said, but she sounded apprehensive. "The white powder on the lip of the bottle was ketamine."

"One of the date rape drugs?" Aiden asked.

"Well, technically it's a general anesthesia," she said. "But yes, it's one of the top three date rape drugs."

Unbelievable. Harper shook her head and stared open-mouthed at Aiden as she tried to process the news. "So he wasn't trying to poison me but knock me out?"

"Exactly," Maya said, her tone laced with disgust.

"But why?" Harper continued to stare at Aiden. "I had bodyguards, and even if I was drugged, he couldn't get to me."

Aiden shrugged. "Maybe he believed he could best us somehow."

She took a long breath and let it out. "Then he really *is* delusional."

"You should also know," Maya said. "I swabbed the side of the bottle too. I found an herbicide. Norflurazon is the trade name."

Aiden's eyes narrowed. "What's it used for?"

"It's a preemergent herbicide. You spread it to kill weeds before they emerge from the soil."

Aiden stared at his phone. "So it could have many uses, including at the produce farm where Gurly works."

"Yes," Maya said. "Likely came from his clothing, and, if the bottle was left by the stalker, this could rule out Matthew, as he's in Vermont."

Aiden looked at Harper. "Unless he had someone do it for him, but that's not typical behavior for a stalker. They want, no need, to see their victim's reaction. So this could further confirm we're on the right track with Gurly. Or could even point to Tanner, right? He works on a farm."

Harper nodded, but her gut cramped at the news. Could it really be Tanner? Was she foolish for writing him off? She didn't see it, but she had to admit that the evidence meant she couldn't rule him out as a suspect.

"Is there any way to track who buys the stuff?" Aiden asked.

"It's banned in other countries, but I don't know how widely used it is in our country. Especially here in Oregon, where so many farms are environmentally conscious. Let me check around and see what I can find."

"Thanks, Maya." Aiden ended the call and looked at her. "If Gurly has herbicide residue on his hands, he has to be working right now. We need to contact farms in the area."

"Oregon is a big agriculture state so the list will be long," Harper said. "Though we can rule out organic farms right away, which is a large number of farms here. And maybe we should talk to Tanner. Just in case."

"*I* need to talk to him. Alone. He might not feel free to talk in front of you."

"But I—"

"If he's your stalker, it would be dangerous to bring you to see him. He could snap." Aiden eyed her with his this-is-not-optional look that she was beginning to recognize. "It's for your own good."

"Okay." She took a few deep breaths and blew them out slowly before she let her disappointment get to her and said something harsh. "But I would still like to look Tanner in the eye. I think I could tell if he was guilty just by looking at him."

"We can't take that risk." He curled his fingers. "After the ketamine, we have to be hyper-vigilant.

"You're the expert." She'd hired this amazing man and his brothers to keep her safe. Even though she wanted to talk to Tanner, she would follow Aiden's advice.

"I wish we could trace the ketamine," he said. "It's mostly used in hospitals and vet clinics. But it's also readily available on the street. Tracing it will be nearly impossible."

She shook her head. "It shocks me that drugs like these

find their way to the streets. But I'm pretty naïve when it comes to that. Well, except for performance enhancing steroids. They're an issue in the sports world for sure."

"I wish I hadn't seen as much as I did as an ATF agent, but when you find firearms and alcohol, you often find drugs."

"I'll bet that's part of the job that you don't miss."

"And you'd be right. The hardest part was seeing families torn apart by it. My heart goes out to every parent who has a child involved with drugs."

Harper could feel his sincere pain, and she wished more people could see the hearts of most law enforcement officers. They really did want to serve and defend the public above all.

"Looks like we have just enough time to check out the enhanced photo from Nick before we need to get ready for tonight. Unless you need more time."

She wanted to look her best tonight, knowing her mother would criticize if Harper hadn't taken great care with her appearance, but she wanted to see this photo more. "I'm good."

She scooted closer to the screen. Aiden opened the image. It was blurry, the person's features just out of reach.

"Recognize him?" Aiden asked.

She squinted. "I don't know. Could be Gurly."

"What about Tanner? Could it be him?"

"Yeah, but I wouldn't testify to either one. It's just too blurry to know."

Aiden sat back. "Tell me more about Tanner. Did he just not make the grade or did something else derail his skiing career?"

"Unfortunately, he never was a top skier." She frowned over the memories of when they broke up. "To compensate, he started taking steroids. He still didn't make the cut, and he was bitter about that. Started selling the drugs and ended up in prison. When he got out, he seemed to put it all behind him. Left the ski world altogether and went to work with his dad."

"How long ago was that?"

She sat back to think. "I guess it would've been around ten years ago."

"They didn't do routine DNA samples back then, but his prints would be in the system and Sierra could use the partial to compare. But even if we get Tanner's prints and there's no match, he could've worn gloves. Just like Gurly could've worn them."

She shook her head. "I just don't see Tanner as being my stalker."

"You could be right." He didn't sound convinced, but Brendan and Erik came down the hallway, taking Aiden's attention.

She ran her gaze over their tuxes. They looked wonderful, but Harper wasn't attracted to them. Not at all. It was amazing how God created men and women to be interested in certain people. That was the only explanation for having eyes just for Aiden when this sea of handsome men were about to be surrounding her.

Brendan walked over to Drake. "Time to go make yourself look pretty. Not that you can, but you can try."

Drake rolled his eyes and reached out to punch Brendan in the shoulder, but he ducked out of the way. After Drake headed down the hallway, Brendan took a seat.

Erik stabbed the elevator button. "I'll go relieve Clay so he can come up and change."

Aiden looked at his watch. "We should get ready too."

"Do you need anything before I go to my room?" she asked.

"I'm good. But thanks for asking."

Silence descended on them, and the atmosphere suddenly turned awkward. She didn't know why but left it alone and headed to her room to change. As she showered, the call from Maya came to mind. Visions of things her stalker could have done to her if he'd succeeded in getting to her played out before her eyes. The steamy air thickened until she couldn't breathe.

Here she'd been thinking about how handsome the brothers were in tuxedos when she should have been focused on the guns under their jackets and how good they were at keeping her safe. Tonight, that was all that mattered.

She quickly dried off and put on a silky black dress with a red lace overlay that her mother had bought for her. Then, she spent a little extra time twining her hair up and putting on makeup, which she seldom did. Thoughts of the stalker continued to plague her as she walked down the hallway to her family room, and she purposefully let them play out to remind herself to be safe.

That was until she got a look at Aiden.

Oh my. He leaned against her counter and was peering at his phone. He looked like James Bond in the tux. She didn't know which version of Bond, but he looked darkly dangerous and incredibly sexy. She felt the need to fan her face.

Breathe. Just breathe.

He looked up from his phone and ran his gaze over her, his expression appreciative. Their eyes met in an explosion of emotion, and that was it. She was a goner. Totally a goner. She would have to fight to keep her mind on her safety tonight where it needed to be. That is, if she wanted to follow any directions he offered to keep her alive.

14

Brendan pulled into the hotel parking garage, and Aiden got a clear view of the lobby swarming with guests on their way to the fundraiser. He didn't like what he was seeing. Not one bit. Looked like chaos. But Gage's team had vetted the guests and the wait staff, and Aiden trusted the Blackwell team to do a thorough job.

Brendan rolled to a stop in front of the locked staff entrance that led to a hallway and gave them access to the staff-only elevator. He looked over the seat at Aiden. "We'll get the door open and call the elevator."

While he exited the vehicle with Clay, Aiden looked at Harper. "Once in the hallway, we head to the right and straight into the elevator. No stopping for any reason. Understood?"

She fidgeted with her hands resting on her lap. "Got it."

He jerked his gaze from her coat before he started thinking about the sheer red lace of her dress. When she'd stepped out of her bedroom, his jaw had hit the floor. The sleeveless V-neck dress clung to her every curve and accentuated her toned body as if it had been custom made for her.

Thankfully, after she'd put on her coat, he handed her a Kevlar vest, which put his focus right where it needed to be.

Clay signaled for them to join him.

"Stay put while I open your door." Aiden jumped out and took a long look through the parking garage. Erik and Drake had already cleared it and manned the entrance gate, keeping anyone from entering until they had Harper in the elevator, but still, Aiden wouldn't let down his guard.

He opened her door, and she slid out her long legs and feet covered in strappy sandals with heels high enough to put her almost on his eye level.

He took her arm and hurried her forward, those heels clicking on the concrete.

"I know we have to go fast, but if you could slow down just a bit," she said. "I'm not used to wearing heels, and I don't want to do a face-plant."

He eased off some but kept them moving, and they stepped into the elevator with Clay, leaving Brendan to have their backs and secure the vehicle.

"We're clear," Aiden said into his comms for Drake and Erik. "Join us in the room."

"Roger that," came their replies.

The elevator opened at another hallway. Clay went ahead while Aiden held the elevator.

"Clear," Clay said.

Aiden looked at Harper. "We're a go. Please make sure you stay at my side at all times."

She gave him a nervous smile. "Glad too."

If he wasn't focused on protecting her now, he'd take time to ponder her response and if it held a double meaning, but he had to pin his whole attention on her safety. They moved down the hallway past uniformed waitstaff and into the kitchen. They approached the checkpoint where

Jackson Lockhart, a big muscular guy with short dark hair, blocked the entrance to the room. Clay nodded at Jackson and eased past him to check out the room.

Aiden shook hands with Jackson and introduced him to Harper.

"Nice to meet you," Jackson said. "Your mother talks about you all the time."

"Some of it good, I hope." She chuckled.

"She's very proud of all you've accomplished."

Harper's forced smile said she wasn't as convinced of that.

"Everything quiet?" Aiden asked.

"Very." Jackson frowned. "Maybe too quiet, if you know what I mean."

Aiden nodded. Jackson was referring to that hinky feeling they often got when something seemed wrong, but they couldn't put a finger on it.

Jackson stepped back. "Your mother's waiting for you."

"I'll take the vest." Aiden held out his hand.

She ripped off the Velcro, and he set the vest on a nearby shelf for the trip back to the car. "After you."

She stepped in front of him and slid out of her coat. He was acutely aware of how her dress plunged in the back, revealing creamy skin that looked very kissable. He snapped his gaze up to his brother Clay. "We good."

"All clear. I've got this covered."

Aiden looked at Harper. "Erik's at the front door with Alex and Riley from Blackwell, along with two of your mother's detail. Coop's with your mother, as are two of her staff. Brendan and Drake will be at midpoint with the last two troopers on her detail. So the room is fully covered. But remember. Operators outside of Nighthawk are all here for your mother. We're the ones you need to listen to."

"Got it," she said with a firm tone, but then nibbled on her lip.

"Let's check your coat and join your mother."

She took a long breath as if she dreaded the meeting, but maybe she just didn't like attending events like this. He sure wouldn't want to, but he admired her loyalty to her mother.

They entered the room, and Aiden inhaled the fresh smell of dill filling the air. They wound their way through round tables covered in white cloth and laid with service for the dinner. Conversations hummed around them as dressed-up partygoers filled the aisles, talking and drinking cocktails. Most were seated at the tables. A good number of them noticed Harper and stared as the buzz of the crowd lowered a notch. Some stuck out a hand to shake and acknowledge her accomplishments.

She smiled and thanked them for supporting her mother. Aiden discovered she used three canned lines that varied as she talked to the guests. Though canned, she delivered them with sincerity that he had to wonder if she felt. He also had to wonder what it must be like to be so recognized. True, she didn't have Hollywood celebrity status, but these people obviously knew who she was and what she'd accomplished.

Took five minutes to reach the coat check and they dropped her coat off. Nearby, the governor had her hand tucked into her husband's arm, deep in discussion with an elderly man who looked like he might drop if she let go. Coop stood next to her, his gaze roaming over the crowd. Two men in suits from the governor's official detail took up a stance on either side of them. Coop nodded at Aiden, who gave a clipped nod in acknowledgment.

Her mother waved a hand, beckoning Harper, who frowned. Aiden didn't know if seeing her mother caused her mood or if it was from the person her mother was talking to.

Her father extricated himself, hurried toward them, and hugged Harper. He stepped back and looked into her eyes. "How you holding up, sweetheart?"

"I'm good." She gave him the first genuine smile Aiden had seen since they'd come into the room. "This is Aiden Byrd."

"Nelson Young. Nice to officially meet you." Her father shook hands but continued to assess her with deep brown eyes like Harper's. "Have you gotten any more messages or gifts?"

She looked at him for a long moment as if deciding what to say. "My water bottle was tampered with at Timberline."

He grimaced. "Tampered with how?"

"We found white powder on the rim. It was ketamine, an anesthesia often used as a date rape drug. And they found herbicide on the outside of the bottle. Norflurazon."

He paled and grabbed her arm. "This is escalating beyond belief. Promise me you won't go back to Timberline."

She patted his hand. "No worries. I've already decided not to. And on the bright side, we're making some progress in finding my stalker."

His eyebrow went up, reminding Aiden of Harper's quizzical looks. "You are?"

She nodded overly hard, maybe trying to convince herself. "We even have a strong suspect. Guy's name is Jeffry Gurly. Ring a bell for you?"

Her dad shook his head, the color coming back into his tanned face, but he still had a sick expression. The guy had to be hurting. Aiden couldn't begin to imagine how hard it must be as a father to have a daughter with a stalker. Aiden imagined being married to Harper and having an adorable daughter that looked just like her. If his child was in this situation, he wouldn't just have a sick look on his face. No. He would want to kill the creep, and a murderous rage would be beaming from his face.

"Who is he?" her father asked. "And what do you know about him?"

Harper clutched her hands together, the only hint that this conversation bothered her. She was doing an incredible job of hiding her feelings. Likely so her dad wouldn't worry. Aiden didn't want to focus on her, but she kept impressing him with her actions. Had been for days now. Which didn't bode well for his no-serious-relationships rule.

"A former ski coach who went to prison for sex with underage skiers," she said. "Now that he's out, he's been accused again."

Her dad shook his head, his gaze wary.

"You're sure you don't recognize the name?" Aiden asked.

"Positive."

The governor excused herself and joined them. She gave Harper a brief hug. "You look exquisite."

"As do you," Harper said, her tone more formal than with her father.

The governor turned her attention to Aiden. "And you and your team all look sharp tonight. Thank you for taking extra care to try to fit in."

Aiden nodded and felt Harper running her gaze over him. He wanted to see what she might be feeling, but he kept his gaze roving the room, where more of the guests had taken a seat, giving him a better view of the entire space.

The governor took Harper's arm. "The program's about to begin. Harper, you're seated at my table."

They started toward the main table on a raised platform

in the front of the room. Aiden, the governor's men, and Coop followed.

Aiden made eye contact with Harper before she sat. "I'll be nearby if you need me."

She smiled at him. For a second, he imagined what it might be like to be dressed up and on a date with her instead of this public gathering.

"Everything going well on your detail?" Coop asked.

Aiden shrugged. "We're making progress. Yours?"

"No additional threats," Coop said, keeping his focus on the governor. "You ever consider our situations are related?"

"I gave it some consideration, but there's nothing pointing in that direction."

"Agreed, but we're not ruling it out."

"Us, either."

Governor Young stepped up to the podium and spoke to her guests. Aiden listened but let his gaze continue to roam the room. Near the end of her talk, she introduced Harper, who said a few words and received a vigorous round of applause. He recalled the first things he'd read about her being a prima donna. He'd seen nothing in her behavior to support that. Perhaps it was just a symptom of being in the limelight. Others got jealous and put negative things out there to sell news. If so, he hated that for her.

The speaking ended, and waiters hustled into the room carrying large trays. Aiden kept his eye on the male serving Harper's table. When the guy lingered a bit too long near Harper, Aiden started for them, but the guy moved on.

"Clay, report," Aiden said into his comms unit.

"All clear."

"Erik?"

"Clear here too. Arrivals have stopped."

Aiden let out a relieved breath but didn't let his guard down. He occasionally met Harper's gaze as he looked around, and she smiled every time. He responded with a quick nod when he wanted to smile back, but it would be unprofessional.

Finally, the meal ended, and, when she got up, he joined her. She gave him one of those luminous smiles.

He swallowed hard. "Ready to go?"

"Not quite yet." She sighed. "I need to greet people and work the room for Mom before we can leave."

He didn't like the answer, but he nodded. "Let me know about ten minutes before you're ready to depart so I can get everyone in place."

"Will do." She moved gracefully among the guests, using the same prepared lines she'd used earlier, and he stayed close to her side. Somehow she remembered which one to use not to repeat herself. He figured she had to do this not only for her mother, but at events she attended for her career. He didn't envy her at all.

After nearly an hour, she turned to him. "Ten minute warning."

He leaned down to his mic. "We're leaving."

Brendan and Drake headed for the vehicles. Erik remained at the front door, and Clay stayed put at the back.

Transport was the riskiest part of this situation, and Aiden sharpened his gaze. That hinky feeling was still with him, but everything seemed to be going fine. Could be the reason for his apprehension. Protective details rarely went off without a hitch.

Harper looked at him. "Let's grab my coat and get out of here."

"Gladly." He moved with her to the coat check, keeping his eye on the room since his brothers' departure had left the middle area unprotected.

"Vehicle's ready," Brendan said over the comms. "I have eyes on the door."

"We're good to go," Aiden told Harper.

"Just let me say good-bye to my parents on the way out." She crossed to them, and he continued to scan the room as she hugged them.

Her mother looked up at him. "Good night, Aiden. Thank you for the good job you're doing in keeping Harper safe."

Would she say the same thing if she knew he'd developed feelings for her daughter? Still, he nodded at the governor and then shook hands with her father.

Aiden's gut was warning him to take care, and he kept moving his focus as they headed for the back door, where they held up while Clay marched into the kitchen to clear the area to the elevator. Aiden retrieved the vest and handed it to Harper.

"We still clear?" Aiden asked in his comms unit while she fastened the Velcro.

"Crystal," Brendan said.

"Clear here too," Clay said.

Aiden liked the sound of that, but it didn't mean he could let his guard down. "Erik and Drake, move. On our way to the elevator now."

They boarded the elevator, and when they stepped off, Aiden took Harper's arm. He moved at a good clip and safely got her settled in the SUV. He wanted to release a breath, but they weren't in the clear yet. "Erik and Drake, advance."

Brendan waited until their brothers were in the other vehicle and let them take lead. The SUV wound down the ramp and out onto the street behind Drake. Aiden let out his breath. They'd safely left the event, and were almost clear of any danger. He still had to keep vigilant until Harper was safely in her condo, but maybe it was time to admit his gut had been wrong.

Odd, because it rarely was.

He kept his head on a swivel on the short drive to her condo, where Brendan curled up the ramps in her parking garage. Brendan stopped close to the door, and Aiden and Clay hopped out. Clay gave Aiden a we-did-it look of satisfaction, but Aiden wouldn't celebrate just yet.

He opened Harper's door and held his hand out. She took it, and Aiden's eyes were drawn to her shapely legs and strappy shoes as she swung her feet out. But his breath stopped when he caught sight of something white peeking from under the floor mat.

"We have something here," he said to Clay and handed Harper off to his care.

Aiden lifted the mat, revealing an envelope addressed to Harper in the same handwriting as the previous letters she'd received. His stomach roiled.

He looked up at her. "It's another letter from your stalker."

Her eyes flashed open, and she clutched her chest. "But how could he access your vehicle?"

"That's what I want to know, and I will find out," Aiden said, knowing this was what his gut had been warning him about. "But just as much, I want to know what the letter says."

Harper rode the elevator to her condo as the chicken she'd eaten for dinner congealed in her stomach. Aiden held the unopened letter in an evidence bag, and Clay, arms crossed, stood near the doors. Drake and Brendan remained with the vehicle, which Sierra was on her way to process for prints, DNA, and any other trace evidence she could recover. Erik had gone ahead to make sure everything was safe in her condo before she entered her home.

Harper stared at the envelope, frantically twisting her ring. She couldn't imagine what the letter said. She wanted to know, and yet, she didn't. She wasn't sure if she could handle another offending message.

"I can open it for you," Aiden said. He was scowling, and anger burned in his eyes. She didn't know if it was due to the actual letter, or because he felt like he'd failed her when the stalker had gotten so close.

"I need to do this myself," she said. "No matter what it says."

The doors opened, revealing Erik, who stood tall and strong just inside her condo. He gave a sharp nod. "Everything's clear here. Unless you need me for something else, I'll head down for lobby duty."

"Go ahead. But keep your eyes open."

Erik nodded. After a long look at Harper that she couldn't interpret, he waited for the three of them to exit the elevator and he boarded the elevator. The doors whooshed closed behind him.

She followed Aiden to her big dining table and sat. Tension was as sharp as a knife in the room and she stared at the letter in Aiden's hands. She just couldn't bring herself to open it yet.

Clay remained standing by the elevator. It whirred into action again, and Clay spun, his hand going to his gun.

The door soon split open, and Brendan stepped inside. He nodded at Clay then joined Harper and Aiden at the table. "Searched the vehicle before I came in. Didn't find anything else."

Aiden let out a long breath. What did he think they might find? She supposed the stalker could've put anything, including a bomb in the car, but she didn't really see that happening. Still, it was possible.

Aiden laid the evidence bag with the letter in it on top of the rich mahogany dining table, and met Harper's gaze. "Are you ready to look at this?"

"I don't know." She shrugged out of her coat and joined him. "I don't think I'm over the shock that he was able to access your SUV."

"It's not surprising he knew where you were," Aiden said. "But it *is* surprising that he managed to get into our vehicle."

"How is it even possible?"

Brendan walked over to them. "Could be a relay attack. Someone would have to have been near Brendan with a device that picked up a signal from his key fob. Then he or she relayed that signal to the stalker, who was next to the vehicle. He then used it to open the SUV."

"How did he get such a device?" Harper asked.

"You can buy them on Amazon," Brendan said.

Aiden gave his brother a sharp look. "Seems like you would've mentioned this when we were customizing the vehicles."

Brendan didn't even flinch at the criticism, telling her he possessed the same inner strength as Aiden and was a confident man in his own right. He held up his phone. "I just read about it while I was on my way up here. We should modify our vehicles ASAP to get rid of the keyless entry system or somehow block the signal."

Aiden fisted his hands on the table. "You can be sure I'll be checking into that."

Brendan pointed at the letter. "Isn't opening the envelope more important right now?"

Aiden turned his attention to her, and the anger fled from his eyes, replaced by concern for her. "Ready to open?"

She lifted her shoulders. "As ready as I can be to see what this creep has to say."

He handed her a pair of latex gloves.

She took her time putting them on, hoping the increasing acid in her stomach that burned up her throat would go away, but it didn't. She took the envelope from the evidence bag, carefully slit it open, and pulled out the letter.

Before she unfolded the paper, she dropped onto a chair for support. She lifted the top fold and then the bottom, pressing the white paper out on the wood.

Aiden peered over her shoulder. Big childish letters in bright red ink said, *Why do you think anyone can keep us apart? We're meant to be together. Ditch the He-men. You are mine. Mine only, and I WILL have you.*

She stared at the words. She couldn't even process the message.

"Finding a letter under the floor mat most likely rules out Matthew even more," Aiden said. "He's still in Vermont, and he would've wanted to be there to see your reaction. Still, I can't prove he didn't find two guys to help him, so I'll ask for the local police to interview him and confirm he has an alibi."

She looked up at him. "Do you think Tanner has the skills to break into our car?"

"Most anyone could do it," Brendan said. "It's not like older model cars where a Slim Jim works. Can't use them on newer cars. He'd just need the internet to figure out how to use the key fob."

"Then I'm going to interview him first thing tomorrow." Aiden's phone rang, and he looked at the screen before answering. "What's up, Erik?"

He listened and scowled. "I'll send Clay down to get it."

He shoved his phone into his pocket and held her gaze.

"A package was delivered for you by courier while we were gone."

Her heart sank. "You think it's from him?"

"I do," he said, his eyes turning darkly angry again. "I really do."

15

Aiden held his breath and curled his hands as he watched Harper look into the box that the team had already checked for any lethal danger like a bomb or poison. The box contained a single folded piece of white paper that lay on the top of crumpled pink tissue paper.

She picked up the letter and pressed it open. Another handwritten message.

Can't you see I know you better than anyone, and we are meant to be together? Please say you're mine.

The sloppy letters matched those from the letter in the SUV. Aiden's gut tightened more.

She lifted out an item wrapped in tissue paper. She slowly ripped the tissue to reveal a miniature John Deere tractor.

She dropped it back in the box and looked at him. "I had a John Deere when I was a kid. Not a miniature one like this, but a pedal tractor that was my dad's from his childhood. He still has it in his barn. I rode it all the time when I was little. Was one of my favorites, and I thought I could pass it on to my child. But now?" She paused, her eyes sad and tortured. "Another memory destroyed."

"I'm sorry about that," Aiden said sincerely. "And I'm sorry that this is making it even more likely we're looking at Tanner."

"Agreed." She gaped at the letter and shook her head. "So, what now? Other than you going to talk to Tanner tomorrow?"

"The package tells us one more thing. Tanner, or whoever your stalker is, didn't deliver the package to the lodge so he knows where you live now." Aiden ground his teeth. "That's not good. We need to move you to a new location."

She frowned. "But can't you all stop him from getting in here?"

He didn't want to dilute her confidence in him and his brothers, but he had to tell the truth no matter how much he hated to answer her question. "I'd like to say we can, but you never know, and it's safest to move to an undisclosed location."

"But where?"

"Normally, I'd say we move you to the capitol with your mother because the security there is top-notch, but, with the threats to her, that would just double the danger for both of you."

"I could stay with my dad," she suggested.

Aiden shook his head. "It's clear by the gift that your stalker knows about your past. Which also means he's likely familiar with the farm. And if Tanner's your stalker, he'd be right next door."

"She could stay with us," Brendan chimed in.

Aiden eyed his brother. "That's not a good idea."

"Why not?" Brendan eyed him right back. "We have state-of-the-art security. Cameras we can monitor, Guards on duty twenty-four/seven. And we'll all be there."

He was right. It was a perfect solution. Except for having

the woman he shouldn't be interested in staying at his condo. Right. He was assuming she'd stay at his place not with one of his brothers. Or even Sierra.

"I need a gym," Harper said. "I might have agreed to stay away from the slopes, but I have to work out."

"We have a gym." Brendan smiled at her. "A nice one, actually."

She looked at Aiden. "I don't want to put you out."

He was being a jerk by making her feel this way. She could stay at the condos, and he could find a solution that worked for both of them. "No, it's fine. You can have my condo, and I'll bunk with Brendan."

Brendan's mouth dropped open. "Hey, I—"

"Will be glad to share." Aiden gave him a pointed stare.

"Right." Brendan grinned. "Just what I was going to say."

She looked between them a few times. "Okay, then it's settled. I'll just go pack."

Aiden watched her leave the room, wondering how it was going to go with her staying at the condos. On the one hand, he liked the idea. But on the other, he knew they could be playing with fire.

Clay stood. "Need to hit the restroom. You guys got this?"

Aiden nodded and sat back to rethink their plans while Clay headed toward the guest bathroom.

Brendan eyed him. "You got a thing for Harper."

"Not a thing exactly."

"And she's got a thing for you too."

Aiden shifted in the chair. "Don't sound so accusatory. I can't help that we're attracted to each other, but I'm not going to do anything about it and blow this gig for us." He hoped. "We need it too badly."

"Yeah, we need it, all right, but maybe God put her in your life for a reason—other than to keep her safe and give our agency the money we need."

"Like what?"

"Like so you can find someone to spend your life with."

Aiden raised an eyebrow and stared at Brendan. "You're the last brother I'd expect to mention finding someone."

Brendan blanched.

Aiden was so wrapped up in his own world, he didn't know when to keep his big mouth shut. "Hey, sorry, man. I shouldn't have brought that up."

"It's okay."

"No, it's not," Aiden said. "You're still grieving."

Brendan folded his hands on the table and stared at them. He had to be thinking about his former girlfriend, Tristen, who died about a year ago after a beating from her former boyfriend. "Not grieving exactly."

"Just blaming yourself."

He looked up, the pain of regret in his eyes. "If Tristen had only told me about that jerk, I could've saved her."

"But she didn't tell you, so how could you have done anything?"

"I couldn't but..." He shrugged.

Aiden got it. He would be feeling the exact same way if he were in Brendan's shoes, but Aiden's job as his brother wasn't to humor him, but to help him move on. As it stood now Brendan had sworn off dating and women all together. Same stance as Aiden held but for a far different reason.

"Hey." Brendan sat forward. "Way to change the subject. We were talking about you and Harper."

"Now's the wrong time for us," Aiden said and hoped to end the conversation. "Completely wrong."

"Not if it's God's timing."

Was Brendan right? Did God have His hand in bringing him together with Harper?

What a question. God had His hand in *everything* good.

"There's my kidney," Aiden added. "I don't know if I can saddle a woman with the risks I face."

"Harper's a strong woman. She can handle it." Brendan locked gazes with Aiden. "I mean, if you don't ask, you can't know, right?"

Aiden stared at the brother he was not only closest in age to, but they'd also hung out a lot when they were young, sharing most everything. But after their time in the military, they'd both clammed up. Still, Aiden was glad he had a brother who was willing to question his actions. Just not right now.

"Pretty wise words for such a punk," Aiden said to lighten the mood.

"Punk?" Brendan grimaced. "Only to an old guy like you."

"Seriously, thanks, bro." Aiden squeezed his shoulder. "I'll give it some thought."

Brendan gave him a tight smile. "Someday you'll see that I'm a competent adult and can give sound advice."

"Nah." Aiden waved a hand. "You'll always be my little brother, even when we're old and gray."

Brendan groaned.

Aiden liked joking with Brendan as it lightened his heart, but he didn't want to continue this conversation, and they had a job to do. "Text Erik and tell him we have a change of plans. I'll call Drake to see when we can use the SUV." He held his brother's gaze. "And let that be the end of this talk about me and Harper. I don't want the other guys to be concerned too."

"Um, bro." Brendan rolled his eyes. "I don't have to tell them anything. They might not be as astute as I am, but I'm sure they've figured it out for themselves." He laughed.

"If they say something, make sure you tell them I've got things under control." Aiden marched off toward the bedrooms to gather his things. Hopefully, he wouldn't make a liar of himself.

~

Aiden hadn't slept a wink on Brendan's couch, so he'd come up to his condo and relieved Brendan. He shifted on his couch to stare at the latest gift sitting on the dining table. All his fault. At least that's how he saw it. He'd tried to keep her from looking at it, but she'd insisted. Sure, he couldn't have stopped the delivery from arriving, but maybe he should've figured out that Gurly had located her address and changed her location before a gift arrived. She wouldn't have had to feel the incredible pain that came with knowing an unstable man knew where she lived.

Aiden curled his hands around his coffee mug and took deep breaths. His dreams—ha, nightmares—had been plagued by Gurly. His hands around Harper's neck, dragging her away. She was screaming, her eyes terrified. Aiden wanted to help, but he couldn't move. His feet were cemented to the ground. He'd tried to fight his way out of the dreams, but he kept sinking in deeper and, when Gurly dragged her into a car, Aiden had thankfully come awake.

Sweating, he'd taken a shower, and then came up to his own condo to relieve Brendan and review the report on the tenants, ruling them all out for the time being. Around four a.m., he started compiling a list of farms in the area.

His phone dinged, and he read the text from Blake. *All quiet at motel. No sign of Gurly. Will keep you updated.*

Aiden typed his thanks just as his bedroom door opened and Harper stepped out. She wore plaid pajama pants, purple fuzzy slippers, and a pink fuzzy fleece. Her hair was messed up, sticking out at all angles, and her eyes were sleepy. She yawned.

"Don't say a word about my hair," she said as she made a beeline to the coffee pot. "After thinking about Gurly last night, I had to shower and went to bed with it wet."

He actually found her messy hair endearing, but he wouldn't tell her that. "It's not bad. If you're a porcupine."

She laughed, and he loved the sound of her laugher in his condo. His home. He could get used to it for sure.

"Cups are in the cupboard above the pot," he said. "Did you sleep well?"

"Pretty good, how about you?" Her back was to him as she reached up for the cup, leaving a creamy strip of bare skin above her waistband. He jerked his gaze up. He'd had that talk with God last night. Not that it had helped. Aiden's feelings on why Harper was in his life or if she would be in his future weren't any clearer. What was clear, however, was that he needed to keep an open mind. To watch for God's hand and not immediately rule out a potential relationship.

Harper turned to him. "I wasn't expecting to see you here. I thought Brendan was on duty."

"Since I was up anyway, I told him to grab some sleep."

She sat on the end of the couch and sipped her coffee. "What are you working on?"

He held up his legal pad. "I'm just finishing the farm list. And FYI, I've read Nick's report on the building tenants and ruled them out. I'd start calling on the farm list, but I have to go to Salem to evaluate the venue for tonight. Unless I can convince you to skip the next event."

She set down her cup on the coffee table. "There are a lot of things I'd stay home from, but this isn't one of them."

She crossed her arms for good measure. "I'm going."

He stared at her, trying to figure out what to do. "Care to share why it's so important to you?"

"I have lots of reasons," she said, looking like she didn't want to share them all. "It's a fundraiser for a leukemia research organization. I'm the charity spokesperson, and the people attending are expecting me. Not only people suffering from leukemia, but the people who give so generously to the cause."

"Couldn't you postpone it?"

"Not without incurring significant costs for the organization."

"Then maybe we can stream a live video of you."

"No. That's not what they paid for, and I'm not going to disappoint them. I'm going." She took a breath. "Most of the time I'm just a PR pawn. Hawking this and that, my name used as an endorsement. But this is the one time of year I can use my name to do good, and it's something *I* choose to do. No one else. Me. It's more important to me than you know."

"Sounds personal."

She took a long breath and let it out. "I had a cousin who died from leukemia, and it would mean a lot to me to see a cure."

"Okay." He held up his hands. "I get it, and I want you to go if at all possible. Let me make sure it's safe."

He started to get up, but she took his hand and stopped him.

"Thank you. It really is important to so many sick people. If not, I would cancel. Honest."

With those open and beguiling eyes looking up at him, he'd promise almost anything, but he couldn't. "I'll do my best to find a safe way for you to attend. I should be back by noon, and then I'll interview Tanner. Drake dropped off one of the SUVs to have the windows retrofitted, and it should be ready by the fundraiser."

"You really think of everything, don't you?"

"Your life could depend on it."

Her smile faded, and he felt bad for making that

happen. But the damage had been done by his statement, and he couldn't change that. "While I'm gone, you can get started calling the farms if you'd like. I'll give you a list of questions to ask. If you don't get to them all, I can finish up when I get back. Plus, we can finally watch those uncut ski videos from the news media."

"I can also get my workout in while you're gone." She looked at the clock. "But how can you be back from Salem by lunch? Roundtrip, you have two hours minimum driving time, and knowing you, you'll want to be very thorough in your review of the venue."

"I arranged to use Gage Blackwell's helicopter. Riley will be heading out soon, and he'll standby to take us tonight. It not only makes the trip faster, but it eliminates a lot of dangerous time on the road."

"That must be costing me a pretty penny," she said.

"Actually, Gage is doing it for free. Says it makes your mother more comfortable, and he wants her to be happy."

"Sounds like a good plan then." She blew on the coffee in her mug.

He was feeling very at home with her here and could easily imagine having a conversation with her each morning. "Before we do anything, I want to cook breakfast for my brothers. To thank them for their hard work the last few days. That is, if it's okay with you."

"Sure." Enthusiasm rang through her tone. "I'd like to help."

"On one condition—you don't judge the quantity of food I prepare. We're all still growing boys." He laughed.

She chuckled. "No judgment on my part. But I would like to get dressed and do something with my hair first."

He nodded, though he liked the rumpled look. It made this moment feel so personal and drew him to her. He reached out to move a wayward strand. "I kind of like the messy Harper."

Her eyes widened. "I can't imagine why."

"Makes you seem more approachable than the all-together skier who has Olympic gold medals to her name."

"And is that good?" She rested her mug on her knee and searched his gaze. "The approachable part when we're committed to ignoring our feelings."

"In this moment"—he met and held her gaze—"it's fantastic."

He slid his fingers into her tangled hair to cup the back of her head. He could smell her minty toothpaste mixed with coffee.

"Aiden, we... I want..." She set her mug on the table, took a shuddering breath, and wrapped her arms around his neck, drawing him nearer.

His gaze went to her full lips then back to her big luminous eyes. "What do you want?"

"For you to kiss me. Now." She leaned closer.

Not a good idea. Not at all, but he was lost in her gaze. In the warmth she was sending his way. At the emotions ignited between them. He should ignore them. Completely.

No. Not now. Just one kiss wouldn't hurt.

He surrendered and lowered his head. Pressed his lips against hers. And kissed her like he'd been wanting to do for days. Letting all of that pent-up emotion drive him and tell her exactly how he felt.

16

Shock traveled through Harper. She'd never been kissed like this. Never wanted a kiss so badly. And never wanted it to end. The urgency. Intensity. A fire burning. Aiden ignited long-simmering feelings inside her.

The door opened. His brothers, joking and laughing, cut through her fog. She'd done exactly what she didn't want to do. Become unprofessional and kissed one of her bodyguards.

She jerked free of Aiden's arms, scooted down the couch, and ran a hand over her hair. Right. As if it would do anything to tame the mess or tame her wayward emotions.

"I'll just get dressed." She fled the room as the brothers stepped into it.

They'd gone quiet, something she'd learned was unusual for them. If Aiden's face was showing the emotions from the kiss like she suspected hers was displaying, she could only imagine what the guys were thinking.

Mortified, she rushed into the luxurious master bathroom. She'd showered in here, but had been too tired to think about the fact that it was Aiden's bathroom. Now she saw his products everywhere. She stopped to touch the plush towels on the holder. Run a finger over the handle of his razor. Stare at his shampoo and soap through the shower door.

"Face it." She touched her just-kissed lips. "You're falling for this guy. Falling hard."

And just what did she plan to do about it? Other than splash water on her face to cool it down?

The cold water snapped her out of her trance. Brought her back to her senses. She grabbed her hair straightener and started pressing out the wrinkles in her hair. Feeling like she was pressing out the wrinkles in her brain at the same time.

She was Aiden's client, and she knew that he needed this job to get their agency going. She wasn't going to ruin that for him or his brothers. No matter how much she was attracted to him. She would just have to swallow her feelings and remain professional. Starting with breakfast.

She put on jeans and one of her favorite worn and soft T-shirts, giving her comfort. She checked her hair one last time, took a breath for courage in facing four big strapping men who likely knew she'd been kissing their brother, and opened the door. The savory scent of frying sausage filled the air, and her stomach rumbled.

The guys were grouped around the island on bar stools, Aiden in the kitchen turning sausage links in a pan, his back to them and her. She stepped closer, and the talk of football ended as the brothers turned to look at her. Five sets of eyes, law enforcement inquisition in them, locked on her.

The power of his gaze reached clear across the room but she ignored it and went to a large carton of eggs sitting by a bowl and whisk on the counter. "So how many of these eggs do I need to crack? I hear you all like to eat a lot."

"All of them," Aiden said.

She fired him a questioning look. "Seriously, all eighteen?"

Aiden nodded and grinned. "Remember. Growing boys."

At his intimate smile, even though they were surrounded by his brothers, her promise to ignore him fled, and she smiled back. She got lost for a moment. Unwilling to look away.

"Need help with those eggs?" Drake asked. "'Cause we're starving."

Feeling the heat of embarrassment on her face, she snapped her focus back to the eggs. "I got it."

She began to break the shells, hitting them more forcefully than required and needing to remove bits of shell from the bowl. The guys went back to talking about the Seattle Seahawks, and she whipped the eggs into a frenzy.

Aiden's hand came over hers from behind. "I think you've got these well mixed."

She jerked free, nearly upsetting the bowl. He took it to the stove and poured the smooth liquid into a large frying pan.

How could he be so calm after that kiss? Maybe it hadn't affected him the same way. After all, he'd probably kissed a lot of women, while she, on the other hand, had experienced very few kisses in her life. It was probably no big deal to him. Sure. That was it. And a good thing, too, as it wouldn't be a problem going forward.

"I can cook them," she said, trying for casual.

"Go for it." He stepped over to a four-slot toaster to drop in thick slices of wheat bread. He went to the refrigerator and got out a giant bottle of orange juice and put it on the island. "Someone get the dishes."

"I got it." Brendan jumped up.

Harper stirred the gooey egg mixture, watching it solidify and form fluffy lumps. She needed things in her life to solidify too. Like, what was she going to do after her skiing career ended? And what was she going to do about Aiden? They would eventually catch her stalker, and then she would be free to pursue her feelings. If he was keen on the idea. But with her crazy travel schedule, she'd never even tried to enter into a long-term relationship. She'd seen plenty of her teammates fail at it even to consider it. Besides, she was totally into training. But she'd never felt this way about a guy before, and that could change things. And, if the kiss didn't affect him, he might not be as into her as she was into him.

Visions of standing here without his brothers in the future filled her mind. Not with a giant pan of eggs but just a few for the two of them. A real domestic scene. Which would be followed by her going away for weeks on end. Months even. And them breaking up.

"Those look about done," Aiden said.

She looked up to find him standing close enough for her to catch the fresh scent of his shampoo. To be able to reach out if she wanted and draw him close. She wanted. How she wanted, but she wouldn't.

"Do you have a bowl, or should I just put the pan on the island?" she asked, working hard to keep her emotions in check.

"We're perfectly fine with the pan." He looked at her like this was more than a statement. Maybe a test to see what she thought about not using a serving bowl.

"Sounds good." She turned off the burner and settled the pan on potholders on the island.

Erik, the closest brother, scooped a huge pile of fluffy eggs onto his plate that already held two slices of golden brown toast and five sausage links.

"Thanks," he said and dug into the eggs like a man deprived of food for months.

She grabbed a glass and poured orange juice, sipping on it and watching the others load their plates.

"Hey," Aiden said when he came to the island with another stack of toast. "Ladies first."

She waved a hand. "Go ahead. I can wait."

"You sure?" Brendan asked, spoon filled with eggs midair.

"Positive. I like seeing you all together like this. As an only child, I never had the joy of a big family event."

"Lucky." Drake grabbed the egg spoon Brendan had laid down. "Growing up, we always had to do things in order of names. All except Sierra. She got first dibs on most everything."

"Speaking of her, where is she?" Aiden asked. "I asked her to breakfast too."

"She said she was finishing up the items you got last night." Clay covered a slice of toast with strawberry jam. "She'll come up when she finishes."

"I appreciate her diligence," Harper said.

Aiden handed her a plate. "You better grab some food before there isn't any left."

"You first." She pushed the plate back his way. "After all, you're a growing boy."

He chuckled. "You sure?"

"Positive. I'm going to grab more coffee." She went to the counter and refilled the cup she'd left before.

No one spoke, and she turned to find them all voraciously eating.

She eyed them in wonder at the speed and amount of food consumption. "I can't even imagine how much money your parents must've spent on food."

Aiden swallowed. "Was one of the reasons my mom always had a big garden. She grew enough to can and preserve things."

"And they had several freezers to store meat when they bought a cow," Drake said.

She rested against the counter across from the island. "I remember when kids in my FFA group raised animals and how their families did the same thing."

"Not yours?" Aiden asked.

"We only grew hazelnuts and then processed them into food products. We produced some of the products ourselves, like chocolate, fudge, caramel."

"Now that's a business I could sink my teeth into." Erik laughed, and his brothers groaned.

Erik looked at Harper. "The youngest never gets any respect."

Drake jabbed him. "Don't tell such lame jokes, and we'll respect you."

The others murmured their agreement through bites of food.

"I guess you're getting to know the real us." Aiden moved back to join her, a piece of toast in his hand. "I hope that doesn't destroy your confidence in our ability to protect you."

"Of course not," she said. "I'm enjoying getting to know everyone better."

"No need," Aiden said. "I can tell you about them in a nutshell. Brendan's the family sniper. He's an expert at shooting down ideas that won't work. Clay is the idea generator. You want to be creative, ask for him. Drake's the devil's advocate, and he's very good at it. Erik's the mediator. Or at least he tries to be. He probably succeeds better at it when it comes to the job than in our personal lives, as we often ignore him. After all, he's the baby of the family. Sierra's the nurturer all the way."

"And you?" she asked. "What are you in a nutshell?"

He leaned against the counter next to her and lowered

his voice, his tone intimate again. "You've been with us long enough. You tell me."

"You're the decision maker. Leader of the group." She paused to think. "And I think you're a bit inflexible and over-bearing."

His eyebrows shot up. "You pegged me for sure. Though I try to be openminded, when I set a goal, I won't let anything stand in my way."

"Like starting this business. You're not going to let your interest in me derail you." She whispered the words to be sure the brothers didn't hear her.

"That makes me sound like kind of a player." He kept his voice low and moved closer. "Which I am, I guess." A dark looked crossed his expression, and his lips pressed together for a moment. "I kissed you when I had no intention of following up on it. I shouldn't have—"

"It's okay," she said, trying not to feel hurt by his blunt admission. "I encouraged you, and I don't have any desire for a relationship, either."

She was only admitting what she'd already determined, but why did it feel like a lie?

Harper finished loading the dishwasher, wishing she could just sit and enjoy the Byrd family—maybe go meet their parents, as they had to be pretty amazing to have raised five terrific men and an amazing woman. They possessed quali-ties, as did Sierra, that many people lacked today. Respect. Dedication. Commitment. Strong communication skills and the ability not to have their faces in their phones all the time. They had it all. But they weren't here to socialize with her. They were here to protect her and find the stalker.

She closed the dishwasher door and looked for Aiden.

He was standing by the floor-to-ceiling windows and looking out, his hand on the back of his neck. He seemed tense and maybe frustrated. She was causing him problems by insisting on going to the charity event. Sure, it was his job to make sure she could safely go about her life, and she knew he would figure out how to keep her safe, but it put a pain in her heart to know she was causing him to work doubly hard and to worry.

And that worry might be a big clue that Sierra's comment about Aiden having feelings for Harper was true. And it was time for Harper to admit that she cared about him too. More than she ever imagined she could in just a few short days.

He turned and caught her watching him. A question on his face, he strode past his brothers working on their electronic devices and into the kitchen. "Riley hasn't texted yet, so why don't we watch the ski videos while I wait for him to arrive."

"Sure," she said, glad to have something to do to keep her wandering mind busy. She went to the couch that faced the TV, and three of the guys got up.

"Thanks for helping make our breakfast," Brendan said.

She smiled at him. "It's the least I can do considering what you all are doing for me."

"Remember," Erik said. "The cone of silence on the quantities of food we can put away."

Harper laughed.

"Good one, little brother," Drake said.

"Wait, what? Was that a compliment?" Erik turned to Aiden. "Quick, give me some paper to write this auspicious moment down."

"Just enjoy it, kid," Brendan said, giving Clay a hand up from a deep chair. "'Cause there won't likely be another one soon."

"You should've quit while you were ahead." Drake placed his hands on Erik's shoulders from behind and headed him toward the door.

Still smiling, Harper watched them leave and then took a seat.

Aiden came to join her.

"I like your brothers," she said.

"I still need to teach them the whole professional thing."

"I don't know. Maybe this personal touch will work for all of your clients."

"Maybe." But he didn't sound like he believed it.

While she and Aiden cleaned up, Erik had connected Aiden's computer to the TV and gave him instructions on how to start the files. She was beginning to learn the brothers' roles in the group, and apparently Erik served as their techie.

Aiden started the video playing from the first World Cup event this fall in Sölden, Austria. Harper had already watched this event over and over, as she did after every competition, looking for ways to improve for the next one, but never had she seen the uncut footage or paid any attention to the crowd.

She searched for Gurly or anyone else she might know but saw no one who seemed suspicious, not even Gurly. The view changed to a shot of her standing at the gate, mentally preparing herself for the giant slalom race.

"You look nervous," Aiden said. "Do you still get nervous?"

"Sure. And especially at Sölden. It's the first race of the year, and to come out with a win? Incredible. I'm a down-hiller, and giant slalom is my worst event. This was my first GS win."

The start clock began the countdown beeps, and she took off.

Harper watched the run with a critical eye.

"You're amazing," Aiden said. "You make it look like it's as easy as walking when I know it's extremely hard."

She pointed at the screen. "My extension isn't as good as it should be there. I came up under that gate well, but then almost lost it."

"No one but you noticed."

"The commentators and my coach did. They don't miss a thing." She scratched her cheek. "Thankfully, I let it go." She stabbed a finger at the screen again. "And carried the speed from here to the end of the pitch and onto the flats. I made up a full second for the win."

When Harper crossed the finish line on the screen, she let out a long breath. "It always makes me nervous watching myself. I don't know why, but even if I know the final results, I see my mistakes and feel like I might fall."

He locked gazes with her, and his interest seemed to build like a pressure cooker. Was he transferring his admiration for the abilities he'd just witnessed in her run into personal feelings for her? She had to be careful when it came to relationships of any kind. Friendship or romantic. People wanted to be a part of her success, and sometimes that meant not being interested in her so much as liking what she accomplished.

But she didn't get that feeling from any of the Byrd brothers. Sure, they praised her skills, but that was where it seemed to end. Even with Aiden's intense interest, never did she feel like he was a hanger-on, and she was drawn to the sincere emotions she was picking up on.

And that was a problem. "We should move on to the spectator video."

He held her gaze for a moment longer before reluctantly turning back to the computer and starting the video.

She took a breath and scanned the crowd, watching for anything unusual.

"There, stop!" She pointed at the screen. "It's Gurly with his arm around a woman's shoulders."

Aiden paused the video. "Her sunglasses and hat make her hard to identify."

"Look at her clothes, they don't look like a young girl's. More like a woman's." She squinted to try to make out anything about her face. "Can you zoom in?"

He ran his finger over the mouse, and the image grew in size.

Harper gasped. "I know her. It's Ulyana Lebedev, a Russian skier who sought asylum in our country and recently joined the U.S. Alpine Team."

Aiden faced her. "You're sure?"

Harper nodded. "She has a gold tooth on the right top, and she got a tattoo of a U.S. flag on her neck after she left Russia. You can see both of them in the picture."

Aiden's eyebrows raised. "Why did she seek asylum?"

"She was rocketing to the top of the standings and was hyped by Russia as their new breed of athlete. But she said the state controlled her life, keeping her captive in a training facility and forcing her to train at a level that was detrimental to her health. She didn't share the details, but it must've been bad enough if she left her homeland."

"She's a U.S. citizen then?"

"Yes. She applied right away so she would be eligible for our team and joined us in about a year." Harper stared at the picture. "She's only seventeen. She's in foster care, but the parents don't travel with her, so she's vulnerable. She might just think of him as a father figure."

"But it's unlikely that he thinks of her as his daughter. Let's see how long the camera keeps them in view." Aiden started it playing again.

The couple soon moved out of camera range.

"Let's finish watching this video in case they return." He continued playing the video, but the couple didn't reappear. He moved on to the next file from an earlier meet. Midway he stopped it. "There in the far left back. It's Gurly, but he's alone."

"Ulyana wasn't on the team yet."

Aiden started it up again, and Gurly took off at the end of Harper's run.

"Seems like he's only watching you," Aiden said.

"Which makes him a likely suspect, but he could just be acting as a scout for other teams."

"Do you think that's likely?"

"Not really." She bit her lip, her fingers searching for her ring. "I can't imagine anyone in the sport hiring him, but I suppose it's possible. Maybe we should talk to Ulyana."

"Not yet." He made strong eye contact. "If she's close to Gurly, that'll tip him off, and we don't want to do that."

"Can I at least call our coach so he can stop Gurly from preying on her?"

"That should be okay, but he has to promise to keep your name out of it."

Harper grabbed her phone, and as she dialed her coach, she was already running through the words she needed to say to succeed in protecting Ulyana from a convicted rapist.

17

Aiden was impressed with the Gidwell wheat farm. Fields of golden grains blowing in the wind spread out before him. Large barns and other outbuildings were neatly labeled with signs. Aiden headed for a guy on a tractor rumbling in from the fields. They made eye contact, and the burly guy slid out. He had tanned skin and wore denim overalls with dirty knees.

"Help you?" He hooked his thumbs in his overall straps.

"I'm looking for Tanner Gidwell."

"I'm Tanner." His eyes narrowed.

Aiden handed his business card to him. "We're looking into an investigation involving Harper Young."

"Harper? I haven't seen her in years." He took off his baseball cap and scratched his head of thick blond hair. "Wait, this the same thing the Portland detective asked about."

Aiden nodded and left it at that, hoping Tanner would be forthcoming on his own.

"Like I told him, I haven't seen or heard from her. Don't follow skiing anymore. No time. Too much to do to keep this place running."

A perfect segue to Aiden's questions. "Is the farm having financial difficulties?"

He jutted out his wide jaw. "That's none of your business."

So he was touchy about his finances. Under different circumstances, Aiden would keep after him, but struggling with money wouldn't likely be related to stalking. "Might you all use Norflurazon?"

"Used to. Years ago." He aimed his jaw at Aiden like a weapon as if he thought Aiden would judge him for using the chemical in the past. "Now we're all organic."

Aiden didn't know why this bothered Tanner, but Aiden wouldn't waste valuable time on figuring out the guy's feelings. "So you and Harper used to date?"

"A long time ago."

"Do you have a girlfriend now?"

"No."

"Recently."

"No."

"Were you upset when Harper broke up with you?"

"Of course I was, but that was so long ago, I don't even think about her anymore, except when you guys come around."

"C'mon, now. Her dad's orchard is right down the road. Don't tell me, when you see the place, you don't think of what might've been if you stayed together."

Tanner firmed his stance. "No point in speculating over something that can never be. Learned that when I washed out in skiing and got involved with drugs. Better to just look at what it is."

A change in direction was what was needed here to get this guy to let his guard down and be more forthcoming.

"Has anyone new been hanging around town, asking questions about Harper?" Aiden asked.

He shrugged. "I don't spend much time in town."

"So you haven't heard any gossip, then?"

He shook his head and looked away.

"What about your mom or dad? Might they have heard anything?"

"You'd have to ask them." Tanner shoved his hands into his pockets.

Great. That did nothing to get him to talk.

Aiden glanced around and saw a newer model pickup truck. "You have electronic locks on the truck?"

"We do."

"Ever heard that vehicles with electronic ignitions can easily be stolen using a device you can get off of Amazon?"

"Nope," he said quickly. Perhaps too quickly.

Aiden met and held his gaze. "Where were you last night?"

"Here."

"Can anyone verify that?"

"I was alone."

"Your parents don't live here anymore?"

Tanner glared at Aiden. "I'm way too old to live with them. They have the big house, and I have a tiny house I built out back."

Aiden really wanted to be able to prove or disprove this guy's alibi, not just be left in a gray area. "Can you see it from the main house?"

"No."

"What about the driveway? Do you share it?"

"Yes."

"Are your parents home?"

"I think so, but I don't want you to go bothering them over nothing." He crossed his arms. "Ever since I went away for the drugs, the cops think I'm good for all kinds of crimes. I'm not, but they come here far more often than I want. One of these days, my dad's gonna take a swing at them."

"Sounds like he has a temper."

"He does and, before you ask, no, I didn't inherit it." He stared at Aiden. "Now, if that's all."

"I'm sorry if you don't like it, but I'll be stopping to talk to them on my way out."

Anger that he didn't inherit flared in Tanner's eyes.

"If you think of anything that can help us find the man stalking Harper, I know she would appreciate it if you would give me a call."

"I will, but only because I once cared about her. She's a special person. Not many can compare."

Aiden gave the guy one last look and walked away. He couldn't stay or he might cross a professional line with Tanner. Aiden was getting something from Tanner's tone that he didn't like. Something underlying that hinted at still having feelings for her. Or, at the very least, disappointed that he hadn't been able to find anyone like her. Aiden strode across the gravel drive to the big white house with tall trees towering overhead and whispering in the wind. He peered in the direction of the small house that Tanner described, but Aiden couldn't see it from his location. And he could hardly go wandering around the place without an invitation.

He climbed the steps to the wide porch and opened the screen door to knock. He glanced back at Tanner, who was frowning at him. If the guy was innocent, Aiden didn't like seeing him upset, but Aiden would stop at nothing to find Harper's stalker.

A woman with a curly cap of gray hair, weathered skin, and worn jeans and T-shirt opened the door. A paisley apron coated with flour covered her knit shirt and worn jeans. The tantalizing smell of fresh baked bread seeped out of the house, and Aiden immediately thought of his mother, who'd baked bread every day to keep him and his brothers fed.

"Help you?" she asked.

He handed her his card and explained his investigation.

"I heard about this on the news." She tsked. "Harper's such a lovely girl. She doesn't deserve something terrible like this."

"Were you disappointed when she and Tanner broke up?"

"Sure. But that was ages ago."

"And how did Tanner take it?"

"He was moody for a while, but he got over her like we all do after a time."

Aiden didn't want to point out that not all people got over someone they once loved.

"Does she ever come around these parts anymore?"

"Harper? Gosh. I don't know. I saw her a few months ago. Ran into her in town when she was getting some dog food for her dad's huskie."

Now Aiden was getting somewhere. "Were you alone?"

"Tanner was with me. I talked to her, but he took care of getting our supplies."

Aiden made a note to ask Harper about that. Tanner must've hidden out, because Harper didn't mention seeing him. And the timing would have been perfect for when the stalking started. "I suppose he wouldn't want to talk to her, since she broke up with him."

"We just had a busy day is all." She eyed him with suspicion. "You don't think Tanner has anything to do with Harper's stalking, do you?"

"We just need to rule everyone out."

"People around here just can't seem to let go of his one mistake. They blame him for all kinds of things now."

"That's unfair for sure." He gave her a tight smile. "So I can rule him out, you don't happen to remember what day you two saw Harper in town, do you?"

"Day? Nah. Just an ordinary day."

"Would you have receipts for the supplies?"

"It was for the farm so my husband would."

He would ask to speak to the husband when he finished questioning her. "Does Tanner have an old-fashioned typewriter?"

"Typewriter? Nah. He's not into things like that. None of us are. We're farmers, not writers."

"You're sure?"

"You ever been in a tiny house?" she asked.

"No."

"The place is so small Tanner barely has room for everyday things like dishes and cooking utensils. More often than not, he comes up to eat with us."

"Did he have dinner here last night?"

"No. It was his pizza night."

"So he was home last night?"

"Yeah, sure. I mean...I think so."

"You didn't see his truck leave the driveway or come back?"

"Did I?" She tapped her chin. "Maybe. I'm not sure." She frowned, but her eyes held a hint of guile. "When you do the same thing most every night, it all runs together."

"What about your husband? Might he have seen Tanner last night?"

"Nah, Nigel wasn't here. He had his monthly Legion meeting." She stepped closer to him. "Which, between you and me, is more of a reason to go carousing with his buddies, but don't tell him I told you that." She grinned.

"Could I talk to him?"

"Sure, but he's in town. Had to take one of the machines

in to get fixed. Another reason to have a beer or two with his buddies."

Aiden would like to track down the dad to see if he'd noticed Tanner's truck when he got home. He looked at his watch. He really should head back to Portland. "Would you have him call me when he gets home? I just want to cross Tanner off my list."

"I'll make sure he does." At her genuine smile, Aiden felt bad about misleading her into thinking this was all about eliminating Tanner as a suspect and more about proving he could be Harper's stalker.

~

Tears swam in Harper's eyes when Aiden returned to his condo from interviewing Tanner. "What's wrong? Did something happen while I was gone?"

She quickly shared information on her call with her coach, her words rushing out like a fast moving river. As she talked, the tears intensified, and she mopped her eyes with a tissue.

"Sorry." She sniffled. "It's just hard to see someone as young as Ulyana be taken advantage of by a creep like this. My coach was clueless about the relationship, but when I told him, he remembered suspicious incidents."

She paused and dabbed her eyes. "He promised to keep an eye out for Gurly."

"That's all we can hope for." Aiden's phone dinged before he could tell her about Tanner. He read the text. "Sierra wants us to come to the lab."

"She probably has fingerprint results. Let's go." Harper jumped up and raced down the hall.

"Hold on!" He charged after her. By the time he caught up to her, she was opening the door. He stepped in front of her. "I need to check out the hallway first. We might be in a secure building, but it's not impenetrable."

"I didn't realize."

"Just don't do it again." He tried to couch his demand with a smile but failed.

"I'm sorry. I don't want to make your job harder." She touched his arm.

Her hand fired off every nerve ending in his arm, and he spun to shake it off. "I'll just be a second."

He shot out into the hallway and took a few breaths. Seriously. He was a grown man who'd been able to control his emotions for years. Harper just did something else to him that he couldn't even put words to.

He scanned the hallway. When he was satisfied that danger didn't lurk out there, and he was back in control, he crooked a finger at her.

"I really am sorry," she said, looking contrite.

"I should be the one saying sorry for shouting at you like that. I just..." He almost said he just couldn't bear the thought of losing her.

"Just what?"

"I need to do my job." He got the elevator open and held the door for her. He didn't really want to bring up Tanner right now, but she needed to know what he'd learned. He recounted the conversations. "So no one can verify that he was home last night. In fact, it seems as if his mother was trying to cover for him."

"But he doesn't have a typewriter."

"At least she doesn't think he does, but if he bought one for this purpose, he would hide it. I know Johnson checked Portland shops for the typewriter, but he didn't likely extend his search out to McMinnville. We can check with the local shops to see if he bought it there." He waited for her to say something, but she looked over his shoulder, her expression pensive.

"Did you see his mother in town?" he asked.

"Yes, but I had no idea Tanner was with her. She didn't say he was, and he didn't show his face."

"It was about the time the letters started arriving, though."

"Was it? Could be. Let me check my calendar, and I can see if I was visiting my dad back then." She got out her phone and swiped several times. "Yeah. Yeah. That *is* when it was."

"So maybe seeing you again is what triggered him."

"Could be." She tilted her head in an inquisitive pose. "Sounds like you're thinking he might be the stalker."

"I'm liking him more for it now than I was before I went to see him. The dad is supposed to call me back. Depending on what he tells me, I may ask Johnson to circle back to Tanner."

The door opened, and he stepped out to check the hallway. He motioned for her to proceed into the hallway and led her to the lab. Before they could enter, his phone dinged, and he reached into his pocket. "Text is from Maya. She says the herbicide is still pretty widely used and would take an army to track down."

"So, that's a bust," Harper said, sounding disappointed.

"Still, it will help us narrow down suspects." He held the door for Harper.

His sister sat at one of the large tables, the boxes from Detective Johnson and the tractor and letter located on white paper in front of her. Harper and Aiden joined her at the table.

"Missed you at breakfast, sis," he said. "But thanks for working on this."

"Yes, thank you so much," Harper said.

Sierra smiled at Harper. "Thanks for coming down here so fast. I have results for you, and I'll start with what I found when I examined the typewritten letters. I agree with the misaligned A findings, and it does demonstrate that all these letters were written on the same machine."

"Did you find anything else?" Aiden asked.

"No, but just wanted to mention that this is enough of an exception to match the letters to an individual type-writer. So if it's found, we can do that. Plus, if the ribbon hasn't been changed it will have the information embedded in it."

"Hard to imagine anyone would use a typewriter these days," Harper said.

Aiden nodded. "Especially to commit a crime, as it's traceable, where computer type isn't as easily traced."

"So maybe this typewriter means something to the stalk-er." Sierra looked at Harper. "Were there any important events in your past involving a typewriter that stand out for you?"

Harper shook her head. "I've never even used a typewriter."

Aiden's phone rang, and he looked at the screen. "It's Johnson."

"Finally," Harper said.

Aiden connected the call.

"Your file is on the way by messenger," Johnson said. "Should be there any minute. Now, what do you know about the guy in the picture?"

"His name is Jeffry Gurly." Aiden explained how they located him and about the guy's past. "We also found the cheap motel where he has a room paid up until the end of the month. Your patrol guys checked him out for Denver police, but he wasn't there. I stopped by, too, but didn't find him."

Johnson let out an exasperated breath. "I suppose you searched the room."

"We wore gloves and didn't disturb anything. FYI, we found boxes of 9mm ammo. No firearm. I figured we should connect you with Detective Walters in Denver, and you could get a warrant to search the place so we can get prints and DNA for comparison to the items sent to Harper."

"I need you to butt out of this." His testy tone didn't sit well with Aiden. "It's a police matter. I'll call Walters and go from there."

"Hey, I get it. I'm private now. But I still have to protect my client, which means I need all the information I can get. We chose not to do prints and DNA in the room to preserve it for you. In light of that, I was hoping to get Gurly's prints from you."

"That will be up to my LT."

Aiden wondered if he needed to get Blake involved with this request. "I can call your lieutenant if you'd like."

"You know I wouldn't *like* that. I'll handle it and get back to you."

"I'd appreciate that as soon as possible, please." Aiden breathed deep. "Now that we know Gurly is grooming other girls, we were wondering if this stalking is limited to Harper. Did you question the other women on Harper's team to see if they'd been approached by anyone or given any gifts?"

"I interviewed all of them, and you'll find the details in my file when it arrives." The guy sounded irritated. "Now, if that's all."

"Did you talk to an Ulyana Lebedev?"

"Name doesn't ring a bell."

"She's in another World Cup video. Gurly has his arm around her, and she's only seventeen."

Johnson drew in a sharp breath. "I'll look into it."

"Also, you should know that Harper received another

letter and package last night." Aiden shared the details, though, with the guy's attitude, he didn't feel much like cooperating. "The items were properly handled and are in evidence at the Veritas Center."

"Any results?"

"We were just about to talk to the trace evidence expert now."

"Loop me in on what the expert finds, and she can add the items to our evidence box."

Aiden was surprised he didn't insist on them being delivered to him. "You should know, I interviewed Tanner Gidwell, and he might not have an alibi for last night when the envelope was delivered. I'm waiting on a follow-up call from his father to confirm, but you might want to talk to him."

"You should have called me out to the scene last night."

"What would you have done that we didn't do?"

"Filed an official report."

"You can file one now."

"You should have called, and you know it."

Yeah, he did know it, but putting Harper through additional stress just for some paperwork? Nah. "One more thing. Someone tried to drug Harper at the ski resort. Her bottle stored in a locker was tampered with. No cameras in the area and we interviewed the employee. The bottle is in evidence here too. We called the Clackamas County Sheriff's Office. A deputy filed a report, and we asked them to coordinate with you. Did you hear from them?"

"Not yet."

"The drug was identified as ketamine. We also found herbicide on the bottle. Norflurazon."

"I would've appreciated a call at the time of the incident."

Aiden resisted snapping at the guy. "I did call you. I left a message."

"But your message was vague, and I figured you were going to hound me about the file, and I couldn't speed up the records people."

Aiden swallowed the smart-aleck response begging to come out.

"Anything else?" Johnson asked.

"Just a request to share anything you recover from Gurly's hotel room, and we'll keep sharing what we find too."

"You do that." He ended the call.

Aiden shoved his phone into his pocket and took a cleansing breath before telling the others what the detective had to say.

"Sounds like you're learning how frustrating it is to be on the other side of law enforcement," Sierra said.

"True that," he said. "But it's the path we've chosen, and in the long run I believe we'll be able to help more people."

"Well I, for one, am glad you formed an agency," Harper said with conviction. "And I'll be glad to give you a testimonial for your website and recommend you to anyone I hear of needing your services. And I'll tell my mom and dad to do the same thing."

Aiden could hardly believe this woman had been so skeptical of their agency just a few days ago. He hoped her enthusiasm didn't have to do with feelings she was developing for him, because, despite kissing her—which had been wrong—he wasn't in a place to pursue her, and he could end up hurting her, when that was the very last thing he wanted.

18

Sierra kept looking between Harper and Aiden, and Harper had no idea what she was searching for. But Harper wouldn't ask as she suspected it was personal, and Harper didn't want to go there.

"Please tell us what you found," she said to Sierra.

Sierra slowly dragged her gaze from her brother to the table. She tapped the box from Johnson. "I recovered various prints from these gifts, and none of them returned a match in the database."

"Then they can't be Gurly's prints or they would be in the database from his prior arrests." Aiden gave a heavy sigh. "So whose prints are on the items?"

Sierra cut her eyes to the evidence. "It's likely the prints belong to people who made or shipped the products."

"That makes sense." His phone chimed, and he got it out. "It's the front desk. Johnson's file is here. Let me go grab it so we can see if the prints you lifted match the ones they recovered."

He bolted for the door, leaving Harper alone with Sierra. Something that should be no big deal, but Harper suspected

Sierra wanted to talk about Aiden, and Harper didn't want to go there.

"I'll wait for him to come back before I share the rest of my findings." Sierra settled on a stool. "Tell me what it's like to race down those mountains."

Harper let out a relieved breath over Sierra's choice of topic. "Exhilarating. Crazy. Scary. But mostly challenging. Your mind is on the work not the danger or fun. You can't lose focus for even a split second, as that's all it takes to fall, which can be deadly at that speed."

"Have people died doing this?"

Harper nodded. "I know several skiers who have."

"Gosh." Sierra's eyes widened. "Have you ever been injured?"

"More times than I can count, but I've been blessed." She took a second to thank God for her health and safety. "Only two serious injuries, both compound fractures. One arm. One leg."

Sierra pursed her lips. "Now that I know you, and know Aiden cares for you, I'm never going to watch you ski. I'd be too afraid to see you fall. I don't know how he'll be able to handle it."

Harper worked hard not to gape at Sierra. "We find each other attractive. That's all."

Sierra looked Harper directly in the eye. "Trust me. I know my brother, and it's more than attraction."

The door opened, and Aiden rushed in. Harper couldn't be more thankful for his timing. She shifted her focus to the large package he carried under his arm. He ripped it open on a nearby table, pulled out a thick binder, and started flipping through the pages.

"Okay, here's the report on prints." He removed the pages and handed them to Sierra.

She read the report before taking out fingerprint cards

and holding them against various pages. "Results are the same for the prints I lifted from the objects. I'd need the actual cards for my comparison to stand up in court, but I'm confident our findings match the ones in the report."

Aiden weaved his fingers into his hair. "And the other items and letters?"

Sierra flipped the page. "I haven't had a chance to process the later items except the tractor, which I did right away. It didn't return useable results. I haven't done the letters yet, but it says here that PPB criminalists didn't recover prints on any of them."

"That's odd, right?" Harper asked.

"Not if the stalker wore gloves." Sierra narrowed her gaze. "But I want to be sure, so I'll use a vacuum metal deposition instrument on every item possible, and maybe it will reveal prints they missed."

Harper looked at Aiden to see if he knew what Sierra was talking about, and his head was tilted, his eyes narrowed. "I'm guessing that's an item not readily used."

Sierra nodded. "And not something PPB has in their arsenal."

"So what does it do?" Aiden asked.

"The physical process coats evidence with a very thin metal film under high vacuum revealing hard to recover prints. The metallic substances don't land on the top of the fingerprint ridges, but goes in between so that the top of the ridge is touched, and that's where we also find DNA." Sierra met their gazes. "But I should warn you, it's used for old prints, so if I find them on the letters, they could've been there before the suspect even thought about using the paper for evil and protecting his hands. Or they could belong to anyone who touched the paper at any point in manufacture too."

Aiden's expression turned stony. "So could be from anyone then?"

"Yes." Sierra had a hitch in her voice. "A roommate. Family member. Or he could even have brought the paper home from work."

Aiden met Sierra's gaze, his eyes dark and intense. "I guess the big question is, if you find any prints, will they match anyone in the database?"

~

After delivering copies of the DNA reports from Johnson's file for Emory to compare to her findings, Harper sat at Aiden's dining table and wished Sierra and Emory could wave a magic wand over the rest of the evidence and find proof of the stalker's identity, or they could get DNA results on the water bottle.

Then they could arrest the stalker, and her life could go back to normal. That wasn't going to happen. No matter how much Harper wanted to find this stalker, she wouldn't try to push Sierra. She'd warned them it would take time to complete everything, and Harper appreciated Sierra's thoroughness. Appreciated that she was on the cutting edge and could use things like the vacuum metal deposition instrument. Ditto with Emory. DNA results took time as well.

Aiden looked at her. "How did you do with calling the farms?"

She slid the list across the table to him. "It was mixed. I crossed off the ones I talked to who didn't know anything about Gurly. I highlighted a few where the owners weren't in and no one else could answer my question. And then I also crossed off a few where they *were* in and wouldn't answer my question due to privacy issues. Then there's a bunch at the bottom of the list that I didn't get to."

"I know I said I would help finish the calls, but now that we received Johnson's casebook, I want to look at the information. I'm going to hand off the farm list to Brendan and Erik to handle."

"Sounds good," Harper said.

Aiden got up and took his notepad to Brendan where he sat near the hallway leading to the exit. "Can you—?"

"Split this up with Erik?" Brendan asked, a sarcastic grin on his face. "It's not like I can't hear everything you say. I see the looks too."

Aiden shoved the pad into his brother's hand. "I'll take over for you. Go ahead and deliver it to Erik now."

Harper wouldn't ask what he meant by the looks, but she took heed of his comment and would do a better job of remembering that he or one of his brothers was listening in all the time.

"I'll be over here until he comes back," Aiden said, totally ignoring Brendan's comment. "A perfect time to give Walters a call in Denver."

"I'm going to get some water," she said. "Do you want anything?"

"Water would be good." He got out his phone and looked at the screen.

She went to the kitchen and filled two tall glasses with ice and water from the refrigerator. She heard Aiden give Walters the contact information for Detective Johnson, sounding cordial at first, but his tone soon became irritated.

Walters was likely turning down his request to share the files. Aiden said good-bye and immediately called Blake, asking him to help get the Denver records.

She took the glasses to the table and the door opened. Aiden pivoted in that direction, his hand going to his sidearm. He had to know it was most likely one of his brothers, but he was being cautious, proving again their worth as bodyguards.

The doors opened, and his shoulders relaxed a bit before he disconnected and looked at Brendan. "I also need you to call secondhand and antique stores in the McMinnville area to ask if they've sold a typewriter in the last six months."

"And if they did?" Brendan asked.

"I want the name of the person who bought it." Aiden strode to the table. He took a long drink of the water, and she watched his Adam's apple bob in his tanned neck. She glanced at Brendan and found him watching her.

He quickly diverted his gaze to the list and got out his phone, but she caught his knowing look before he did. She had to come to grips with the fact that she was in a fishbowl until the stalker was caught. Even more of a reason to keep her thoughts where they belonged.

"Walters refused my request." Aiden sat. "So no records or DNA and prints for Gurly. But Blake hopes he can get them."

"That's good then."

"Yeah. If he can do it." Aiden opened the rings on Johnson's binder, removed sections, and made several document stacks on the table. "A separate incident report was created each time you received a letter and item from your stalker. Plus, there's an overview of the entire investigation broken down into victim and witness statements, plus interviews, lab reports, and crime scene information, including responding officer reports and photos."

"Sounds like a lot of information to review," she said.

He nodded. "It would help a lot if you went through the documents too. Seeing the files from your point of view might give us something to go on."

"Okay," she said, though she wasn't sure if she really wanted to read these files.

"We can go chronologically through each section. I'd like to start with interviews, and you take the incident and crime scene reports to make sure they're accurate."

She nodded and picked up the correct stack, starting with the very first letter she received. She read it carefully, looking for any hint that might suggest the author, but it was a pretty generic letter praising her skiing and was signed A Big Fan. Four other letters followed in the initial report, each one getting a little more personal, but she forced away the anxiety they brought.

She looked at Aiden. "He mentions ski terms in these letters that only a skier or someone very familiar with the sport would know."

"That could point to Gurly or to Tanner since he was once a skier too. Or even Matthew, though we've basically ruled him out because he's still in Vermont." Aiden made a note on his legal pad.

"So, which guy is it?" She shook her head and moved on to the next letter. The stalker described her body and the excitement he'd experienced while watching her ski. The ick factor nearly had her tossing the paper down, but then she noticed the poetry in the words and thought about Tanner.

"You know," she said. "I doubt this letter is from Tanner. It's gross to read, but it's also filled with poetic phrasing. Tanner wasn't creative. More straightforward. And he's not into artistic endeavors at all. One of the reasons he had a hard time excelling in skiing. He didn't get his skis on edge well enough, and that was because he didn't look at it as anything more than a muscle sport. Didn't consider that it took grace and finesse to win. That you couldn't just power through it all. And so he didn't want to do the work on slower slopes to master his body posture and pole positions."

Aiden's shoulders drooped. "You really don't think he wrote that letter."

"I don't. I mean, he could have changed, but I doubt his time in prison made him more poetic."

"Likely not. Still, we can't rule him out until the prints are done."

"I wish processing forensics was instant like you see on TV and in movies."

"Don't we all." He smiled and went back to his stack of pages.

She read through the remaining letters in this batch and found nothing else to note. And the report was complete, so she moved on to the second one. It was the beginning of the explicit items sent by the stalker that Sierra hadn't processed yet, and Harper had a hard time reading the report. She made sure it was thorough and had the details right but then moved on.

She picked up the report for Betty Spaghetty and remembered playing with Tanner and the doll. He'd had a GI Joe doll from his dad, which he kept insisting wasn't a doll but an action figure. She remembered teasing him and how mad he got, stomping across the field to his house. Of course, she didn't really know back then that she was hurting his masculine pride, but could those kind of actions have messed with his psyche and caused him to do something like this? Nah, that was really a farfetched thought, and she didn't believe it was Tanner. Not at all.

Aiden's phone rang, and he grabbed it from the table. "It's Emory." He answered. "Harper's here, and I'm putting you on speaker."

"I have DNA results on the water bottle and jacket," she said. "Only Harper's DNA on the jacket, but we got another result from the bottle. Didn't return a match in the database."

Harper sighed.

"Means Gurly didn't touch that bottle," Aiden said. "At least not with bare hands."

"Exactly."

"Okay, thanks, Emory." Aiden hung up and looked at Harper. "We have to face it. We've been proceeding as if Gurly is our guy, but we have little evidence to back up our theory and need to keep digging."

19

Aiden had settled back in the helo that smelled like the aviation fuel used to power it, and taking the time during their quick flight to relax because, barring a missile launch or mechanical failure, Harper was safe in the air. He hadn't had a moment to relax since the team had taken on her detail, and he was enjoying the freedom to chill for a bit. Reminded him of the many ops as a SEAL. In spec ops, operators had to take whatever moments they could to unwind and even sleep, as they had to be on for the mission. For themselves sure, but even more for the guys depending on them.

He sat back and watched out the window, appreciating the view. The lights of Salem soon appeared, and they wound their way steadily toward the Salem Municipal Airport located two miles from downtown and their venue for the night.

"ETA, three minutes," Riley announced over their headsets.

Aiden sat up straight, moving out of relaxation mode and into warrior mode. He surveilled the landing area. The governor had gotten permission for them to have two vehicles waiting at the helipad, and they sat near the landing circle. Riley flew steadily toward them, descending as they moved. He set the aircraft down in the circle, and the helo bounced once then stilled.

The guys filed out. Aiden took off his headset and shifted to Harper to help remove hers without messing up her fancy hairdo. He'd helped her put it on too, and he'd had a hard time not touching a soft tendril dangling by her ear. So he'd purposefully taken a seat across from her where he wouldn't be tempted.

And now he had her safety to think about so he concentrated on the transport ahead. "The vehicles are waiting. Follow Drake to the SUV just like we planned. Don't stop unless one of us instructs you to hold."

"Got it." She grabbed his hand. "Thank you for everything you did so I could attend this event tonight. It means the world to me."

He nodded, but the SEAL in him didn't like this event. He didn't like it one bit. Sure, he'd done his recon and planning, but anyone who wanted to find out where Harper was tonight could do so as she never missed this gala.

She covered her head with a scarf to prevent the wind from the rotor airflow from messing up her hair. He hopped down and helped her out. She wore a plain black coat that was fitted and, thankfully, hid the basic black dress with the split skirt revealing her very toned leg and leaving her shoulders bare. And if, he lost track of his mission for a moment and focused on her, the sight of the tactical vest she wore over the coat would reel him back in.

He put his head on a swivel and moved her quickly to the black SUV where Drake was opening the back door, and Brendan sat behind the wheel. Aiden took one last look and climbed in behind her. The moment he closed the door, Brendan took off, and Aiden watched carefully out the windows on the way to the hotel, looking for anything out of the ordinary.

They passed the main entrance to the Grand Hotel and proceeded to the parking garage shared by the Salem Convention Center. Thankfully, the convention center didn't have any events going on right now. If they had, Aiden would have tried hard to get Harper to agree not to attend.

Brendan pulled up to the staff door, and they entered in the same fashion as they had the Radisson, passing Blackwell Tactical members on the way to the large ballroom with orange-and-beige patterned carpet and contemporary pendant lights that didn't go with the historic hotel at all.

He almost sighed when they reached the room entrance, and he had Harper hold while the team got into position, but Harper wasn't much safer out here. Sure, the governor was attending the function and Blackwell team members were manning the door and looking for Gurly to show, but that didn't mean he was their guy. Could also be Tanner or someone else they hadn't discovered yet.

The room was already filled to capacity, the guests sitting at round tables with sparkling place settings. A large screen was mounted at the front of the room, rotating through pictures that included Harper visiting sickly young children in the hospital, and her compassion for the kids shone through her eyes. Her mother stood on the dais waving at Harper to hurry.

"Your mother looks a bit frantic," he said. "We're not late."

Harper wrinkled her nose. "We are according to my mom. She believes to be on time is to be late."

"As much as I don't want to disappoint her further, we stay here until the others have walked the room and gotten into place."

"Gurly couldn't have gotten past the Blackwell team,

right?" She removed the gauzy scarf and shoved it into her coat pocket.

"Not likely, but we aren't positive Gurly is stalking you, and we have your mother's threats to consider too."

"Oh, right. I didn't think about that." She removed the vest and handed it to Aiden, then shrugged out of her coat and draped it over her arm.

He averted his eyes so he didn't stare at her bare shoulders and lose focus.

"We're clear." Clay's voice came over Aiden's comms unit, and his brothers echoed the sentiment.

"We're good to go." He looked at Harper. "I'll be just off to the left side. Brendan's on the right. Clay and Drake, the middle of the room. Erik, the front. Any one of us gives you an instruction, you follow it. Okay?"

"Roger that." She saluted and gave him a cute grin. "I'll bet you were something as a SEAL. I wish I could've seen it."

"Be thankful you didn't. Those who did were either being rescued from danger...or in danger from us."

Her smile fell, and he felt bad about causing it, but now was not the time for flirting. Actually, never was the time for the two of them to flirt.

"Let's move." He set up at a fast pace but slowed when she had to trot to keep up. He wasn't running a military op here but guarding a woman who wanted to enjoy her night. He slowed, but he didn't relax.

She climbed the two steps to the dais, where her mother grabbed her arm and pulled her close, whispering something in Harper's ear. He wanted to know what that something was, but if it pertained to safety, Coop would have informed Aiden of the problem. Plus, the governor's men stood like robots, and if they ran into trouble, they would be moving.

The program started with a tuxedoed emcee, who introduced the governor. She took the podium and spoke about the charity and gushed over Harper's involvement. She held out her hand for Harper to join her.

Harper glided across the platform, and her mother circled her arm around Harper's shoulders, drawing her close as she continued to speak.

Aiden listened but shifted to watch the room, his gaze going over the crowd, honing in on the men. Checking. Re-checking. Over and over. His brothers and the Blackwell team were doing the same thing.

Near the front, a woman got up and turned toward the exit. She was likely heading to the restroom, but she didn't have a handbag. Not even a tiny little thing only big enough for a phone and a tube of lipstick like Harper was carrying.

Odd. Aiden tracked her movements. She moved casually but looked back at the table where she'd been sitting twice.

"Erik, stop the woman who's leaving," Aiden said into his mic and looked at Coop who was connected via the same comms unit.

"The woman," was all Aiden had to say, as Coop's focus was already on her.

"Drake, check the table to see if she left something behind." Aiden started moving up the steps toward Harper, Coop trailing behind.

His brothers stepped into action, Drake reaching the table at the same time as Erik blocked the woman's path.

"She left a large purse," Drake reported.

"Check the bag." Aiden picked up his pace, making a beeline for Harper. "Erik, don't let her leave."

Drake knelt to check the bag and guests started watching him instead of the governor. Fine, as far as Aiden cared, as he was moving in on Harper and didn't want to draw attention to himself.

"We have a device." Drake's voice came over whisper-quiet, as Aiden knew he was trying to keep the nearby people from hearing. "Cell phone for remote detonation."

Rage welled inside Aiden. "Restrain her, Erik. Make sure she doesn't have access to a cell or device to detonate. Brendan, you're in charge. Evacuate the room."

He reached Harper and took her arm. "Come with me. You too, Governor."

Surprise flashed on their faces, but they didn't argue.

He turned to find Coop right behind him, and he stepped in front of the governor, vying for position with her two men.

"We have a device at one of the tables," Aiden told the governor's protective detail.

"You have anyone with the right experience?" Aiden asked Coop as he whisked Harper toward the exit, fully aware that whatever Drake found could be a dummy device meant to make Aiden and the governor's team take Harper or the governor out the way they'd come in, leaving them as sitting targets. Risk either way.

Coop lifted his wrist to his mouth. "Jackson, move in on the table. Potential device."

None of them needed to utter the word bomb, as they didn't want to panic the people who were scraping back chairs and hurrying for the exit. A low hum of conversation filled the room and footfalls sounded, but Aiden tuned them out. He only had one thing that should hold his attention. To get Harper safely out of the room.

In the back, he tossed the vest to her and hurried her down a hallway to the main exit while she slipped into it, Coop hot on their heels.

"But that's the outside door," Harper said.

Aiden didn't respond, just shoved the door open and took a look around. The street was empty, and an emergency vehicle they'd parked for just such an incident sat ten yards away. He wished his brothers were here to help, but he had Coop and the governor's detail.

Aiden looked back at Coop and the men. "Ready?"

"Go."

Aiden clicked the remote and unlocked the vehicle doors. He stepped out with Harper at his side and got the back door open.

"In coming," Coop shouted. "Behind you. On the left!"

Aiden spun and drew his sidearm. A man on a small motorized platform about the size of a laptop came zooming down the road.

"Gun!" Aiden yelled as he shoved Harper into the back-seat of the SUV.

One of the troopers launched himself at the assailant, who was whirring up to them on the strange motorized device.

The trooper hit the man hard.

The gun fired and skittered across the lot.

The trooper landed hard on top of the man.

Coop took the governor's arm and propelled her into the vehicle.

The other trooper grabbed the man's hands behind his back.

"Go! Go! Go!" Coop shouted.

Aiden jumped into the driver's seat, took off, and spoke into his mic. "We have one armed assailant in custody. The protectees are in the vehicle. Coop too. Heading to rendezvous point."

"Roger that," Erik replied. "Woman in custody. Brendan emptying the room. Jackson working device. Police have been notified."

Aiden glanced at Harper, who was shaking in the back seat beside her mother. He hated that she was so afraid and wished he could comfort her, but his only task right now was to get her and her mother out of danger and do so as quickly and safely as possible.

~

Harper clutched her mother's hand, holding tight. Neither of them spoke as Aiden raced through the streets, winding in and out of traffic. Occasionally looking in the mirrors. He took several left turns, blowing lights and careening around corners and other vehicles.

Her instincts wanted him to slow down. To take his time. But he must possess defensive driving skills from his SEAL and ATF days and know what he was doing. She trusted him completely. Her mother seemed to as well, or maybe she was just in shock.

Coop sat at attention near her mother, not speaking either, his gun in hand. His darting glances and intensity raised Harper's tension.

She pressed a trembling hand over her hair, smoothing it back into place, but several strands had fallen out of the sparkly clip she'd used to pin it up.

Aiden finally slowed down. "I've made enough turns to be sure we weren't followed, and I'm heading to our secondary rendezvous point that both teams agreed on."

"Which is?" her mother asked.

"Police department," Coop said. "Your detail will meet us there."

"They're going to be upset," she said. "Cutting them out like this is going to make them look bad."

"They stopped the gunman," Aiden said as he entered the parking structure. "I'm sure when the media gets wind of this, you can direct their focus to the success."

Aiden looked in the mirror at Coop. "You ever see what the guy was riding before?"

"Not me," Coop said. "It was so small. Never seen anything like it."

"Looked like it was controlled by the way he moved his feet."

Harper had to wonder who this guy was. "Do you think he was there for me or Mom?"

"Now, that's the question of the hour," Coop said.

"Hopefully one we'll get an answer to." Aiden parked.

A contingent of officers hustled out of the building and escorted everyone inside, down a long hallway, and into a conference room that smelled like a mixture of coffee and microwave popcorn.

Aiden got out his phone. Harper watched and listened, her fingers twisting her ring as she waited.

"Brendan, report." He listened, that intense look on his face. "Roger that."

"What's happening?" Harper asked.

"Device disarmed," he said. "Police on scene. The rest of the teams are heading this way in five minutes or so."

"I'm so glad." She let out a breath and nearly sagged to the floor.

He took her arm and helped her to a chair. "You okay? I didn't hurt you when I pushed you into the SUV, did I?"

"Maybe a little, but it had to be done."

He grimaced.

"Hey." She touched his arm. "Don't worry about it."

One of the troopers from her mother's detail busted into the room, a glare on his face for Coop and Aiden. He marched up to her mom, and Harper caught a whiff of mint. "We're ready to head back to the capitol. Come with me."

Coop moved over to them. "I'll be going with you."

The trooper looked like he wanted to argue, but one wilting look from her mother, and he kept silent.

She turned to Harper and kissed her on the forehead. "I wish I could stay, but they're in charge now."

"I get it." Harper gave her mother a tremulous smile. "They have to make sure you're safe."

Her mother looked at Aiden. "Thank you for keeping Harper safe."

He gave a sharp nod but turned his attention to the trooper. "Are the woman or the shooter known to you?"

"Woman no," he said, and Harper was surprised he answered. "Shooter, yes."

"What's his name?"

"He's not carrying ID, and his prints didn't return a match, so we'd rather not release his name until we have a positive ID."

"But you know who he is?"

"We believe he's a person of interest in the threats made against Governor Young, but had no evidence to back it up until now."

Aiden looked at her mother. "This was about you. They were trying to kill you."

"Oh, Mom." Harper shot to her feet and hugged her mother, drawing in her flowery scent that she'd worn since Harper was a child. "I'm so sorry. Thank God you're all right."

Her mother trembled in Harper's arms, something Harper had never experienced from her rock solid mother. But when she pushed back, she had her iron will in place again. "Please let me know when you get safely back to Portland."

"I will," Harper promised.

"I'll call your dad and tell him we're both okay." She gave a sharp nod and marched to the door, the trooper quickly slipping in front of her.

Harper turned to Aiden, suddenly realizing they were

alone, and her first thought was to throw herself into his arms and cry like a baby. Not a good idea. Not good at all. She had to find a way to handle her emotions on her own. She'd done it for years. Was the only way she'd succeeded in the competitive sports world. She might want Aiden to help her through this, but when they found her stalker and she parted ways with Aiden, she would be on her own, and she couldn't come to depend on him. She just couldn't.

20

The trip home was made in silence. Aiden was concerned about Harper's mood, but she'd shut down any of his attempts to try to help her work through it. Fine. She didn't want his help. He got it. She was a strong, independent woman, and he had to leave it alone. At least for now. But he had other things he could do to help move the hunt for her stalker forward.

So when they arrived back at the condo, he left Harper with Erik and went to Nick's lab. Even at this time of night, he was seated behind his computers. A pizza sat to the side, the tangy smell lingering in the small room.

Aiden approached him. "I need your help. Now. It's really important."

Nick's hands still hovered over the keyboard. "What's up?"

Aiden moved closer. "A guy with a gun showed up at a charity event that Harper attended with her mother. Looks like he was going for Governor Young, but I want to make sure."

Nick's eyes narrowed. "Are they all right?"

"Fine. The guy was riding a thing that looked like a small laptop with four wheels. Controlled it with his feet."

"I think I know what you're talking about. I saw an ad for a prototype for one of those in Japan on my honeymoon." His fingers went flying over the keyboard.

"I think they called it a walk car or something like that." Nick pulled up a website with a large picture of the device. "Yeah, look. Is this it?"

Aiden peered over his shoulder. "That's it."

"Never seen one in person, but man, I sure would like to." Nick rubbed his hands together. "What happened to it?"

"I assume it's in evidence with the police," Aiden said. "The state troopers on the governor's detail arrested him, and they claim he's known to them and this was an attack on her."

Nick narrowed his eyes. "But you don't believe them?"

"It's not that I don't believe them. The guy didn't have any ID on him, and I need to be certain he is who the troopers think he is." Aiden took a breath. "Can you pull up any CCTV in the area? Then, if it captured the incident, run the guy through facial recognition software."

"If it exists, I'll have it to you within the hour." Nick turned to his computer.

"Send me the footage even if you don't get a hit on the ID, okay?"

"Will do." Nick flicked his fingers, dismissing Aiden like swatting away an irritating bug.

When Aiden first met Nick he'd thought the guy was kind of rude, but he really was a great guy, just very focused on his work.

"I'll be in my condo if you need me." Aiden left the room, but he didn't think Nick had a clue he'd gone.

Back at his condo, he looked for Harper, but she wasn't in the room. A bolt of unease hit him until he heard his shower running. He totally understood that she wanted to wash off the night. So did he. He'd come close to losing her. Too close. And it was a good thing she'd gone to bed, or he would've let her know how much seeing her in danger had bothered him.

Erik stared over the back of the couch. "You look worried."

"I am." The collar of Aiden's tuxedo shirt was strangling him, and, even when he unbuttoned it, the fabric felt too restrictive. He stripped down to his undershirt and settled next to his brother. "We almost lost someone tonight, and I can't let it go until I know for sure the man they arrested is who everyone thinks he is."

Erik shifted on the couch, setting a bag of potato chips next to him. "You think they got it wrong?"

Aiden grabbed a chip, and the salty crispness dissolved in his mouth as he crunched. "I'd rest easier if the shooter had ID in his pockets, and we weren't relying on the troopers' ID. You know how adrenaline can cause people to make mistakes. Maybe the troopers made this guy for someone else, and he really was there for Harper."

Erik's eyes narrowed. "Is it common for a stalker to escalate to murder like this?"

"It's not uncommon," Aiden said. "But from the content in the letters, I honestly never believed he would move this fast."

Erik shook his head. "So you're thinking he's our guy and Harper could be in the clear."

"Isn't the guy they arrested who they say he is?" she asked from the mouth of the hallway.

Aiden chastised himself for not being more careful. He had his back to the hallway and didn't hear her enter on her bare feet. He turned and forced himself to lighten up. "I'm sure he is. I just want proof."

She stepped into the room. "How are you going to get that?"

He told her about his conversation with Nick, and she gave a sharp nod, but that worry in her eyes remained.

"You guys mind if I go change?" Erik ran his finger along his shirt collar and mocked gagging.

"Please go ahead and get comfortable like I did." She smiled at him. "If Aiden says it's okay, that is."

"Fine," he said, knowing it would seem petty if he refused, though he didn't want to be alone with her. Or maybe he did, too much.

Erik took off, and Aiden reached for his tuxedo shirt.

"Don't bother," Harper said. "I don't mind."

But he did. Oh, he did. He minded all right. She was wearing a delicate pink tank top and matching silky pajama pants, and he wasn't about to be too relaxed around such temptation. Better to put on the shirt as a reminder of the professionalism he wanted to maintain. He got up and slipped it on.

"No relaxing for you," she said. "Mr. Professional at all times."

"I'm not here to relax." He started working the tiny buttons on the shirt. "I'm here to protect you."

"Which you did an amazing job of tonight." She cast him an admiring look.

The way she was looking at him, he couldn't even come up with words to say. He just wanted to pull her close and hold her.

She took a step toward him, and he hurried to the kitchen. What was he doing? He was supposed to be the professional she'd just accused him of. Not running like a scared little boy. He opened the refrigerator and pulled out a single-serve orange juice. When he turned, she was standing right there. Her wet hair clinging to one of her shoulders.

He didn't think but brushed it away with his free hand. "Tonight, I..."

His voice broke, and he stopped to take a long drink of the juice. The sweet liquid cooled his throat, but that was all.

"So you aren't the total professional you're trying to make me believe." She moved closer and twined her arms around his neck, her delicate fingers running gently over his skin. "I could've died tonight. We could've died tonight. I just want to feel alive."

"Harper, I can't. We can't." He set down the orange juice. "You know that."

"But we already did once before." She pursed those red lips. "Didn't you enjoy our kiss?"

He took a long breath and inhaled the sweet smell of her shampoo. "You know I did."

"Then, why?"

"You could've died tonight. It's my job to be on duty twenty-four/seven to be sure you stay alive. No time for flirting. Kissing. Anything else. Just focus on the job." He gently took her arms down and set her away.

She blushed bright red. "And here I am throwing myself at you."

"Please don't misunderstand," he said, still feeling the softness of holding her. "If it were any other situation, I would let you throw yourself at me all you want. But until that stalker is behind bars, we need to be extra careful, and distractions like this can cost lives."

"I get it. But one question. What happened to you not wanting to get involved at all?"

As of now, all she knew was that he was physically attracted to her, but it was more than that. He liked the whole package. Her determination. Her kind heart. Her competitive nature and desire to work toward a goal. Her compassion. And he just plain liked being with her. Sharing things with her. He could imagine much more. Coming home to her. Sharing his day. His life.

Dangerous emotions. At least dangerous if he wanted to stay single and get this business off the ground.

He looked at her and was going to tell her exactly that, but she was peering at him with wide sincere eyes, and she deserved his honesty. "You happened to me."

"What does that mean?"

"I'm attracted to you. You know that. But it's become more. When I saw the gunman, I..." He shoved his fingers into his hair. "My heart nearly stopped, and that has never happened to me before. Never."

"I felt the same way when you pushed me into the car, and your back was exposed." She took his hands, her skin soft and still warm from the shower.

"But see, this..." He lifted their joined hands. "This is what we have to put aside."

She smiled at him, and he nearly jerked her to him and showed her how much she meant to him. But in addition to her being a client and him needing to remain professional, he still hadn't had a chance to think about or even tell her about his missing kidney. He hadn't been involved with a woman since the transplant and never really considered what it might mean in that scenario. He didn't think he'd really let it impact his life other than reducing dangerous activities, but what about his future?

Sure, he'd pondered that before donating. Weighed the risks. But they were just facts and statistics then. No names. No faces. But now that he'd fallen for Harper, everything was becoming clear. Was he willing to saddle a wife with the extra worry? Could he ever marry? He just didn't know right now.

He heard a key sliding into the lock, and he dropped her hands and spun, going for his weapon. The door opened, and Erik entered with Nick behind him.

Aiden took a moment to let the shock of surprise flow out of his body. He'd been caught up in her again, and it had to end. For her safety.

He reminded himself of his life's creed. *The ability to control my emotions and my actions, regardless of circumstance, sets me apart from other men.* It was time he displayed the control he'd learned to master.

"This is exactly what I meant," he whispered to her. "I can't be surprised by someone coming to the door. I need to focus and be ready to act at all times."

She looked disappointed, maybe hurt, but he wasn't going to change his mind. He mentally put up a wall between them and then looked at Nick. "Must be important if you came all the way up here."

"I wanted to see your face when I gave you the information I found." He handed a packet of papers to Aiden.

The front page read Confidential Report on Dewitt Urbina. "This the guy they arrested?"

Nick nodded. "Or at least he's the guy in the video."

Aiden was impressed. "How'd you get his name when his prints didn't return a match in the database?"

"Database of Facebook." Nick grinned. "I simply uploaded his image to Google and ran a search."

Aiden shook his head. "We have all these law enforcement tools, but in today's world Facebook often trumps all."

Nick nodded. "You can read the report for details, but, in a nutshell, he's a local farmer who is also into skiing. And he's very vocal on gun control, opposing Governor Young's stance."

Harper joined them. "So he *was* out to get my mom."

"Could be."

"Could?"

Nick frowned. "I found something else that might put his motives in question."

A warning bell went off in Aiden's head. "What's that?"

"Just look at this photo." Nick held out a picture.

Aiden's heart dropped, and he flashed his gaze up to Nick. "He thinks he's quite the poet and has an antique typewriter."

"He does indeed," Nick said, looking proud of discovering the picture with Urbina sitting behind a manual typewriter. "Question is, does it have a misaligned A?"

Harper punched the pillows as she made the bed. She hadn't slept. Not one bit. She'd tossed and turned all night in the luxuriously soft sheets, her mind torn between Aiden's admission of his feelings for her and the fact that Urbina fit many clues in their hunt for the stalker. She'd immediately called her mother, who'd insisted that the police get a search warrant for his place to look for the herbicide and test the typewriter. Which they were going to do, but were taking their time in getting back to her mother.

Harper took one last look at her appearance and winced at the dark circles under her eyes that not even her cover-up could hide. She wouldn't have to worry about putting Aiden off. Her *Walking Dead* look should do that all on its own.

She headed for the living room and heard the low hum of conversation. Good. Aiden wasn't alone. She turned the corner and found all five of the brothers in the living area. They were seated and holding plates with bagels slathered in cream cheese and mugs of coffee. The nutty scent perfumed the air, and she was almost drawn across the room to the pot that was gurgling the end of its cycle.

Aiden looked at her from next to a portable whiteboard, black marker in his hand. As he laid eyes on her, a genuine smile lit his face. "Good morning."

She could get lost in that smile, so she looked at his brothers instead. "I'm surprised to find everyone here when some of you should be sleeping."

"What can we say? We're gluttons for punishment." Erik grinned.

She laughed at his boyish smile. "What's going on?"

"We just started reviewing our suspects and leads on your stalker," Aiden said. "You're welcome to join us."

"Let me grab some coffee first." She went to the kitchen but caught the names listed on the board as she passed. Gurly, Tanner, Matthew, and Urbina. Right now, her money was split between Gurly and Urbina, but she could only rule out Matthew.

She poured her coffee and added sugar this morning for something sweet to brighten her day. Bagels and cream cheese sat by the pot, but she couldn't eat anything while discussing her stalker. Plus, she hoped to get in some time at the gym and she would eat after her workout.

She went back to the living room and sat on the end of the sofa by Erik.

"Let's start by listing reasons each person is a suspect." Aiden tapped the first name. "Starting with Tanner."

"Access to herbicide," Brendan said. "Former boyfriend. Skis."

"No alibi for when the letter was put in our vehicle," Clay added.

"The dad hasn't called back." Aiden wrote it all down and added *call the father* next to the point on the board. Aiden turned. "Anything on Tanner buying a typewriter?"

Brendan shook his head. "Called every store I could find

in an online search. No one has had a typewriter in years. Or, if they did, they don't remember."

"Figured that was a long shot." Aiden added a note to that effect, and then tapped the next name. "Gurly?"

"Convicted of rape," Erik said.

"Wanted for another rape." Drake frowned. "Not sure of his alibi, as we haven't found him."

"And don't forget the items we found in his motel room," Brendan added. "Plus, he may work on a farm. We're still waiting on a few callbacks, so we can't rule that out. Lots of farms use migrant workers and don't check IDs very carefully. He could be using an assumed name."

Drake set down his empty plate. "And he was in all those videos watching Harper."

Aiden noted that. "And Urbina?"

"Herbicide," Clay said. "Skis. Typewriter."

"And poet," Harper said, glad to be able to add to the discussion that was leaving her unsettled. "At least one of his letters suggests that."

Aiden noted it on the board then wrote *Alibi?* "Not for the shooting, but for the other events."

"And Matthew?" Aiden asked.

Clay leaned forward. "I keep checking in like you asked me to do, and the guy's been in Vermont the whole time. He could've hired someone to do his dirty work, but like we've discussed, that's not typical for a stalker's need to see their victim."

"Is everyone agreed he's a no-go?" Aiden asked.

The others nodded, and Harper did too. She'd never thought Matthew was a viable suspect. True, she was probably too close to the situation to be objective, but it sure appeared to be a long shot at best.

Aiden struck through Matthew's name and tapped the top three names on the board. "It could be any one of these guys. Which means we need to concentrate on our outstanding items and hopefully narrow the field."

"My mother is still trying to get info on Urbina's typewriter and checking on the herbicide." Harper rested her mug on her knee, the heat seeping into her skin. "I'll let you know the minute I hear from her."

Aiden added that to the board.

"Ditto on my calls for the farm list," Brendan said. "But you already have that noted."

"The only other outstanding item I can think of is the special fingerprint test Sierra is doing," Harper said.

Aiden nodded. "I'd like to check in and try to push her along, but—"

"Big mistake, bro," Drake said. "She won't appreciate it, and you know what that means."

Aiden's forehead wrinkled. "She'll turn the tables on me and start talking about my personal life."

"Exactly." Drake faked a shudder. "No one wants that to happen."

"Not to mention that she'll contact you the second her tests tell her something, and trying to push her won't make the results go faster," Clay said, his tone matter-of-fact.

"You're right," Aiden said. "I'd only be asking for trouble I don't need right now."

"We're also waiting for DNA on the gifts and letters sent to Harper, right?" Clay asked.

"Right." Aiden turned to the board to write it down. "No point in following up with Emory either. The results take at least twenty-four hours, and we're not there yet."

Harper's phone rang. Hoping it was her mother, she dug it from her pocket. Drat. Not who she was expecting. She looked up. "It's my dad. I should take it."

She stood and went to look out the window with the fabulous view of the downtown Portland skyline, the sun

228

glinting off buildings and the river. She tried to put a cheerful note in her tone. "Hi, Dad, What's up?"

"He killed...she's in the...oh, no." His voice broke, and he panted like he was hyperventilating.

Her stomach clenched, and she wished her hand was free to reach for her ring. "Dad? What is it? What's wrong? Who killed who?"

Aiden jumped up and charged over to her. "Killed?"

She shrugged and held out the phone so Aiden could listen too. "You're scaring me, Dad."

"Sorry, I—" His voice faltered. "A woman. In the barn."

"What woman? What happened to her?"

"I don't know her." His voice was barely above a whisper. "I found her. She's dead. Her throat cut. And she has a note pinned to her shirt."

"Note?" Harper looked up at Aiden, her heart in her stomach. "What does it say?"

"It...it says"—he sucked in a noisy breath—"it says, "I thought she could be a substitute for you, Harper, but you're the only one for me.'"

21

Brendan turned into the long driveway of Harper's family home, and her gut tightened when she saw the place was swarming with police. Lots and lots of uniformed officers and white-suited forensic staff. She clenched her hands as they drove past her mother's car and two black SUVs that had Blackwell Tactical guys leaning against them. She'd come to support her father and seeing the chaos, she knew he would need comfort.

Brendan stopped at the yellow crime scene tape strung across the drive and tied to the big maple tree with the rope swing she and Tanner had spent hours on during their childhood.

Tears of sadness mingled with fear, and she didn't know which emotion was going to win out. She should pray, but she struggled for the right words.

Where are you, God? How could you let this happen?

Her father was sitting on the back of an ambulance with one of those shiny blankets over his shoulders, his face haggard and stressed. She gasped then bit her lip to keep from crying.

"What is it?" Aiden asked.

She took a breath. "My dad. He looks awful, and it's all because of me."

Aiden swiveled to look at her, fixing his concerned gaze on hers. "You can't blame yourself for what some crazy person does. None of this is on you."

He was right, but she still felt responsible. She wanted to help him, but she knew it was going to take time for him to get over finding a dead woman in the barn. Maybe he'd never get over it and have to move. To leave his precious orchard. That would kill him.

"I just don't get it," she muttered. "Where's God in all of this?"

"He's here," Aiden answered when she was really more talking to herself.

"Where?" she challenged.

"All around. You just have to look for Him."

She shook her head. She couldn't imagine the loving, all-powerful God she knew would allow this to happen or even allow the stalker in her life.

"I get what you're going through." Aiden gestured at his brothers. "We all do. We've been there many times on the job and in the military. And at times, we've lost sight of God."

"So what did you do?"

"I went back again to the last place where I saw Him and started from there to rebuild."

Last place. When was that? "I'm not even sure I know when or where that was. Definitely not since this all began."

"It's hard right now, but when you find some quiet time, I know you can figure it out."

"What makes you think that?"

"Because I know you, and I know God. You both have the same goals. You won't give up until you find Him again, and He won't give up on you either. He'll keep after you until He gets your attention."

Aiden's words comforted her. For the moment anyway, but long-term, she would have to find that quiet time Aiden mentioned and get before God to have a long talk.

Aiden released his seatbelt. "I don't suppose I can convince you to wait here while I find out what's going on?"

"Sorry. No." She slid out of the car, the fresh country air hitting her the minute she stepped down. She took a deep breath, drawing in so many memories with it, pulled her shoulders back, and marched up to the uniformed deputy standing by the fluttering tape. "I'm Harper Young. Detective Voight is expecting me."

Aiden came up behind her.

The deputy held out a clipboard. "She's over by the barn talking to your mother. Just sign in first."

"He's with me." She nodded to Aiden as she scribbled her information on the sign-in sheet and handed it to Aiden, not giving the young deputy a chance to argue.

"I'll let her know you're here." He got out his phone.

She opened her mouth to argue. To tell him that this was her home and she had every right to access the property, but this wasn't her home right now. It was a crime scene. A murder scene at that. And she didn't want to make a fuss. It would embarrass her mother and stress her father.

Aiden's hand brushed hers, and she flashed a look up at him. He offered her a comforting smile, and she knew the touch had been intentional. She appreciated his concern and stepped closer to him. "Thank you."

He nodded, his gaze once again focused as Detective Voight strode toward them. She was a petite woman with short gray hair in a blunt cut to her shoulders and a trim figure in black dress pants, gray blazer, and white blouse. She wore serviceable shoes and had a no-nonsense look.

She shoved out a hand. "Detective Kathy Voight. You must be Harper." As she shook hands with Harper, she lifted her gaze to Aiden. "And you are?"

"Aiden Byrd, Nighthawk Security." He handed a business card to the detective. "We're providing protection services for Ms. Young, and I'll be escorting her through the crime scene."

He sounded so professional and looked it, too, and Harper was impressed with his quick transition from supportive man to bodyguard.

Voight frowned. "I'd like to keep the people on scene to a minimum, so you can wait here, and we'll see to her safety while she's on the property."

His shoulders lifted, and he looked even more imposing. "I'm sorry. That's not negotiable."

Detective Voight hunched her back and looked like an angry cat that was about to hiss and spit.

"Please," Harper said, trying to make peace. "I would like him to accompany me."

Voight gnawed on the inside of her cheek and looked like she was going to say no.

"And I'm sure my mother, who hired them, would like it too." Harper hated to play the my-mom's-the-governor card again, but she had to put up with all the inconveniences of being the governor's daughter, so she might as well take advantage of the connection when it was important.

Voight scowled and lifted the tape. "Stay close together and right behind me."

"I served as an ATF agent for years, so I know crime scene protocols," Aiden said.

That made Voight's scowl deepen, and she turned to march off. They followed, but, when they reached the barn, her dad launched off the bumper and jogged over to her.

"You shouldn't have come," he said, clutching her arm. "It's horrible, and I don't want you to have to see her."

She patted his hand. "They need me to take a look in case I know her."

"I'm so sorry." His eyes were haunted.

"You have nothing to be sorry about." She squeezed his hand and released it to look at her mother, who was approaching.

Escorted by two troopers on her detail along with Coop and Jackson, she was dressed in one of her power suits and high black pumps, her makeup and hair perfect. She looked out of place on the farm, and especially at a murder scene.

She gave Harper a short hug. "I heard they'd called you in."

"They think I might know this woman."

"Do you have any thoughts on who it might be?"

Harper shook her head.

"I didn't recognize her," her mother said.

Harper grabbed her mother's hand. "They made you go in there?"

"They wondered if it might be related to the man threatening me."

"Have you learned anything about Urbina's typewriter?" Aiden asked.

"No." The governor released Harper's hand and gave her troopers a very disappointed look. "I would have expected to hear something by now."

Mirrored sunglasses hid the troopers' eyes, and their faces showed no reaction.

She looked back at her mother. "Since the Blackwell guys are with you, does that mean you don't think the threats against you are resolved?"

"It's too soon to know, so we're being cautious."

"I'd like you to accompany me now, if you don't mind,"

the detective said, looking at Harper and then at her mother.

"Sure," Harper replied.

Voight started for the barn. Harper and Aiden followed. She'd been thankful for him almost since he'd started working her detail, but, except for when he'd saved her life in Salem, she'd never been more thankful than now.

They entered the space that smelled like a mixture of grease and oil laced with horse manure and hay. Her horse, Pepper, whinnied from one of the four stalls in the back of the open barn. The green-and-yellow John Deere tractor parked in the middle, very familiar to her, yet the forensic staff in white suits hovering next to the closest stall were foreign.

They stepped out of Voight's way as she approached the stall.

Harper stopped to take a breath. Aiden gave her hand a quick squeeze, and she let out the breath and swung around the wooden gate. A woman with purple lips and a distorted face lay on a bed of hay saturated with crimson blood, her throat sliced from ear to ear. The metallic smell of blood mixed with hay, and Harper's stomach churned.

"Do you know her?" Voight asked.

She nodded and opened her mouth to speak but couldn't get the words out.

Aiden stepped forward. "It's Ulyana Lebedev. One of Harper's teammates on the U.S. Alpine Ski Team."

Aiden felt out of place in the large farm-style kitchen with a big worn table in the middle. Harper and her parents each cupped mugs of hot coffee while he stood to the side with the troopers from Governor Young's DPU and Coop from

Blackwell. Aiden had started to think of himself as more than Harper's bodyguard, but, honestly, that was all he was. Just like these other guys. Hired hands.

He didn't like the thought and wanted to sit down at the table with them. To talk through the incident. To take Harper's hand and offer comfort.

She'd burst into tears in the barn, and then run from the space and into her father's arms. When she told him Ulyana was the deceased, he'd started sobbing with her. Not the governor, though. She remained outwardly calm. The unflappable governor. But she twisted her wedding ring, round and round, telling Aiden she was upset too. It also told him that Harper shared more traits with her mother than he'd first thought.

Now, the governor sat calmly, staring at Harper, who looked distraught and pensive.

Harper set down her mug. "I have to call Coach. Tell him about Ulyana."

"I can do that for you," her mother said before Aiden could offer the same thing.

Harper shook her head. "I'm not a kid anymore, and you need to let me handle it. It's my responsibility."

Her mother frowned. "I'm not trying to treat you like a kid. I just want to help."

"I think the best thing you can do is go back to Salem with your guys. They're making me nervous."

Her mother looked at the men assigned to her protection. "Would you mind waiting outside?"

"No problem, ma'am," the one next to Aiden said.

Coop departed with the guys, and Aiden wondered if he should be going with them. He looked at Harper to take his cue, but she was staring at her mug. He shifted his focus to the governor, but she was watching Harper.

Nothing for it, but to ask. "Would you like me to go with them?"

Harper looked up at him, her forehead scrunched. "I would like you to sit down with us."

He took a seat at the end of the table and felt the governor eyeing him, but he wouldn't look at her. He didn't want to inadvertently transmit his feelings for Harper. He should have remained standing. Kept that professional distance.

Harper looked at him. "Where do we go from here? Other than to notify Coach."

"Since Gurly's looking good for your stalking and this murder, we need to call Detective Johnson so he can coordinate with Voight."

"Will you do that?" she asked.

"Of course." He stood. "I'll do it right now."

Thankful for a reason to get away from the governor's continued study, he went to the corner of the room, made the call, and told Johnson about the murder.

"I'll get with Voight and compare notes," Johnson said.

"I've got Harper's safety to worry about," Aiden said, looking at her as she twirled her ring around her finger. "Will you keep me updated on new developments?"

"I'll loop you in on anything I can."

Aiden ended the call and headed back to the table.

Coop came to the door. "We have a Tanner Gidwell who wants to see Harper. He says he knows something about the murder but will only tell her."

"Odd," she said and looked like she was going to invite him in.

Aiden stepped up to her. "He's a suspect. He needs to be searched before he comes in."

"I'll see if he'll submit to one." Coop exited.

Aiden looked at Harper. "Are you up to talking to him?"

"I never really thought he was my stalker anyway, so sure." She locked gazes with Aiden. "As long as you're with me."

"Trust me," he said, his hands going to his hips. "I'm not going anywhere."

The room fell silent, and he could hear the clock shaped like a teapot mounted above the range, ticking away. It grated on his nerves, but he remained watching the door.

Coop returned. "He agreed, and I've cleared him."

"Then send him in," Aiden said, acting like he wasn't troubled, but in fact, he was. Very.

He went to the door and watched as the guy who Aiden still hadn't cleared stepped into the room. He wore jeans and a baggy T-shirt along with that same dirty baseball cap he'd worn when Aiden questioned him.

He pulled his shoulders back into a hard line, showing more backbone than Aiden had given the guy credit for. "I'd like to talk to Harper alone."

"Not going to happen." Aiden eyed the guy. "I'm not going anywhere."

He shifted his focus to the table. "Then, begging your pardon, Governor Young, but could you and your husband leave?"

Harper's mother looked at her daughter. "Is that okay with you?"

Harper nodded.

Her mother frowned. "We'll go, but only because you said you know something about the murder. If I find out you don't know anything, be prepared for my wrath."

Tanner cringed. "Yes, ma'am, but I do have information to share."

The governor and her husband got up slowly and took reluctant steps toward the door.

"Can I sit down?" Tanner asked, looking like he'd lost his confidence.

"Sure," Harper said. "It's been a long time."

He dropped into a chair across from her. "I know, right? I...we..." He removed the hat, ran his hand over his head, and replaced it. "I thought we would've gotten back together a long time ago."

"You did?"

Tanner nodded vigorously.

"What do you know about the murder?" Aiden asked to move them along.

That gained him a dirty look from Tanner, but Aiden didn't care. He didn't like seeing this guy with Harper. He'd kissed her once upon a time. Maybe fallen in love with her, and maybe she loved him back. And that didn't sit well with Aiden.

Tanner folded his hands on the table. "I was up late. Couldn't sleep. Went to our shop to work on my Mustang."

"You still have it?" Harper asked.

He nodded and smiled. "We had some good times in that car, didn't we?"

"Absolutely," she said.

Aiden stifled a growl.

"And you saw what?" Aiden pressed.

Tanner kept his gaze on Harper. "I saw a light in your barn. Not like the overhead light had been turned on, but like a flashlight."

"And you didn't think to check it out?" Aiden asked.

Tanner glared at Aiden. "I was going to go over and take a look, but the light went out. Then I heard a car door close, and I saw a pickup rolling down your drive, no lights on and the engine off. Just coasting. I thought again about going over, but the truck reached the road and took off without lights. I couldn't see the plates or anything to ID it. But the engine didn't run particularly well, and I might be able to identify it based on that."

"You were always good with engines," Harper said, a hint of praise in her voice.

"And that's it?" Aiden asked. "That's all you saw?"

Tanner nodded.

"And what time was this?"

"I didn't look at the clock after I got up, but that was around three a.m."

"Why couldn't you tell this to the police?" Aiden challenged. "Why insist on seeing Harper?"

"I could've." He turned back to Harper. "I could...it's just...I wanted to see you before you went back." He jerked a thumb at Aiden. "After this guy's questions and innuendos when he came to interrogate me, I didn't think you'd agree to see me unless you had a good reason."

"Why did you want to see her?" Aiden asked.

"Would you please?" Tanner lifted his chin. "This is between me and Harper so butt out."

Aiden didn't like the guy's tone and took a step toward him.

"Please," he said.

Aiden widened his stance and nodded. "Go ahead."

Tanner looked at Harper. "After this guy talked to my mom, she asked me why we split up and why I never fought for you. I didn't have an answer. But I got to thinking about it. It was why I couldn't sleep last night. I realized I've compared every girl—every woman—to you since then. So maybe I still have a thing for you."

He took a long breath and peered intently at Harper, whose eyes were wide with shock.

"You don't have to say anything," he went on. "I just wanted you to know that I do. I do have a thing for you, and I would like to try to get back together."

Her mouth fell open for a second, and then she shook her head. "But it's been, what? Ten years. I'm not the same person anymore, and neither are you."

"Still, in your off-season, we could try to reconnect, couldn't we? And if it's the travel you're worried about, I'm okay with that until you retire. Then you can come back to the orchard, and we can combine our two businesses and run them together."

"That's—"

He held up a hand. "Don't say anything right now. Just think about it, and I'll call you."

"I don't want to lead you on, Tanner." Harper gave him a sincere smile. "There's someone else in my life right now."

Aiden's turn for a jaw drop. This was the first time he was hearing about another guy. She wouldn't lie to Tanner, that much Aiden knew, so she wasn't making this up. And she sounded very sincere. Why hadn't she told him?

Tanner's shoulders hunched. "Are you serious about him?"

"All I know right now is that I have feelings for him that you and I never experienced." She patted his hands. "I hate to disappoint you, but please, don't hold out hope. There's someone out there for you, and I know you'll find her."

Time for Aiden to step in. "I'll see you out, Tanner."

Tanner got up reluctantly, took a longing look at Harper, and left the room. Aiden stood at the doorway until Tanner exited the house. Then Aiden turned back to Harper to ask about this man in her life, but Harper's parents returned, and then Brendan came to the door.

Brendan glanced at Harper then back at Aiden. "I hate to interrupt, but can I speak to you outside for a moment?"

Aiden followed his brother outside but stayed by the door to protect Harper if needed. "What's up?"

"I got a call back from a manager at one of the farms I had to leave a message with."

"And?"

"And they use Norflurazon on the farm and have a guy working for them who fits Gurly's description. He's living in their bunkhouse with the migrant workers, but his name is Steve McKinney."

"And you think it might be Gurly using an alias?"

"I do." Brendan firmed his stance. "I texted her a still of Gurly from the video, and she made a tentative ID."

"Way to bury the lead." Aiden shook his head. "Where's this farm?"

"Less than twenty miles from here."

"And is McKinney at the farm now?"

"She said he isn't expected back until tomorrow morning. He was off yesterday and today. Left first thing yesterday morning, and she says he never returns from his days off until he's scheduled to work the next morning. She told me she would let me know when he came back."

Aiden pondered the news for a moment. "Gurly's had plenty of time off to kill Ulyana."

"Yeah, my thoughts too."

"Did you warn her not to talk to him about your call?"

"I did, and I told her he could be dangerous and to call us immediately when he shows up, but, if she felt threatened, to call local authorities. Or maybe you want to leave this up to them."

"Are you kidding? With no proof he's our guy or even Ulyana's murderer, Detective Voight will insist on talking to him first, and by the time Voight gets to Gurly, it could give him a chance to flee. There's no way I'm letting that happen."

"Figured you might say as much."

"Let's get Harper back to Veritas and then come back and sit on the place."

"Sounds good to me." An eager expression brightened Brendan's face.

"I'll go see if Harper's ready to leave, and, if not, encourage her to go." Aiden looked at his brother. "If McKinney really is Gurly and the killer, he could be hiding out in the woods watching everything go down. So keep your head on a swivel and tell the others to do the same. Including Blackwell."

"Roger that." Brendan strode down the driveway.

Aiden went back into the house, forcing himself to appear calm when his insides were jittery.

Harper met his gaze. "Is everything okay?"

"We have a lead on Gurly." Aiden took his seat at the table. "He might be at a nearby farm going under the name of Steve McKinney."

"Wait." Harper grabbed his arm, her mouth hanging open. "Steve McKinney? Don't you recognize that name?"

Aiden shook his head.

"He's a pioneer in the speed skiing world. I'll bet Gurly is using the name as a joke."

Aiden's gut cramped hard. "Then it really could be him, and we should get going so we can stake out the farm."

22

Aiden kept his gaze pinned outside on the way back to Veritas, but his gut was another matter. That remained firmly in a knot. The first thing he would do when he got back was to get Harper alone and ask about this mystery guy. How pitiful was that? They'd just found a murdered young woman, and he was concerned that Harper was in love with another guy. If she had a boyfriend, she should've told him. Not only as the person providing her security, but also as a guy who was falling for her. She said she hadn't dated, so maybe it wasn't a boyfriend but a guy who didn't return the feelings. Maybe that's really why she didn't date.

He stepped into the elevator at Veritas and turned to his brothers. "Let's take fifteen minutes to regroup and then we'll meet back in the office to plan our approach for the Sunny Acres Farm. I've got Harper."

He received a nod from everyone but Drake, who opened his mouth, but Aiden silenced him with a look. He was not in the least bit interested in one of Drake's barbs. Aiden punched the right buttons for his brothers' condos and leaned back while they got off on their respective floors.

On six, he checked out the hallway then stepped back to let Harper exit the elevator.

"How are you doing after the discovery?" he asked as he hadn't really had a chance to see if she was okay after such a shocking development.

"Better." She shuddered. "But it's going to take some time to get over seeing Ulyana like that."

"I hate to say this, but you won't ever get over it. Just learn to live with it."

"I suppose you would know."

He nodded but didn't elaborate, as she didn't need to know the things he'd seen as a SEAL or while with ATF. He unlocked his door and held it open. "Wait in the hallway while I clear the place."

"Is that really necessary?"

"You should know by now I don't take chances." He twisted the deadbolt and tugged on the door then made quick work of checking every room and returned to the hallway. He looked to her. "Did you mean what you said when you talked to Tanner?"

"Of course." She shrugged out of her jacket.

"You told him there was someone in your life," he said. "You didn't mention this boyfriend to us."

She looked him square in the eye. "There's no boyfriend. I was talking about you."

"Oh...oh!" The intensity in her gaze floored him. "I didn't...I mean, I knew we had something, but you made it sound like you were in love. Anyway, that's the way I took your comment about feelings you never had for Tanner, and I assumed you loved him at one time."

"Yeah, sure, as much as a teenage girl can love a guy. But what I'm feeling now, for you? It goes beyond that, and I honestly want to see where it might lead."

He was shocked to his core and didn't know how to

respond. "You know my position on that. I mean, I've been clear, right?"

"Very. But positions can change. Clearly, mine is changing."

"You still want to be the best at skiing though, right?"

"Yes. I think I can have both."

"Look," he said. "Even if we have feelings for each other. Even if I gave in, I can't be responsible for interfering with your dream. You'd grow to resent me, and that would end badly. So you need to keep thinking about skiing and only skiing, the way it takes to succeed. About getting right back to practice so you can win your second slalom and all the other World Cup races you have scheduled."

She didn't look happy with his pronouncement.

"I'm the one who decides what's good for me."

"You're right. I just don't want us to grow to resent each other."

"I get it, but we'll just have to see how it plays out."

He wasn't as certain, but talking about it wouldn't change anything. "I'm gonna go get cleaned up, and then we can head over to the office."

In his bathroom that smelled like her sweet hair products or perfume, he made quick work of washing his hands and face but took a moment to glance at himself in the mirror. He looked fine on the outside, but he was a mess on the inside. He was letting his responsibility to his brothers and their business ruin his life. Maybe letting the kidney issue do so too. When was he ever going to find another woman as incredible as Harper?

Was he going to be ten years down the road and look back, like Tanner had just done, and regret letting her go?

But long-distance relationships didn't work. Did they?

Do they, God? Could Harper and I handle that?

Aiden shook his head and stowed his thoughts. He had a

stalker—now a murderer—to catch. That was all he needed to focus on.

His phone rang, his screen displaying an unknown caller, but he answered in case it was related to the case. "Aiden Byrd."

"Yeah, it's Nigel Gidwell." The gruff voice carried a hint of irritation. "My wife said you wanted to talk to me."

"Yes, thank you for calling back." Aiden explained the situation and asked about Tanner's alibi.

"Um...well...let me think."

"Your wife said you were at your Legion meeting that night," Aiden said to help jog his memory.

"Oh, right. Yeah, I remember now. No, I didn't see Tanner when I got home. Sorry. I just hit the hay and didn't wake up until morning."

"What time did you get home?"

"Around ten."

"And you're sure you didn't see or hear Tanner's truck in the driveway? Either coming or going from somewhere?"

"Positive."

"Positive you didn't see anything or you're positive his truck was home?"

"I didn't see anything, but then from our house I can't see his place, so don't know if he was home or not."

Aiden didn't want to end the call because he hoped Nigel would give him a lead, but there was nothing else to ask. "Okay, thank you, Mr. Gidwell."

"Sure thing."

Disappointed, Aiden disconnected and headed for the family room. He found Harper leaning against the wall by the door, her expression pensive. Just fifteen minutes ago, he would've asked her what she was thinking about. But after her declaration, he held his tongue.

"Got a call from Tanner's dad," he told her. "He didn't see Tanner the night of the letter delivery."

She pushed off the wall. "So Tanner remains a suspect then."

He nodded and went to the door. "Hold here."

He stepped out to check for anything out of order. His phone chimed. He looked at the text from Sierra and turned back to Harper. "Sierra said she got additional prints from the earlier letters you received but doesn't have a match for them. However, they're different than prints previously recovered."

Harper stepped into the hallway. "So additional people touched the papers."

He nodded.

"Does this mean it's not Gurly?" Harper asked. "Because his prints aren't on anything."

"It's a possibility for sure, but again he could've worn gloves." Aiden led the way down the hall to the skybridge. "Hopefully, we'll find him at the farm and be able to answer that question today."

When they stepped into Nighthawk's office, his brothers were already gathered around their big table, a large aerial map of Sunny Acres Farm and the surrounding area in front of them.

"I see Nick came through with the map," Aiden said as he joined them.

Harper sat at the end.

He leaned over the map and used a red marker to put an X on the bunkhouse at the far end of the driveway. He was reminded of his SEAL days when the team planned an op like this. Though they would drill over and over, but this op wasn't nearly as complicated.

Now Harper was another story altogether. He'd never planned a SEAL op with a woman in the room before, much less a woman he cared about. Sure, he'd gone on ops with female ATF agents, but they were trained in assault and wouldn't be sitting, hands clenched and chewing on their lip, like Harper was doing.

If Aiden hadn't wanted all his brothers in on the planning, he could've asked her to stay in the condo with Drake or Erik, who weren't going on the op as they would stay with Harper, but he wanted all eyes on the aerial map so they didn't miss anything.

Harper's phone chimed, and she grabbed it. "It's from my mom. The A on Urbina's typewriter doesn't match the unusual A on the letters I got. She also said the detectives are interviewing him to ask questions about me."

Aiden nodded. "Looks like he might be in the clear, but I'm glad they're following up."

"Me too," she said. "And that's exactly what I'm going to tell my mom."

She started typing on her phone, and Aiden looked back at the satellite photo.

"So, what are your thoughts on the plan?" Drake asked.

"I'd like to hear suggestions for our approach." He already had in his mind the best way to handle the op, but it would be good practice for the others to weigh in.

Erik trailed his finger down the long driveway past the manager's house, a barn, and a small outbuilding. "We need two approaches. One for if he's already arrived back at the bunkhouse, and one for if he's not on the property."

"What do you suggest?" Aiden asked, though in his mind they only needed one approach.

Erik tapped his finger down the road from the property. "If he's home, looks like you can pull over here and approach on foot."

"Why can't we take this approach no matter where Gurly is located?" Brendan asked.

"You could, I just figured OGs like you wouldn't want to hike that far." Erik smirked.

"Old guys." Clay sat forward, looking like he might deck Erik. "Who're you calling an old guy?"

"Well, the three of you *are* all over thirty." Drake chuckled.

Clay rolled his eyes. "Says the guy who turns thirty in a few months."

"Focus," Aiden said, though he was smiling inside.

"What I meant about a second plan," Erik said. "We need a plan for breaching the bunkhouse in case Gurly gets there before us and there are people inside with him."

"You're right," Brendan said. "There are other workers on site. It could turn into a hostage situation if we're not careful."

Drake looked at Aiden. "Maybe you should sit this one out."

Aiden crossed his arms. "Not happening."

Drake raised his chin, glancing briefly at Harper. "One of us has to say something."

"Don't," Aiden warned.

"What?" Harper asked.

"He donated a kidney to our dad last year," Erik said.

"Erik." Aiden fired his youngest brother a warning look.

Drake ignored Aiden and focused on Harper. "It's one of the reasons we all got out of law enforcement."

"Drake," Aiden said again.

"Well, why'd we make the change if you're going to risk your life anyway?"

"We're not discussing this." Aiden rose to his full height and looked each brother in the eye, ending with Brendan. "If Gurly *does* get there before we arrive, could you convince the manager to call him up to her house."

"She's cooperated so far, so I don't see why not." Brendan

furrowed his forehead. "As long as we assure her that we'll take him into custody before he reaches her."

"We can do that," Aiden said.

"How can you be so sure?" Harper asked. "He's killed someone."

"Allegedly killed someone," Brendan said and got a raised eyebrow in response.

"It's not the first time any of us has apprehended a murder suspect," Aiden said. "We're trained to do so, and Brendan will be on overwatch, so he can take Gurly out if needed."

She gasped.

"Hey, hey," Aiden said. "That's the last resort, and it's not going to come to that. I just wanted you to know everything's under control."

"If you say so." She placed her hands in her lap and twisted her ring.

He wanted to offer more comfort, but he'd wait to do that after they finished this assault plan. And, lesson learned. Next time he had to plan an op, no matter the reason, he wouldn't do it in front of their protectee.

"Why didn't you tell me about your kidney?" Harper asked, trying her hardest not to let Aiden see she was hurt when her nerves were raw and her emotions right on the surface ready to explode.

He dropped onto the stool at his kitchen island. "It's not important."

"Not important. If you hurt this one, then what?" Just the thought nearly closed her throat.

"Then I'll deal with it." He grabbed his water and chugged.

She appreciated his brothers giving them a moment alone, but, honestly, it didn't seem to matter to Aiden. He wasn't going to talk about this with her any more than he did with his brothers.

Well, *she* wanted to talk about it. And do so before he went into danger. "Is this part of the reason you don't want to start a long-term relationship?"

He shrugged and looked at his glass. He turned it in circles in the moisture ring on the countertop.

"Come on, Aiden. Talk to me."

His head snapped up. "What do you want me to say? I love my dad, so I gave him a kidney. Yes, that means I only have one. Yes, that puts me at greater risk if I get injured. So I gave up the things I love. Skiing. My job. And yes, I haven't quite come to grips with it. All right?"

He pushed off the stool and marched to the door.

She watched in horror. She didn't want him to go into a dangerous situation with this being their last conversation.

She opened her mouth to call him back, but he stopped at the door and rested his forehead against it. She hurried down the hallway to him.

"Aiden." She took his arm to turn him around.

"I'm sorry I snapped," he said, his tone soft as he gazed into her eyes.

Emotions welled up inside her, nearly overflowing. "It's okay. I understand. At least I'm trying to."

"Most guys take their identity from their work. From their physical prowess. And I've recently lost both of those, so I'm trying to reinvent myself, and I don't want the new Aiden to fail you." He brushed her hair over her shoulder and rested his head against her forehead.

"That was hard for you to admit."

"Yeah."

"Can I remind you of something you told me?"

"Sure."

"God's got this. You just need to find Him, and you'll know everything's okay."

"Wise words." He smiled.

"Wise man." She pressed her hands against his chest. "And a man who will succeed."

"How do you know that?"

"I know you," she said to repeat his words again. "Things might be tough right now, but you're right where God wants you, and that's a very good place to be."

Nightfall. The beginning of the end of every day. In some places—dangerous places—the beginning of the end of safety and civility. But also, the best time to find cover, to find bad guys.

It was all in how you looked at it.

Aiden had to hope tonight it brought good things, because dark had descended on them by the time he got Harper settled with Drake at her side and Erik at the door, and then pulled into the ditch near Sunny Acres Farm with Brendan and Clay. Brendan had checked in with the manager to see if Gurly had arrived, but he hadn't come back yet.

They'd passed the Youngs' orchard on the way. Lights illuminated the property, and various sheriff's vehicles sat in the drive. Aiden half wondered if Gurly was still somewhere in the woods watching the chaos he'd created. Maybe hoping to get a glimpse of Harper again. But she was safely tucked up in his condo at Veritas, and they'd made good and sure they hadn't been followed back to Veritas.

Aiden looked at Brendan, who was on the phone talking to the farm manager.

"We're at your property now," Brendan said, picking up his rifle. "Three of us. All wearing black, so don't be alarmed when you see two of us approach the bunkhouse from the south side and one head into the barn."

He listened for a moment. "No need to call me. We'll be able to see any vehicle that turns onto your property."

Aiden slipped out of the old truck they'd borrowed from their dad so they would fit into the surroundings and quietly closed the door. Brendan and Clay followed suit. They all wore tactical vests and clothing to blend into the dark. The night was cool, the wind sharp and biting as he eased around the front of the pickup.

"Ready?" he asked his brothers.

He got a nod from each of them, and they started forward, keeping to the brush that ran along the property line. They had to cross a small creek. The water, icy at this time of year, trickled into his boots and wetted his ankles above. He reached the other side and heard a vehicle slow on the road. He held up his hand and lifted his binoculars to see if it was the blue pickup the manager had described as Gurly's truck.

But it wasn't Gurly. Far from it. A patrol car slowed to look at their truck. The deputy got out and pointed his flashlight inside the cab. He flashed the beam on the license plates and leaned down to his mic. Aiden figured he was running the plates. It's what Aiden would've done if there'd been a murder nearby. He waited and watched, hoping the deputy didn't come looking for them.

The officer flashed his light in the brush and on the other side of the road then shrugged and got back in his car and drove off. Aiden waited until his taillights disappeared over a hill and let out a breath.

"Good thing we took Dad's truck," Clay said. "If the

officer ran plates for the agency's SUV, he wouldn't have given up so easily."

"Agreed." Aiden turned his attention back to the op and started forward. They had to battle through fallen trees and knee-deep grass but finally came to the back of the main clearing.

He stopped and glassed the area with his binoculars. He paused on the bunkhouse, a run-down building that needed repairs.

"Outside lights on the bunkhouse. Probably motion-activated, so be sure to stay out of range." Aiden turned to his brothers.

Brendan lowered his binoculars. "It's clear for me to move. I'll let you know when I get to the loft and have a shot."

Aiden nodded, and Brendan moved ahead. Ducking down, he bolted for a tree then paused. He moved to the next one and then, giving the bunkhouse a wide berth, disappeared into the dark.

"Nothing better than this." Clay's voice burned with excitement. "Making a difference but doing it our way."

Aiden agreed to a point. "Let's just hope this all goes down peacefully and no one gets hurt."

Harper paced the wood floor in the condo behind Drake, where he sat on the couch, his phone in hand. He wasn't looking at it but was waiting for Aiden to call with a status update. They'd been gone for hours and could be gone for many more if Gurly didn't return home until the morning.

If so, she'd be nuts by then. Certifiable. Wild visions of Aiden or his brothers getting hurt kept racing through her mind. Especially Aiden. Two reasons. He only had one kidney, and she cared for him. More than she thought. But mostly, the kidney, right?

Wrong. She'd let herself fall for him. She blamed it on being away from the slopes. From not keeping her focus on her goals. From the stalker breaking down all of her resolve. Or it could be one other thing. God. He had this sneaky way of infiltrating her life, and she didn't even know. And before long she'd done something He wanted to have happen in her life when it was contrary to her long-term goals.

So, God, is this you? Truly. Do you want me to be with Aiden? Are you working on his heart too? 'Cause you're working on me. At least I think you are.

Sneaking in. Taking over. Guiding her in the right direction for her own good despite her wants.

If so, you better show me the rest of the plan, i.e., skiing because I can't hang up my skis now, can I? Not when I'm this close to setting a new record.

The night fell deeper into darkness, and Aiden hunkered down against a large tree trunk, Clay at another trunk not three feet away. The wind had picked up and was washing over them at a strong clip. He only hoped it wouldn't interfere with Brendan's shot, should he need to take one. He could account for the wind, but it made the shot harder to land.

Aiden stretched his arms and legs, getting stiff in the cold, and looked at Clay. "You change your mind about how great this is yet?"

"Maybe a little. Stakeouts were never that exciting, but the ending could be."

"True that."

Clay fell silent for a few minutes. "So you gonna let me take the lead here?"

"No."

"No matter what we all told you."

"Yeah, no matter that." Aiden made sure there was no doubt in his voice.

"Because Harper is more than a client."

"Could be," Aiden admitted. "But right now she *is* a client, and that's all that matters."

Clay shook his head. "Right. Professional at all costs. Even your future."

Aiden fired his brother a testy look, though he likely couldn't see it in the dark. "We need to be professional or we won't have a future. At least not as an agency."

"I'm pretty sure Harper doesn't care if we put a professional front up. She's gotten to know the real brothers over the past few days, and she's not going to run screaming if we're authentically ourselves."

"Actually, if I didn't rein you all in she *might* go running." He grinned at Clay. "Even I'd go running when faced with that."

Clay snorted.

A vehicle hummed from the highway. One with an engine that was chugging like it was on its last legs.

"Be alert," Aiden warned Brendan in the barn as he ran his binoculars over the property. "Suspect might be approaching the driveway."

"Roger that." Brendan sounded watchful and ready.

The truck slowed and turned in.

"Suspect vehicle in sight," Aiden said into his mic. "I repeat. Suspect vehicle in sight. We're a go."

23

Aiden had just texted Drake, saying Gurly had arrived, and Harper's stomach clenched tight. She could barely handle thinking about Aiden and his brothers in danger. She could only imagine this must be what the significant other of a law enforcement officer must feel every time the person they cared for went to work. If so, she was thankful Aiden had left the ATF and faced danger less often in his current duties.

"Come on," Drake said, rising from the couch. "Let's put all that energy into something productive."

"Like what?"

"Like let's finish going through those ski videos and maybe find more info on Gurly so when Aiden brings the creep in—and he will—we have more ammo for his conviction."

"Okay."

He grabbed his computer from the table and connected it to the TV.

"Don't tell Erik I know how to do this, or I'll get stuck with the job." He grinned.

She was struck with how much he looked like Aiden, and it made her heart hurt.

"What? You don't think I'm funny?" He mocked pulling a knife from his chest.

"Your smile. It reminds me of Aiden's."

"Ah, that." He opened his computer but looked at her. "I'm kind of known in the family for being straightforward. Telling things like they are."

"Yeah, I noticed that."

"So then you won't take offense when I say you need to give Aiden a chance. He's a great guy. Honest. Dedicated. And loyal. Man, the guy's loyal. To his family. His law enforcement brothers. To his SEAL team, whose backs he still has." Drake took a long breath, looking like he was getting a bit emotional. Probably due to the lack of sleep, as otherwise she doubted he would reveal this side of himself to a woman he hardly knew.

"When we found out Dad needed a transplant," he continued, "Aiden stepped up right off the bat. He told all of us not to bother getting tested. If he was a match, he was donating, and he wouldn't hear of any of us doing so. We all owe him big time for putting his health at risk to save our dad, which is why we formed the agency. To keep him out of those high-risk ATF raids. He would never have left that job otherwise."

"And you're telling me all of this because..."

"Because, he's never said so, but I think he's letting the one kidney thing impact his life. I mean, how could he not, right? Whether consciously or subconsciously. And now, he's also taken on the full weight of getting the agency off the ground. He's the big brother. Always in charge. Has to be the one to make the business succeed."

He paused, a frown finding its way to his face for a moment. "I have to admit, there are times we all just let him take it on because we know there's no point in arguing. But put that together with the missing kidney, and it spells disaster to his personal life. When this is all over and he feels free to go after you, I can see him pushing you away because he has to put his family first."

"He's alluded to both of those things."

"Don't let him get away with it." He firmed his gaze. "You're a goal-oriented person. An over-achiever. Set your goal on Aiden, and don't let him get away."

"I'll think about it."

"You do that, and I'll talk to my brothers. Maybe we can figure out a way we can step up and alleviate some of Aiden's responsibilities. Even if we have to tie the guy up and stage a revolution."

He laughed, but Harper could see how serious he was and how much he loved his brother. She respected him for his willingness to have this conversation with her and could easily imagine becoming part of this amazing family.

The thought shocked and scared her, but it also thrilled her. She wanted to be with Aiden. To find a way. To make the long-distance relationship work. Or to retire. One or the other, she wanted a relationship with him. *If* she could get him on board, and she suspected that was going to be an even bigger challenge than winning an Olympic gold medal.

Gurly's truck puttered down the drive and stopped in front of the bunkhouse as the sun began to climb and striations of red and orange burned in the sky. Aiden would love to enjoy the beautiful sunrise but he had a job to do and no time for distraction. He signaled to Clay, and they crept out of the brush toward the truck.

Whistling, Gurly hopped down and headed for the

bunkhouse. He jingled his keys in his pocket, the sound mixing with birds starting to chirp in the trees.

Aiden charged ahead to get to Gurly before he reached the bunkhouse, and Clay circled behind the man.

"I'd like to talk to you, Gurly," Aiden called out, his hand ready to go for his gun.

Gurly spun, eyes wide, panic wedged in the dark orbs. "Not sure who you mean. Name's McKinney."

Aiden scoffed. "You're going by that name sure, but your real name is Jeffry Gurly."

Gurly arched an eyebrow. "Do I know you?"

"Doubt it." Aiden moved closer. "But I have some questions for you."

"About?" Gurly inched toward the bunkhouse.

Aiden increased his speed, now ten feet away. "Harper Young."

Gurly blanched but quickly recovered, his expression going blank. "Who?"

Aiden suspected Gurly would be hard to get information from, but this was ridiculous. "You're a former ski coach, so you know who I mean."

Gurly narrowed his eyes. "You must have mistaken me for someone else. Like I said, my name's McKinney."

"A name you took from a former speed skier."

Gurly shook his head and moved closer to the bunkhouse door.

Aiden couldn't let the guy get inside. He picked up his speed. The door opened, and a Hispanic male, arms raised and yawning, walked out. This guy interfering was the last thing Aiden needed. It was time to grab Gurly and sit him down for a talk where no one else could get hurt.

Aiden motioned for Clay to move in. Gurly caught sight of him. He bolted ahead. In one swift move, Gurly grabbed the unsuspecting man and flicked open a switchblade. He put it to the guy's throat.

"Back off," Gurly said. "Or he dies."

Aiden didn't want to back off. He wanted to charge.

"I could take him," Brendan said. "Just let me know."

Aiden gave a quick shake of his head, telling Brendan not to act. They weren't officers responding to a hostage scene and wouldn't kill someone unless their lives were threatened. Not when, if they did as Gurly asked, he would let the man go. Sure, Gurly would get away, but they had no other choice.

"Please," the man pleaded. "He'll kill me. I know him. He's brutal. He'll do it."

Aiden signaled for Clay to halt. Gurly backed away with the guy, dragging him toward the wooded area behind the bunkhouse. Aiden moved forward, keeping Gurly in sight, but also keeping his distance so Gurly didn't slice the knife across the man's throat.

Gurly moved quickly toward a small storage shed near the woods.

"Open the door,' he snapped at his hostage.

The guy opened it and the pair disappeared inside.

Aiden's brain raced for what to do now. "You have eyes on them, Brendan? Any hole anywhere you can see in?"

"Negative."

Clay stepped over to Aiden. "What do you want to do?"

"Circle around back to make sure there's not a way out."

"Roger that." Clay took off toward the shed.

He reached the side when a large two-seater ATV crashed through the door.

Gurly was in the back of the two-person machine and had a loose hold around the guy's neck, the knife in place. He raced past Aiden, the man casting a terrified look at Aiden. The rumbling roar of the machine echoed through the morning quiet. Birds took flight, squawking and flapping their wings.

"Faster!" Gurly shouted.

The machine picked up speed. About one hundred yards out, Gurly pulled back and shoved the man into the mud then slid down behind the handles and roared off.

Brendan could easily take a shot and bring him down, but they couldn't shoot a fleeing man in the back. Or even shoot out a tire. Gurly would lose control of the machine and crash, potentially killing him without a helmet to protect his head.

Aiden looked around. Spotted a smaller machine in the shed. He raced for it and was thankful Gurly left the keys. Aiden fired it up.

"No!" Clay shouted. "Let me go."

Aiden wouldn't even consider it. Gurly was his man to get. To bring in. To make pay for hurting Harper. No one else. Him.

"Check on the hostage," he yelled to be heard over the high-pitched engine. "Make sure he's not injured."

Aiden hit the gas and roared off down the track running along the woods. He had to go. Just had to. Even though it was suicide in the cold light of dawn where Gurly could easily turn a gun on Aiden and take him out.

Harper sat next to Drake, trying to concentrate on the videos as time ticked by slowly. She appreciated his willingness to try to keep her mind occupied. He might be a no-nonsense kind of guy, but there was compassion and caring underneath. She'd found the same trait in all the brothers, and she gave their mom and dad kudos for raising such fine men.

His phone dinged, and he grabbed it. "Text from Clay. Gurly took a hostage and disappeared on an ATV. Aiden went after him."

"Alone?" She gaped at him. "Did he go alone?"

"Text doesn't say."

"Then ask."

"Sorry." He took a long breath. "No can do without one of them telling me they're clear to receive two-way communication."

"But I don't understand." She clutched her hands together. "I need to know."

"If they're engaged in a shoot-out or hostage negotiations, a text from me might distract them and someone could get hurt."

"A shoot-out! You think...?" She couldn't even continue her statement.

He held up his hands. "Calm down. I'm speaking hypothetically. These are procedures we've put in place for just such a situation."

She jumped up and stared at him. "How can you sit there so calmly?"

"Trust me." He gritted his teeth. "I'm far from calm, but I'm used to it."

"There must be something we can do to help."

"We can pray." He locked gazes with her. "And then it's all up to Aiden and God."

Going full throttle, Aiden rose up on his feet to see farther ahead. The wind beat him in the face, and he had to blink hard. In the early dawn light, he could still see the taillights of Gurly's vehicle and smell the exhaust, but Aiden wasn't gaining on the guy at all. He needed more speed. Unfortunately, even open wide, the smaller machine just didn't have the power that would allow him to catch up with Gurly.

Aiden sat and lowered his head to streamline his airflow and ran the machine full out. The wind buffeted his hair. The engine growled, and the machine vibrated beneath him as if it might fly apart at any moment from the high speed. He bounced over a deep rut, nearly losing his balance and doing a header. He had to be careful. No helmet. Falling off and knocking himself out wasn't going to stop Gurly.

"Aiden, report," came Clay's voice over Aiden's earbud.

Aiden would be glad to report, but he couldn't afford to take a hand off the handlebar to push his mic. If he'd known in advance that he would be flying down a muddy trail at top speed, he would've turned off the push-to-talk feature and could report without touching anything. But who knew this would happen?

At least Gage wasn't here to see this fiasco. He would be most disappointed in them, but not as disappointed as Aiden was in himself. He thought he'd planned for every possible situation. But why didn't he check that shed in the back?

"Okay, so you can't talk," Clay said. "I hope you aren't injured and can hear me. We found out where the trail leads, and we're on the road, planning to cut Gurly off at the crossing ahead."

Good. Great even.

Aiden rose up again to take a look. He'd made some progress in closing the distance but didn't see a road ahead. He dropped back down and wound the machine through the wooded path. Mud splattered over his legs. Trees snapped at his body, but he let the branches take their bite and kept hauling himself closer. Closer. Until he could hear the snarl of Gurly's machine more intensely.

He rose up again. The crossing was just ahead. Gurly

was slowing to cross the road. Aiden would keep going and come right up to Gurly. Hopefully, his brothers were nearby and would block the way.

Aiden dropped onto the seat and churned the machine closer. The terrain changed beneath him. The mud lessened. He looked up. Gurly was at the road. His brothers approaching from the side.

Gurly turned. Gave a sick grin and lifted his arm. He had a gun.

Aiden released the throttle. His machine decelerated beneath him, and he reached for his weapon.

Gurly fired.

24

Harper's phone rang, and she grabbed it. Her dad's picture popped up on the screen. *No!* It was supposed to be Aiden. Not her dad. She bit back her disappointment and answered the video call.

She tried to put a smile on her face, but her lips trembled. "How are you doing, Dad?"

"Still pretty shook up." He frowned and the stress of finding a murdered woman made him look far older than his sixty years. "How are you?"

"Okay," she said and made sure she sounded like it. "Aiden and his brothers found Gurly. They're going after him right now."

"Good. Good. The guy needs to be put behind bars." His adamant tone brought some color to his face. "And you deserve to have the stalking come to an end."

"It will when Gurly is caught."

He looked skeptical, but she didn't know why. Maybe he didn't trust that Aiden and his brothers could end this nightmare.

"And then you can go back to skiing," he said, his voice holding the same skepticism.

She nodded, but she honestly wasn't looking forward to it. Spending time with Aiden when no one was threatening her, when he wasn't being paid to be with her—that was what she wanted to do.

"How many more days do you have off before they expect you back?" he asked.

"Two. We have that last event with Mom, and then I have a flight out the next day."

"Right. Your mom. Her DPU said the guy they arrested is the one behind the threats against her, and she's going to release Blackwell. She wondered if you would want them to replace Nighthawk."

Odd thought. "Replace them? Why?"

"More experience."

Harper wouldn't even consider it. She wanted Aiden with her until the end. "I'll stay with Nighthawk and see this out. It looks like it's almost over anyway."

"Whatever you want, sweetheart." He offered a tremulous smile. "That's what we want too."

Her dad had always been so supportive and accommodating. Her mom, not as much, but they both loved her and, for the most part, would do what was best for her. Or, in the case of her mom, what she thought was best for Harper. Of that she was certain.

Drake's phone rang. Had to be Aiden.

"Gotta go, Dad. Love you." She ended the call and rushed over to the couch.

"Where?" Drake listened, his mouth turning down in a frown as he came to his feet. "How bad is it?"

Someone was hurt. She could feel it. She stood next to him and kept her gaze pinned to his face.

"We'll be there as soon as we can." He ended the call and took in a big gulp of air. "Aiden's been shot."

She grabbed Drake's arm. "Shot. How bad?"

He frowned. "Bad enough to be rushed to the ER."

⁓

Aiden didn't want to worry anyone, but they were all hanging over his bed, focused on him, their expressions filled with fear. Not just his brothers and sister, but his mom and dad and Harper. Worst of all was seeing the fear in her eyes. His family had years of living with law enforcement scares, but she was new to the trauma, and it showed in her tortured expression.

Sierra took his hand. "You gave us a scare."

"Sorry."

Her husband, Reed, stepped up behind her. "He's okay. Let's focus on that."

She looked up at him, her eyes aglow with love for this man. "Spoken like a law enforcement officer who can face the same kind of danger." She shook her head. "Why, after being raised with a crew of law enforcement officers, did I marry an FBI agent?"

"Because I'm irresistible." He grinned.

She rolled her eyes, but Aiden saw her take his hand and hold it tight. He was truly jealous of what they had. He'd never really experienced the deep raw pain of jealousy until this moment. Sure, Harper had given him a moment of unease when he thought she had a boyfriend, but nothing like this.

His mother turned to Harper and put an arm around her shoulders. "It's okay, honey. He's got the best doctors, and he'll be fine."

"The gunshot was just a graze," he said, patting his bandaged upper arm to lighten her worry.

Her frown deepened. "But you bruised your kidney when you bailed off the ATV. That's what I'm worried about."

"You know what?" his mom announced and clapped her hands to get everyone's attention. "We need to let Aiden and Harper have a moment alone."

His father looked at his mother, then at him, and a knowing look spread across his face that was an older version of the same look on the faces of most of the men in the room.

"Okay, boys, out you go." He started shooing everyone toward the door that his mom held open.

She gave Aiden a pointed look before closing the door.

He glanced at Harper, who was still staring at the closed door.

"Mom and Dad weren't too subtle," he said.

She turned to look at him. "I'm learning that the words subtle and Byrd do not go together."

He grinned at her. "You're right."

She sat on the edge of his bed. "So, now that they left us alone, you can tell me you'll never do anything like that again."

He didn't like the desperation in her tone, but he couldn't do anything to ease it. "I wish I could, but I can't. If someone's life depends on me, then I'm going to act."

"But no one's life was on the line when you went after Gurly."

"Wasn't it?" He held her gaze. "If he'd gotten away, another woman would likely have suffered. I couldn't let that happen." He took her hand. "And I especially couldn't let him get away to continue to stalk you."

She continued to let him hold her hand. "He's behind bars now, so that can't happen."

Aiden nodded. "I only wish I could be in on his interrogation."

She lifted an eyebrow. "Do you think he'll say anything?"

Did he? "Probably not, but at least Johnson promised to get his prints to us so Sierra can compare, and maybe we'll know once and for all that he's behind everything. Plus, they're searching the bunkhouse and his truck now, and they could find the incriminating typewriter."

She frowned when he'd expected his statement to cheer her up. "And then you and your brothers will ride off into the sunset, and I'll go back to hitting the slopes."

"I wish it could be different for us."

"Do you?" She searched his face, looking for what, he didn't know. "Do you really? Because if you did, I'd think you could turn on that incredible determination you're known for and come up with a solution."

He didn't like the way she was looking at him now. A mixture of disappointment and a challenge. "I can't let my brothers down. They need me."

"Right." Her gaze dug deeper. "You have that incredible loyalty too. A great trait I admire. Except when it's carried so far that you give up on what you want for yourself."

He opened his mouth to argue, but a knock sounded on the door. He could ignore it, but he wasn't going to change his mind, so why prolong the conversation and hurt Harper even more.

"Come in," he yelled, earning a frown from her.

Detective Johnson stepped into the room. "Heard they brought you here and wanted to check in on you."

"I'm good. Just a scratch. They're keeping me overnight to keep an eye on me."

"Good to hear." He held up the folder. "Gurly's prints."

Aiden grabbed the folder before the detective changed his mind. "Thanks for coming through with this, man."

He nodded and dug in his pocket. He pulled out a flash drive. "Thought you might want to see this too."

"What is it?"

"Gurly's first interview."

Aiden worked hard to keep his mouth from falling open. "Hey, thanks for bringing it. That's great."

Johnson's eyes tightened. "You didn't get it from me, and it better not go any further than the two of you."

Aiden nodded.

Johnson turned to Harper. "And you should know, we're closing your investigation. We found a typewriter in a storage box in the back of his truck, and it's already been delivered to Veritas. I figure they'll get a much faster result than our lab. After those results are in, I'll send your mother a long report and copy you on it."

"So, Gurly's our guy for sure, then," she said.

"He is indeed." Johnson gave a tight smile. "And we recovered enough physical evidence at the barn to charge Gurly with murder too." He clapped his hands. "Okay, I'm taking off. You get well. You hear?"

He strode away. When the door closed, Aiden held up the flash drive to Harper. "If Johnson thinks this is important, we need to look at it right now."

Harper had wanted to keep talking to Aiden about a potential future, but he was too focused on getting a computer from Erik and loading the interview with Gurly on it. Not that she blamed Aiden. After all, that's what she'd hired him to do. His only concern was to protect her and find her stalker. Not to fall in love with her and give her the happily-ever-after she hadn't known she wanted until she met him. But now, she wanted that more than almost anything. Still, no point in thinking about it because Aiden didn't want her.

And she couldn't be mad at him for that either. He'd told her right up front that he didn't want a relationship. He was sticking to his guns and doing what he believed was right for him and his family. She couldn't fault that when *she* was the one who'd changed her mind. Didn't mean it didn't hurt. It did. Like a hot poker plunged into her heart. She'd stick to thinking and talking about the investigation so she didn't hurt so much.

Aiden's phone chimed, and he looked at it. "It's from Sierra. The typewriter from the bunkhouse matches the letters sent to you. Not only the wonky A, but the ribbon has the text on it."

"That's great. Now he'll be convicted for sure."

He nodded. "Yeah, really brings closure to the investigation."

"That's good too," she said.

They sounded like polite strangers instead of two people falling in love with each other.

"Okay, here we go," he said and scooted over on the bed so she could sit next to him to watch the interview.

She climbed up next to him and was instantly aware of every spot where their bodies touched, but he didn't seem to notice and clicked play. She focused on the screen. Johnson and Voight were both in the room, sitting across from Gurly, who didn't have a lawyer present.

He was stocky, just like in the video, and his head was shaved. He had dark circles under equally dark eyes that focused on Voight as if he wanted to kill her. *Gross.* Harper couldn't imagine having to sit across from him. She'd lose it for sure.

Voight didn't seem bothered by it but nodded at Johnson, who leaned forward. "Tell us about Harper Young."

"The skier?" he asked, looking baffled. "I once saw her on TV when the migrants had turned on the only channel we could get in the bunkhouse."

"Come on, Gurly," Voight said. "Don't waste our time.

You know who I'm talking about. We've matched your prints to your real ID. We know you were once a ski coach and have you on video at her World Cup events."

He let out a low growl of frustration. "Fine. I know about her. Doesn't mean I *know* her."

"But you want to, don't you?"

"She's something to look at, that's for sure. I wouldn't mind a tumble with her." He grinned.

Harper felt Aiden's muscles stiffen at the remark, and she was grossed-out even more by the man.

Voight leaned forward. "But she has no interest in you, does she?"

Gurly crossed his arms. "She would if she knew me."

"But she doesn't want to have anything to do with you. Not when she's surrounded with good-looking bodyguards." Voight paused. "Why would she want a washed-out has-been coach like you?"

He glared at Voight. "She's not into those guys. Her mother's making them keep me away, and now they're just in the way."

"Maybe I'm wrong, and she would find you attractive," Voight said, sounding like she was choking on the words. "Maybe you should tell her how you feel."

"I have. Like a zillion times." Gurly jutted out his jaw. "Even sent her gifts. She just doesn't listen."

Voight nodded, having the guy in the palm of her hand now. "So uncool of her."

"I know, right? After I took the time to order gifts for her, she could at least show her appreciation like Ul—" He suddenly sat back and crossed his arms. "Not saying anything more."

"You were going to say Ulyana," Voight said. "What happened with her?"

"I don't know who you mean."

"We have you on video with her. And your DNA all over her murder scene."

"She wasn't murdered," he stated with resolve.

"Really?" Voight took out a photo of Ulyana in the barn and laid it in front of him. "What do you call this? She sure didn't slit her own throat."

He sat forward and touched the picture, his gaze softening. "She wanted me to be with Harper. Wanted it so badly that she didn't want to compete with her anymore, but she knew the only way for that not to happen was if she wasn't alive."

"So you killed her," Voight stated.

"No. No. It was her wish to leave this world. I just helped her. Not murder. Not murder at all."

Harper shuddered. "He's crazier than I thought. Thank God you kept him away from me."

Aiden closed the laptop. "We've seen enough. He admitted to stalking you and killing Ulyana. That with the physical evidence is enough to bring charges against him. It's all over, and you're safe now."

She should get up and leave, but she couldn't move. She rested her head on his shoulder. "Thank you, Aiden. I'll never forget what you did for me."

His good arm came around her, and he held her tightly. Held her as if he didn't want her to leave.

She closed her eyes and reveled in the warmth of his solid body. In his strength. In his touch. Remembered their kisses. The passion. The tenderness. The love. And pretended that she wasn't going to get up and walk out of his life. But that was what would happen, and her heart was heavy. So very heavy.

25

The next morning, when Harper returned from jogging, reporters swarmed her building's doorstep. She battled through the loud questions thrown at her about Gurly until she reached the front door of her condo. She wanted to collapse in the lobby, but they followed her, their questions more urgent. The guard stepped out from behind the desk, blocking the reporters, and she hurried to the elevator.

Inside, she let out a long breath and wished she could be anywhere but here. Mostly, she wished Aiden had been with her to keep the mob at bay. Or that he'd been with her at her mother's event last night. It seemed so lonely without him. But she was alone again. On her own. One more day at least, and then back to her teammates and skiing to take her mind off Aiden's rejection.

The elevator doors split wide, and her mother rose from the sofa. Her two bodyguards stood on either side of the elevator.

"What a surprise, Mom." Harper forced her voice to not reflect her frustration in having her mother show up unannounced. True, Harper had given her mother one of the new keys to her apartment the day before to be used for an emergency, but no emergency existed right now.

She searched Harper's face. "You look distraught."

"Press. They're in full force out there."

She frowned. "We should have expected that to happen once the murder broke on the news. It was only a matter of time."

Harper heard the commotion through her window, and she clapped her hands over her ears. "Just when I needed some peace and quiet."

Her mother took Harper's hands down. "You can't let it bother you. You've got work to do to get back in the mindset of a champion. You're going to do that, right? Get your head on straight?"

"Yes, of course." Harper raised her chin. "I always do, don't I?"

"Yes, but I sense something different here. Not the stalking. Not the murder. You're distracted by something else."

Harper was. By Aiden. But she waved off her mother's concern. "I'll be fine."

"It's Aiden, isn't it?"

Harper didn't answer because she might start crying, and that would make her mother press in even more. Harper couldn't handle that right now. Couldn't handle the pressure she would exert. Couldn't handle anything. "I need to get away from everything to get my focus back."

Her mother watched her for an uncomfortable moment. "What about the beach house? No one will bother you there, and you can have peace and quiet."

"Great idea. I can get out of here right away. I'll go pack now." She started for her room.

Her mother took her arm to stop her. "Be sure that's why you're going. To clear your head for competition."

"It is," she said, but as she went to pack her bag, she had

no idea the real reason she was going except she knew she had to escape. She looked over her shoulder. "Once I ditch the press, I'll stop by to say good-bye to Dad and then head to the beach. I can leave for the airport from there."

"I'll be watching your heats. Do me proud."

"Don't I always?" She turned and went to her room.

Aiden pulled on his jacket, sliding the bloodstained arm over his hospital band so he could go home. The hole in his vest and blood were a reminder of his close call. He didn't tell his brothers, but Gurly was using a large enough caliber bullet that if Aiden hadn't bailed from the ATV at the last second, his injuries would be far more severe. If he'd even survived.

The door opened, and, hoping it was Harper coming to check on him, he looked up. Brendan strode in, and Aiden's hope fell. He didn't know why he thought it might be her. He'd made it quite clear that he wasn't available, and she'd planted a sweet kiss on his forehead and told him to have a good life.

"Guess you were expecting someone else," Brendan said.

"Let's go."

"Don't you need a wheelchair?" Brendan asked.

"They told me I could walk out if I was able, and I am. I'm fine."

He headed for the door, wincing when the pain in his back and flank from the bruised kidney hit. So he wasn't completely fine, but he would be. And that was all that mattered.

They strode out together and got into Brendan's truck. It was immaculate, like everything Brendan owned. He never lost his army neatness or, maybe as a sniper, he just liked precision. Either way, he was a neat freak. Kind of at odds with his daredevil personality.

He got them on the road. "Mom was hoping you'd stop by so she could lay eyes on you again."

Aiden really wanted to go home, but he wanted to relieve his mother's mind. "Fine. It's not like we have any jobs waiting for us."

Brendan glanced at him. "Actually, we got a few calls after the news story broke about our citizen's arrest of a murderer and stalker."

Just what Aiden had hoped for when he'd taken on Harper's protection. "Then after we see Mom, let's head back to the office so I can follow up on them."

"No need. Clay and Drake already have meetings scheduled for the afternoon."

"Seriously?"

"Seriously."

"Well, then." He didn't know what else to say. Part of him was glad they'd stepped up, but the other part of him wanted to be there so he could be sure they landed the clients. No. He had to let them fly on their own.

Brendan pointed his truck toward their parents' house, and Aiden sat back for the ride. When Brendan pulled into the driveway, Aiden took in the two-story traditional home painted a crisp white with black shutters. A big house, it had six bedrooms. He and Sierra were fortunate to have their own rooms, but the other brothers had shared, leaving one room for guests.

He got out at the walkway lined with orange and yellow mums he'd helped his mom plant way too many years in a row. His dad kept the yard putting-green neat and the house in good repair. After retiring from law enforcement, he'd been lost at first, but now he was content with his security-officer job three days a week.

Aiden didn't knock but unlocked the door and stepped in. The air smelled of banana bread, one of his favorites, and he went down the hallway to the kitchen, where he knew he would find his mother. She stood at the island, dumping a golden-brown pan of bread onto a cooling rack. She was tall and slender and he had no idea how she stayed in shape with all the baking she did. She'd recently cut her hair short and wore it with little tufts sticking up. The gray mixed with the blond, looking like fancy highlights from a salon.

She looked up and beamed a loving smile his way as she came around the island. "You're here. Let me look at you."

She took his wrists and pulled him closer, then turned him around. "You look good."

"I *am* good. Fine, in fact."

She eyed him. "But you'll still take a few days off, right? Maybe stay with us so I can spoil you."

"I'm needed at work."

"He thinks he's indispensable." Brendan shook his head.

"He is to me." She smiled and drew him close for a hug. He let her fuss over him and inhaled the smell of vanilla that always seemed to linger with her. As a stay-at-home mom, she was always baking either bread or rolls or desserts. They'd often devoured everything she made in one sitting. But she loved it, and they loved her. He loved her. Wanted a wife like her. Not necessarily someone who stayed home, but someone who lived her faith and embraced her family with unrivaled passion.

He started to get weepy but wasn't sure of the reason so he pushed free. He wasn't a mama's boy by any means, but no matter how old a guy got, his mother held a special place in his heart.

He slid onto a stool next to Brendan, who'd already cut off a large chunk of the bread and was devouring it.

She came past Brendan and thumped his head. "I made that for Aiden."

"I know." He grinned up at her.

"I know you know." She kissed his head and shook hers, then went to a second pan and emptied it out. "How about you take that and a piece to your dad? He's out in the garage tinkering with who knows what."

Brendan got up and plated two pieces of bread.

"He only needs one," she said. "He's not as active as he used to be."

"The second one's for me. I'm plenty active." He winked at her and took off out the back door.

"So," Aiden said. "What do you want to talk to me about?"

"That obvious, am I?" She sliced a piece of bread for Aiden and handed it to him.

"Totally." He took a bite and groaned over the rich, moist bread with the smooth banana flavor. "Thanks for this."

"I..." She came around to sit next to him, bringing her coffee with her. "I could have lost you." She held up a hand. "I know. I know. I didn't. But I thought, when you left ATF, that you would be safer. And here we are."

He set down his bread and took her hand. "I'm sorry, Mom. All of us have expected a lot of you to accept our choices in life. You've handled it so well that we don't really think about the position you're in."

She patted his hand. "All I want is to see you happy, and if that means you risk your life, then I can live with that." She took a long breath. "But you should also find some balance. A partner."

He rolled his eyes. "I should've known we were headed in this direction."

"I want to see you happy."

"I am."

"Not as happy as I know you can be with a woman like Harper." She held up a hand again. "Before you deny it, I saw the way you looked at her. Haven't seen that look in your eyes since you fell for that girl back in college."

He picked at the bread, pulling out the nuts and biting them. "Neither one of us is in a place for a relationship right now."

"Hogwash. It's just an excuse. No matter where you are in life, you can find an excuse not to get involved."

"But the business is just—"

"You have four brothers to help get that business off the ground," she snapped. "It's not just your responsibility."

"Harper's not going to quit skiing for a few years."

"So you do the long-distance thing." She looked him square in the eye. "The point here is that, if she means enough to you, you do the relationship. No matter the distance. No matter the time. You make it work. You've never failed at anything. I know you can do this. Just take a chance."

Aiden's phone rang. Seeing Emory on a video call, he answered. "What's up?"

"I'm here too." Sierra's face came on the screen. "How are you doing? Taking it easy?"

"I'm fine," he said, wanting to get to the information he knew they must have. "Do you have something for me?"

Sierra nodded. "I got Gurly's prints that you sent over to me, and they don't match the partial on Harper's water bottle."

Aiden sat up. "All the other evidence points to Gurly as the stalker, so how can that be?"

"I can't explain it, but maybe someone touched her bottle before she filled it."

"Yeah, that's the only explanation."

"Just as odd," Emory said, "I got the DNA back from the

items sent to Harper, and we have a familial match to someone in the database."

Aiden planted a hand on the countertop. "To who?"

"Tanner Gidwell."

Aiden's mouth fell open. "What did you say?"

"The results are a familial match to Tanner Gidwell. Matches to a male. Since he doesn't have any siblings, the match has to be his father, and he was likely the person who touched the paper."

Aiden's mind was spinning with the news. "But we have Gurly for the stalking, and PPB didn't have any DNA matches."

Emory's eyes narrowed. "I recovered the DNA from one of the handwritten letters Harper received a couple days ago."

"Sierra, did the partial print from the bottle match to Tanner?" he asked, trying to figure this out.

"I couldn't make a positive match," she said. "But I couldn't rule it out either. So, inconclusive."

"Maybe Harper has two stalkers," Sierra said. "I know it sounds bizarre, but it could happen. That the second guy took over and sent the handwritten notes."

"As far as we know, Nigel Gidwell has no reason to stalk Harper, but Tanner does," Aiden said.

"So maybe the dad touched the paper in the past, and then Tanner wore gloves and used it to write the letters," Sierra suggested.

It was a long shot, but possible, and the thought that Tanner could be after Harper put fear into Aiden's heart. "Then Harper isn't safe, and I need to find her and warn her now!"

Harper's father stood in the driveway wearing his favorite flannel shirt over a T-shirt and dirty work jeans. A shirt he'd always claimed to be his favorite. He was talking to Tanner's dad, who was dressed similarly, except he wore a jean jacket with patched elbows in lieu of the flannel.

They were engrossed in their discussion and didn't seem to hear her pull into the drive. Their body language was tense.

Were they arguing?

She got out of the car, letting the familiar scents of the orchard wash over her, and approached. "Dad?"

He spun, his eyes dark and angry at first, but blossoming into tenderness when he laid eyes on her. "Your mom said you were coming to say good-bye."

She nodded. "I'm going to spend the night at the beach house, and then I have a flight first thing in the morning."

"Hello, Harper," Mr. Gidwell said, his tone kind, but his expression still tight. "Tanner said he recently talked to you."

She nodded and hoped that Tanner hadn't given his dad the details. "Good to see you, Mr. Gidwell."

"Please," he said. "You're all grown up. Call me Nigel."

"Sure," she replied, doubting she ever would as it would feel weird. She faced her dad. "I'll let you two get back to whatever you were discussing and head out."

"Are you sure?" her dad asked. "I could put on some coffee."

"I need some time to clear my head." She glanced at the barn. "The beach house is the perfect place for me to do that."

She grabbed her dad up in a hug, taking a long sniff of his usual scent of hay and the outdoors. She pushed back. "I'll text you my schedule so you know when I'll be back for a visit."

He nodded, his eyes sad.

She touched his cheek. "Love you, Dad."

He gave her a sad smile. "Drive safely and enjoy yourself."

She turned to leave, not sure the word *enjoy* was relevant to her trip. Improving her mental health was the goal. A goal she knew how to achieve to overcome and win. She climbed into the car and, after a stop at a grocery store, made the one-hour drive over the winding mountain roads to the Oregon coast. She tried to empty her thoughts of everything, but visions of Aiden kept plaguing her.

Their kisses. Their laughter, though it wasn't often. The intense looks. His brothers, Sierra, and even his mom and dad. She could easily become a part of their family, and it seemed as if they would welcome her.

By the time she climbed out of her car into the salty ocean air, she was wishing he was here with her. But she was alone and needed to accept that. If she couldn't accept it now, how was she going to do it when skiing down a mountain, when every bit of concentration was needed to keep from falling and potentially killing herself?

She sighed, grabbed her bag, and headed for the side door.

The oceanfront house sat at the end of a long line of houses on the beach, most of them looking deserted for the season. If it was the weekend, the area would be hopping with tourists, but not on an off-season weekday.

She opened the door. The place always smelled a bit musty when she first arrived, and she'd grown to associate that smell with fond memories. She went back for her groceries and put them away, then threw the sheets in the washer so the fabric had a fresh aroma for the night.

She poured a tall glass of water and sat on a stool at the counter to do what she'd put off doing since yesterday. She grabbed her phone. She noticed several missed calls from Aiden. Must've happened while she'd been out of cell range on the drive.

She briefly wondered what he wanted, but she didn't have the mental strength to talk to him right now. Instead, she called her coach.

"Any word on Ulyana?" he asked right off the bat.

Not being in town, he wouldn't have heard about Ulyana yet, and he relied on Harper to give him the news. She should've called him sooner. "I'm sorry. I have some tough news."

"Is she okay?"

"She was murdered."

"Murdered? Really? She's dead?"

"Yes."

"That's just awful." Silence filled the phone, and she could imagine him running his hand over his head of nearly white hair then letting it slide down and clamp onto the back of his neck. How many times had she seen him do that when she'd messed up? Way too many.

"Has anyone notified her foster family or family in Russia?" he asked.

"The police are doing that."

"I know they didn't get along, but still... Are you coming back tomorrow?"

"Yes."

"Good. Good." He sighed. "This is going to mess with everyone's psyche, and having our top skier back will help."

Her spirit was destroyed. How much could she help the team cope in her current state?

"Okay, well thanks for calling," he said. "See you tomorrow."

"See you then." She hung up, feeling as down as she

expected from making the first call she'd ever had to make to tell someone that a person had died. She needed air.

She bolted from the stool, grabbed a Bible from the shelves lining one wall of the family room, picked up a beach chair and blanket, and headed out onto the empty beach.

Ah. Solitude. And cold. The frosty wind razored over her like a sharp knife scraping against her skin. Oregon beaches never really warmed up, but, at this time of year, they rarely crested sixty degrees. Today was much colder.

She settled into the chair, snuggled in the fluffy blanket, the damp salty air blowing over her. She closed her eyes and just breathed. In with the good thoughts. Out with the bad. She wasn't surprised the good thoughts included Aiden. He was going to be her biggest challenge today.

Hah! What was she thinking? Getting him out of her brain and focusing on skiing was going to be the biggest challenge every day for quite some time.

She closed her eyes and tried to remember the last time she and God had really talked, just like Aiden had told her to do. It'd been far longer than she'd first believed. She used to at least pray before every competition, but in the last year, she hadn't. She'd taken God for granted until the stalker when she'd asked for safety for the Byrd brothers and herself. But for the most part, she believed He would be with her no matter what she did. And He would. She just wouldn't know it or take comfort and advice from Him because she didn't look for Him. Didn't include Him.

I'm sorry. So sorry. Is that why you let the stalker invade my life? To get my attention? And was that the reason for Aiden too? So he could give me solid advice regarding you?

She opened the Bible and read. Searching for answers. Not an answer on how to change Aiden's mind, but one on how to change hers. To leave the hurt. Leave the pain and pin her focus where it needed to be.

The skies darkened, threatening a heavy downpour. Soft misty rain began to fall. She packed up her things and raced over the cool dunes and into the house, dropping everything by the door and sliding it closed against the rain now blowing sideways. She grabbed her water glass and took a long drink, cooling her throat. Setting it down, she noticed white powder on the counter.

What in the world?

Was it the same white powder they'd found on her water bottle?

She spun. Looked around the room. Had the powder been on the counter before, and she hadn't noticed it, or was someone in the house with her?

She heard a noise by the front door and reached for her phone.

She didn't wait to see who it might be. She couldn't. Not when she wasn't expecting anyone, and the powder could be a drug. She bolted for the sliding patio door. A hand grabbed her jacket from behind and jerked her back. She squirmed free. Spun. Saw Mr. Gidwell.

"It's you." She let out a long breath. "You scared me."

He didn't say anything, just stared at her.

She started to feel lightheaded. "You. Did you...did you drug me?"

"I'm sorry." He frowned. "You didn't do anything wrong. But I have to get your father's attention."

"But why?" She slowly reached behind her back to grab the door handle.

"He's spraying herbicide that's drifting over to our farm. We're going to lose our organic status. Going to lose the farm if he doesn't stop. He doesn't care. Not even after I sent those gifts and letters to you. He knew they were from me.

And he laughed at me." Tanner's father gritted his teeth. "Well, I'll make him care now."

She gaped at him. "You sent me gifts? Letters?"

"The things from your childhood. Things he would recognize. Things that would make him know it was me. Know I could get to you."

Dawning broke in her growingly muddled brain. That's when the handwritten letters started. Why there were two kinds of letters. Why the gifts changed.

She had to get away from him before the drug took full effect. She wrenched the door open and charged into the slashing rain. She'd surprised him enough that she had a head start. She raced across the slippery deck. Jumped down the stairs. Her muscles started to feel weak, her legs rubbery.

With the drugs on board, she couldn't make it very far. Hiding was her best chance. She ran around the side of the house. Slipped inside the outdoor shower and crouched in the corner. She got out her phone and cupped her hand over it to hide the light. She dialed Aiden.

"Harper? Thank goodness you called me back I—"

"Help. It wasn't just Gurly. Another stalker. He drugged me." She looked through the cracks of the boards and saw his shadow approaching.

"He's coming," she whispered. "Help me, Aiden. Please help."

26

Aiden jumped up from the chair in Nighthawk's office and looked at his brothers. "Someone's drugged Harper. Another stalker. She just called. I don't know where she is. You gather tactical gear in a vehicle while I get her location from Nick."

"You think he can find her?" Brendan asked.

"He has to." Aiden bolted for the door. He took the stairs down to Nick's lab three at a time, maybe four, and burst through the door. "Harper has another stalker. He's drugged her. I don't know where she is, but she has her cell phone. I don't care if you have to break every law in the book, but I need you to find her for me."

"No worries." Nick remained calm. "I put a tracking app on her phone when you had me check it out. Just in case."

Aiden stared at Nick. "I should let you have it for doing something like that without telling us, but right now I could kiss you. Find her. Now!"

Nick turned to his computer and brought up tracking software on the screen. "She's in Pacific City."

"What in the world is she doing there?" He racked his brain for a clue but couldn't come up with anything. All he knew was he had to get to her, and she was an hour away.

So how was he going to do that?

Think, man, think.

Gage.

"Is Gage still here meeting with Maya?"

"Let's find out." Nick dialed Maya.

"Gage still with you?" Nick gave a firm nod. "Then Aiden wants to talk to him."

Nick handed his phone to Aiden. "Harper's in trouble, and I need to get to Pacific City now!"

"Coop's standing by at the helipad," he answered calmly. "I'll call him and tell him to expect you. Need any assistance?"

Aiden would love to have Gage at his side. SEAL to SEAL. But Aiden's team had to stand on their own and not go running to Gage for every need. Plus, Aiden trusted his brothers with this op. They could do it. "We got this."

He tossed the phone back to Nick. "Get me everything you can about that address and text it to me."

"Sure thing. Maybe you should call the cops in Pacific City."

"Right." Aiden made the call and requested a car be sent to the vacation house.

"We'll respond as quickly as we can," the dispatcher said. "But you should know there was a serious accident on the highway with downed power lines and all units are responding."

Aiden said goodbye and shoved his phone into his pocket. "They don't have any units available. Let me know if her phone moves."

Aiden raced for the door and to the parking structure, where his brothers were loading the car. "Move! Move! Move! We're taking Gage's helo to Pacific City."

He slid in behind the wheel of the closest vehicle, his back hurting from the bruised kidney. A good reminder to be careful, but would he follow it? No way. Not if Harper needed him.

~

Harper's muscles relaxed, and her brain swam with confusion. She hadn't swallowed that much of the water, but the drug was kicking in. She suspected she would soon be asleep, and Nigel's pawn. Hah! Nigel. He'd asked her to call him that, and now she had to think of him by his first name because Mr. Gidwell was a friend. Someone who'd cared for her as she'd grown up. Someone her family knew and trusted. This guy wasn't Mr. Gidwell. He was Nigel all the way.

She peeked under the wall and watched as his feet moved past the shower and toward the road. Had she fooled him? Did he think she'd run off?

She held her breath and listened, but the slashing rain and sharp wind hitting the shower's wood slats was all she heard. She was already soaked head to toe, and she was surprised she wasn't shivering. From the cold, yes. But more so from fear. Maybe the drug prevented it.

How was this happening? Her next-door neighbor—Tanner's father—had been the one who'd sent her the last gifts. And he'd likely been the one who'd tried to poison her at Timberline.

Worse, her father must have known about it. Why hadn't he told her? She couldn't even fathom his silence.

She didn't see any sign Nigel was nearby, and she couldn't sit around and wait for him to find her. Wouldn't take him long to realize he hadn't checked the shower. She tried to get up. To move. Her legs were weak. She grabbed the wood braces on the wall and pulled herself up.

Yes. This was okay. She could do this.

She took a few steps. The area swam before her eyes, and she suddenly felt at peace. Oddly at peace. She dropped back down, hitting the shower's metal pipe, the sound clanging out.

No. No. No. She'd likely just pointed out her location to Nigel.

The shower door creaked open. Nigel stood there, his body highlighted by a nearby street light. A dark shadow. A foreboding shadow.

"Hello, Harper," he said, his voice calm yet lethal. "Time to come with me."

The helo winged through the storm, bouncing and swaying. A former army ranger, Coop was an experienced pilot, and Aiden had complete confidence in him, including the fact that he could hover this craft in a storm as the brothers fast-roped down to an open field near the beach house. It would be easier if Coop could touch down, but he didn't have permission to land on the beach, and they didn't want him to get into legal trouble.

Aiden looked at his brothers and pressed his mic on their comms unit. "Everyone clear on their assignments?"

His brothers nodded. Aiden had no idea who this stalker was. His bet was on Tanner because Voight had gone in search of him but hadn't found him home. If he was armed, Aiden would take no chances.

He and his brothers would land one at a time, the first having the second one's back and so on. Then they'd split up. Brendan would get a sniper view of the area at an outcropping of nearby rocks and assess the situation before they moved in. He'd report, they'd compile every known fact, and then they'd wing it from there. Aiden hated winging anything but didn't have time to plan. Not when Harper could be in the hands of a crazy person.

"ETA three minutes," Coop's deep voice startled Aiden.

His nerves were strung so taught, he feared they would snap. He wanted to be the first one out of the chopper, but Brendan convinced him that due to Aiden's latest kidney injury, someone needed to lay down cover fire if warranted. So fine. Aiden gave in. Not for himself. For Harper. He didn't want to take a bullet and not be able to help her.

Aiden looked out the window at the beach houses. The one they were targeting belonged to her parents, another property inherited from her grandad. At least that's what Nick said in an earlier text. He'd also sent the blueprints for the inside, which would be extremely helpful in the rescue.

The rhythm of the helo changed, and Aiden put on Kevlar assault gloves to keep from burning his hands on the rope. So did his brothers.

"You're a go," Coop said.

Aiden offered a quick prayer, then slid the door open. Rain slashed into the helo, wetting his body. He didn't care. He turned and placed the wench in place, checking to be sure it was fully locked into position and secured the rope.

He turned to Brendan. "You're up."

He swung the strap of his rifle over his shoulder and grabbed the rope. A wide grin claimed his face. He was eating this up. Right in his wheelhouse. "See you below."

He swung out into the rain, the rope sliding out with the wench, and disappeared into the clouds. When the rope loosened, Aiden grabbed it.

"Stay safe," he said to his brothers and swung out too,

making sure to get his knees and boots in the right position and not hold too tight with his hands. He slipped through the rain. Brendan waited below, his rifle out. Scanning the area.

Aiden dropped next to him and took position for Clay. Once Clay safely hit the ground, he nodded at Brendan to take off for the outcropping. Aiden kept searching the area around him as did Clay while their last two brothers descended.

"Will be waiting for your report." Coop said.

Aiden wanted a helo available in case Harper was injured, so Coop would hover nearby until Aiden dismissed him.

He signaled for his brothers to move, and they started down the beach. Thankfully, the homes between them and Harper's beach house were dark and looked unoccupied. If the residents were home, they would be sure to see them and call the police. The last thing Aiden wanted.

Clay and Erik split off and climbed up the dune. Clay would cover the side entrance. Erik would run the license plates of any vehicles in the driveway with a buddy at PPB.

Aiden and Drake approached her house through the driving rain biting into their faces and took a knee behind tall scrub grass. Using his binoculars, Aiden ignored the rain and scanned the property. Glass made up the entire back wall of the house, and he could see inside. Harper lay on the couch, a man pacing in front of the window.

She wasn't moving. His heart clenched.

Was she drugged or dead? He didn't know. Couldn't know until he got close to her. He wanted to bolt to the house and take the guy down, but that would be foolish. He swallowed his rage and focused on the man, trying to identify him.

"C'mon, turn so I can make out your ugly mug," Aiden

muttered, but the man crossed the room to look down on Harper.

Aiden's heart nearly stopped beating.

"Get ready to breach," he said into his mic in case the man tried to hurt her. "Brendan, you have a shot yet?"

"Not yet. These rocks are crazy slippery in the rain."

"Suspect standing over Harper, who looks like she's asleep on the couch," Aiden reported and prayed that she was alive.

"Got a truck plate," Erik said. "Belongs to Nigel Gidwell."

"Tanner's dad?" Aiden sat back but kept his eyes on the house. "That seems odd."

"Tanner could've taken his dad's truck," Erik said.

Aiden's gut churned.

The man inside turned and marched to the window, phone to his ear. Aiden zoomed in. "It's the dad. It's Nigel. Not Tanner."

"Why in the world would he want to drug Harper?" Drake asked.

Aiden released his mic and looked at Drake. "Call Nick. Ask him to look up the dad. See if he can find a reason."

As he made the call, Aiden scanned the suspect's body, looking for a weapon. He didn't see one. The wind picked up, howling over the dune and swamping the grasses in front of them.

"In position," Brendan said.

Aiden almost sighed. They wouldn't shoot Gidwell unless there was no other choice because, even if it was a clean kill, Brendan would still likely be charged with manslaughter and they didn't take a life when they could resolve things any other way.

"Zoom in," Aiden said. "Let me know if the suspect is armed."

"Roger that," Brendan said.

Aiden swiped the rain from his binoculars as he waited for his brother to use his high-power scope to search the room with great detail.

"Handgun on the kitchen counter," Brendan said. "He must not be worried about it with Harper passed out."

Or dead.

No. Don't think that way. Think about the layout of the house from the blueprints.

He mentally figured out the shortest path to the counter, other than the patio door where the suspect stood. "Clay, you got eyes on that side door?"

"Affirmative."

"Can you breach silently? Get to the gun?"

"Let me try the door."

Aiden was thankful that Gidwell remained on the phone, staring out at the water. If they had additional operators on their team, Aiden would set up their electronics and intercept the call to see if he could get a lead on who he was talking to.

"Door's locked. Could go in through a window."

"Hold on that." Aiden glanced back at Drake, who was stowing his phone.

"First blush, the guy's clean. Nick will keep looking."

"The house is what, fifty feet away?" Aiden asked. "We could get another twenty feet without being seen. That leaves thirty or so. You think we can make that thirty before the guy gets the gun?"

"If it wasn't raining maybe," Drake said. "In the rain, no."

"Yeah, my take on it too, so we'll need to approach from the other direction." He handed the binoculars to Drake. "I'm going to join Clay. Keep your eyes on the place. Let me know the second anything changes, including if Nigel ends his phone call."

He didn't wait for Drake to argue, as he most certainly

would want to keep Aiden out of a gunfight, but took off up the dune, his boots digging into the wet sand. Rain pelted his face, and wind whipped sand into his eyes. He hardly noticed. Not with his mind on Harper lying there. Defenseless. Not in control. Gidwell planning something Aiden couldn't even imagine.

He reached Clay. "Give me the glass cutter. I'm going in while he's still on the phone and distracted."

Clay gave him an irritated look but passed Aiden the cutter. He put his rifle over his shoulder and went straight to the best window for entry. He cut a small circle by the lock and released the latch. Thankfully, it slid open without a sound. Aiden shimmied over the sill and into the room. Landing as silently as he could, he signaled for Erik and Clay to hold and took a moment to let his eyes adjust.

He entered the hallway that led to the kitchen and listened. Gidwell was still talking, so Aiden moved in. One foot in front of the other on the tile floor, his tactical boots as quiet as he needed. When he could see into the room, he paused and listened to the conversation. Sounded like Gidwell had rented a cabin in the mountains, and there was a problem with his reservation.

Had he been planning to abduct Harper and take her to the mountains?

That wasn't going to happen. Aiden moved forward. Inching closer to the gun.

"Then I'll find another one, and you can expect a lawsuit for not following through." He slammed his fist into the patio door, and the glass reverberated, shimmering in the light. Aiden held his position, waiting for the guy to make another call.

"Stupid rental agency." He shoved his phone into his pocket and turned. He startled and locked eyes with Aiden. His gaze shifted to the gun, and he bolted ahead.

"Stop." Aiden lifted his gun and planted his feet. "Don't give me a reason to shoot you. Another one, that is."

Gidwell stopped.

"Hands on your head," Aiden ordered.

Gidwell looked around, took a step. Aiden dropped his finger to the trigger.

Gidwell winced and lifted his hands to his head.

Aiden pressed his mic but kept his gaze and gun pinned to Gidwell. "Move in. Search the rooms."

Aiden stood waiting, desperately wanting to go to Harper, who hadn't moved. Just to look at her, to see if she was breathing.

"I wasn't going to hurt her," Gidwell said. "I promise. I just needed to take her for a few days so her dad would listen to me and stop spraying the herbicide. It's drifting to our property. We're going to lose our farm if he doesn't stop, and it's been in our family for generations." He shook his head under his hands. "And I can't be the one responsible for losing it. I just can't."

"Behind you," Clay said.

"Restrain him so I can check on Harper," Aiden said.

"She's fine," Gidwell said. "Just a little ketamine."

"She's not fine!" Aiden snapped. "You terrified her. First with the gifts and letters and now by taking her hostage. I'm going to see that you go away for a long time."

"But I—"

"Didn't think," Aiden finished for him. "If you had, you would've realized you could never have let her go without her reporting you. And then what? You'd kill her."

"No. I..." He started crying, and Clay took his arms, one at a time, and zip tied them behind his back. He had the guy sit against the wall and stood over him with the gun.

Aiden didn't want to feel sorry for the man who'd hurt

Harper, but he did, and he offered a prayer for him and his family.

Drake came in through the patio door, Erik behind. Confident this creep wasn't going anywhere, he pressed his mic. "Stand down, Brendan. Gidwell's in custody."

"Affirmative."

Aiden hurried to the couch and knelt on the floor. Harper's chest rose and fell in rhythmic breaths, and his heart swelled with happiness. The happiness his mom talked about.

Question was, what was he going to do about it?

27

The earth moved under Harper's body, but she couldn't raise her head or even pry her eyelids open. Where was she, anyway? Not in her bed. The place smelled of antiseptic instead of cinnamon, the scent that lingered from her perfume in her condo.

"She has to be okay," a deep male voice said from nearby.

Something about the tone of the voice pricked at her memory, but she couldn't place it. Place him. It wasn't her dad, that she was sure of. So who? And what did he mean about her being okay?

"We got to her in time," another low rumbling voice said. "Chill and let the doctors do their thing."

Doctors? Was she in the hospital? Nah. This was just a dream, right? One where you can't open your eyes, and it feels so real, almost like you're hallucinating.

She listened carefully. Heard a few beeps of a machine. Tried to open her eyes again. Couldn't.

"Ms. Young," a man said, and a big hand shook her shoulder. "Can you hear me, Ms. Young? It's Dr. Lindsey."

Yes. Yes. I hear you. But her mouth wouldn't move.

"Looks like we'll need to wait for the drug to wear off," the doctor said.

"Wait? How can you stand by and do nothing?" the first male asked, the voice sounding so familiar.

"We aren't doing nothing," the doctor replied. "We're monitoring her vital signs and will address any issues that come up. Based on how long it's been since she took the drug, she should be coming around any time now."

I don't do drugs. Please. You must be wrong.

"The creep said he gave her a second dose when she started to come to, and he doesn't know how much." That guy again who sounded so concerned. But who was he?

Come on, think, Harper.

She tried. Hard. Then harder. Her brain hurt from the effort, but everything was still fuzzy. Wait. A handsome face came to mind. A smiling man who was drop-dead gorgeous. Strong and compassionate all at the same time. *Aiden. It was Aiden. Aiden Byrd.*

The last few days came flooding back. He was her bodyguard. Her hero. No, not now. He was done with that. And done with her. Her heart ached.

"Sit tight, and I'll check back in a few minutes," the doctor said.

She heard his footsteps move away.

"Please let her be okay." Aiden's voice sounded tortured.

"She will be, and then you need to quit being so stubborn and tell her how you feel." That other deep voice. *Brendan*, she thought.

"No point in it when we're not going to get together."

Her heart ached that he still felt that way.

"Another thing you need to get over."

I agree.

"No can do." Aiden sounded resolute, and she could just imagine his tight posture, those broad shoulders pulled back into a straight line. "I have the business to think of, and then there's the long-distance thing. It might not work, and it could distract Harper. Cause her to lose some of the competitions she needs to win to set the record. She's driven. Focused. I can't interfere with that."

"She'd get over it."

"Yeah, she probably would. But what if we stay together and, years down the road, she starts resenting me for keeping her from reaching her goal? I don't want to be responsible for that or live with such resentment."

I won't. Honest.

"Want to know what I really think?" Brendan asked.

"Can I stop you?"

"You've always achieved what you set out to do and have never failed in anything big. I think you're scared to make a commitment because of the kidney, or you're afraid to fail."

His comment was met with silence, and Harper wanted to see Aiden's face to know what he was thinking, but her eyes remained glued closed, and sleep beckoned. She tried to stay awake, but why? To hear more of Aiden's reason's not to be with her? Why would she want to hear that? She would sigh if she could, but instead, she let go, and the darkness took her.

Aiden was glad when the governor and Harper's father arrived because she was waking up, and he didn't want to be alone with her to see the hurt in her eyes over his unwillingness to begin a relationship. He wanted her. How he wanted her. He'd given Brendan reasons, but it was the kidney that was stopping him. He'd been sensitive about it before, but bruising it in the accident gave him a glimpse of how vulnerable he was. He couldn't saddle Harper with a man who was less than one hundred percent. Not when she had so much she needed to do on the alpine ski circuit. She couldn't be worried for him as she had been when he'd gotten hurt. He wouldn't do that to her.

He moved out of the way to give her parents access and rested a shoulder against the wall.

Her mother rushed across the room and took Harper's hand as her eyes fluttered open. "Are you okay?"

"I think so." She blinked a few times, her gaze unfocused. She closed them and kept them closed for a long moment. When she opened them again, she cast a fuzzy look at her dad. "How could you?"

He came closer, his eyes narrowed. "Could I what?"

"Let Nigel Gidwell stalk me like that," she spit the words out, pain in her eyes.

"Nelson, is this true?" Her mother eyed her husband.

An accusing stare Aiden would melt under.

Her father swallowed hard, his Adam's apple bobbing. "I didn't know it was Nigel. Not for sure. He hinted at the fact that he could get to you, but he didn't admit to sending you things. He couldn't because he knew I could've had him arrested."

"But you had to be pretty sure when the personal items from my past started arriving," Harper said.

He blanched. "I wondered, but I couldn't tell you."

"Why not?"

"I thought you might ask questions, and then—" He glanced between his wife and daughter, his expression so tortured, Aiden didn't know if the guy could continue.

"Spit it out, Nelson," his wife said.

"I didn't want you to find out the orchard isn't doing so well. Financially, I mean. That's why I kept using the herbicide. I didn't want to hurt Nigel's business, but I had a bunch of the Norflurazon in the shed, and I couldn't afford to buy anything else. Especially not the organic stuff. It's all way overpriced. And I couldn't afford to hire workers to take care of weed issues." His voice broke, and he put his hands over his face. "I didn't want you to think I was a failure."

"I wouldn't have thought that," Harper said. "I would have offered to help."

"Me too," her mother said.

He lowered his hands and fired a pain-filled look at his wife. "What, bail out your pitiful husband when you lead such a super successful life? I couldn't even stomach the idea of you offering me money, much less letting you give it to me."

Aiden thought there were some serious problems in this relationship that they would have to work out.

"Don't worry, Dad." Harper held out her hand. "I understand why you did it."

"You do?" He took her hand, his expression shocked.

"I don't like it and it's going to take some time to get over the hurt, but I forgive you and want us all to move on."

Aiden was just as shocked as her dad. He didn't think he could forgive so easily. But Harper was an incredible woman who could do anything she set her mind to. So if she'd already thought this through and decided to forgive, then she would do her best to do so.

She looked at her mother. "And neither of us holds you responsible for what happened. Life's too short to hold a grudge. Being taken hostage and stalked by a crazy man told me that. It's all over now, and we'll go forward."

Her mother didn't respond right away but pushed the hair back from Harper's face. "Are you sure you're okay?"

"I think so." She released her dad's hand. "I was in a fog for a long time after they brought me in. It was so weird. It was like I was in a dream. Everything out of my reach, but I could hear most of what was going on, and I heard the doctor say the drug just has to clear from my system."

Aiden looked at her. Had she heard his conversation with Brendan? If so, she knew what he was planning to tell her.

"Do you mind if I talk to Aiden alone for a minute?" she asked as if she'd read his mind.

"Of course." Her mother turned to face him. "If I was a hugger, I'd give you one for saving Harper. Just know we are forever in your debt."

"You don't have to thank me," he said. "I was glad I could be there when she needed me."

"You have my gratitude anyway." She glanced at Harper. "We'll be right outside."

She marched out of the room, shoulders back, and her husband followed at a slower pace.

"You're very forgiving," he said when the door closed. "I'm not sure I could forgive my dad so easily if he did that to me."

"I didn't want to. Trust me. But after all I've been through in the last few months, I need my family around me. If I held a grudge against my dad, so would my mom, and then what? They'd get a divorce for sure. This way, maybe they'll at least stay married."

He stepped closer. "Still, you're sacrificing your feelings for the good of your family. I'm impressed by that."

"You would do the same thing. You might not think so now, but you're even more a family person than I am. You'd do everything you could to hold them together."

"You could be right." He grabbed a chair and pulled it close. "And you were right on the doctor. He did say you'd be fine once the ketamine got out of your system."

"I can't wait until it's fully gone. It was so weird. I could hear Nigel and what was going on, but I couldn't move or do anything about it." She shuddered. "I couldn't stop him from his crazy plan."

He resisted growling, but that was what he wanted to do. He wished he could go back in time and stop Nigel from getting to her. "That must've been tough."

"It was, but I didn't think Nigel would hurt me until you pointed out that he would've had to."

"I'm sorry I was the one to make you feel that way."

She waved a hand. "Are you kidding? You came to my rescue even when we weren't paying you. That means a lot to me."

"I'm just glad you called me." He couldn't bear to think about what might have happened if she hadn't. "FYI, right before you did we figured out the Gidwells had something to do with this. Emory found familial DNA on one of the letters. It was a match for Nigel. We got it wrong, though. Since we had no reason to think Nigel might be stalking you, we believed he touched the paper in the past, and then Tanner used gloves when he wrote the letter. So we thought Tanner had taken you."

"Either way, you arrived in time." She reached for his hand, and he offered it. "I know this doesn't change things between us, but I want you to know I appreciate what you did."

He held her hand, feeling the softness. Knowing that holding this hand over the years would enrich his life so much, but only if he could resolve his issues. Which, so far, he hadn't been able to overcome. He would have to let her go and say good-bye. Again.

28

Three weeks later

The celebration at Nighthawk's office wasn't Aiden's idea, but he was attending to support his mom, who'd planned the event. She wanted to acknowledge the four-month anniversary of the agency. To acknowledge that, since they'd successfully protected and then rescued Harper —their workload dramatically increasing after making all the news outlets—they were not only in the black but doing extremely well.

He wanted to celebrate both of those things, but his heart wasn't in it. Not without Harper. He'd been thinking about her nonstop since she'd gone back to skiing. But he couldn't bring himself to ask her to be his. He'd wanted to when he'd seen her lying defenseless on that sofa. But he never made long-term decisions in the heat of the moment. Not even ones that involved his heart.

Especially ones that involved his heart.

"You don't look much like you're in the party mood," Brendan said. "We've got a lot to celebrate. I mean, hiring our first employee is huge. Really huge."

Aiden nodded. "It'll be good to have a receptionist to handle all the calls we've been getting."

"Especially the loony ones." Brendan grinned.

Aiden conjured up a smile.

"Come on, man," Brendan said. "If you're going to mope over her all the time then why not go after her?"

Aiden shrugged.

"Is it the kidney thing? Or the agency?" Brendan eyed Aiden. "The agency's under control."

"Yeah. You've all really been stepping up. Some days I almost feel unnecessary." Which gave him even more time to think about Harper.

"And then there's this." Brendan drew folded papers from his back pocket and handed them to Aiden.

He unfolded them but didn't know what to make of the medical report. "What's this?"

"We didn't want you to worry about your kidney or let it slow you down. We all got tested to see if we'd be a match in case you needed one someday. Now you know there are three of us waiting in the wings to replace yours if needed. Sierra and Erik's aren't a match, but no surprise there. They totally take after Mom. Guess they do in this matter too."

Aiden didn't know what to say, and good thing, because he was choking up.

"No more using that as an excuse. Oh, and this too." He took an envelope from the same pocket and gave it to Aiden. "Flight to Finland in time for World Cup Alpine Skiing. Have a good trip."

Aiden stared open-mouthed at his brother. "I can't go just like that."

"You just said that you felt almost unneeded at the office." Brendan eyed him. "And there's this thing called a telephone. It's a device where we can check in at any time, day or night. Sort of like you'll be doing when you and

Harper decide to quit being such idiots and get on with a relationship."

Aiden was half mad, half thankful for his brother's intervention. "You think you have this all figured out, don't you?"

"We do." Brendan smirked. "Only variable we can't control is if you'll listen to your wise brothers and take the flight."

"Go, son." His mother joined them. "She's what you want in life, so go after her."

"But the long-distance thing," he said.

"So you try it." His mom rested a hand on his arm. "What's the worst thing that could happen? You fail. But at least you tried. And that's what I've always taught you boys. You can't get in the game unless you try."

He looked between his mom and Brendan. Then around the room to find his brothers watching him. Clay gave a thumbs up. Drake a sharp nod. Erik made a kissy face.

He laughed, as his younger brother had planned, and suddenly it all made sense. He'd been fighting his feelings for no reason. Well, for a dumb reason. He didn't want to fail. But his mother was right. He couldn't get in the game without trying, and the game of life with Harper was well worth the try.

The crowd was buzzing with excitement, and adrenaline raced along Harper's nerve endings as she made her way to the starting gate. She was up next on the giant slalom, and, after winning the first race of the season, expectations were high. Not only her own expectations, but the crowd's and the news media's too.

Sadly, despite the adrenaline, her heart wasn't in the race. Her heart was back in Oregon with Aiden. Her coach had chastised her all week in practice, telling her to get out of her head and into the game, but she'd struggled for the first time in her skiing career. Really struggled. Sure, she'd had tough times in the past, but nothing like this. It was hard to love someone who didn't love you back enough to want to be with you.

She sighed and moved into position, sliding into the gate and taking a deep breath—seeing the run in her mind's eye. She would hit speeds of ninety miles per hour or more. She had to be in the game. Her life depended on it.

Please help me. I want to win. Sure. But more importantly, I want to be present enough not to get hurt. Give me the single-mindedness I need to run a safe race.

She moved forward, her skis on the precipice. She planted her poles.

You can do this. You have to do this.

She listened for the countdown beeps. Held her breath. Took off, digging in with her poles. A good start, especially for her mindset. She forgot everything except the icy snow beneath her skis and the gates ahead. She sliced by them, getting her skies on edge in the turns. One at a time. Going faster. Faster. The sharp wind in her face. Her body working on muscle memory. Down the hill she flew. She hit the flats and really dug in. Whisked over the finish line and executed a perfect stop.

She breathed deeply, her chest burning with exhaustion. She checked her time. *Good. Good.* She'd made second place. Not bad for her first run. Not bad for her distracted state. Not bad at all.

She skied toward the exit. A man stepped out, stopping her. She lifted her goggles to ask him to let her pass. But she got a good look at his face and could do nothing but stare.

"Amazing race," Aiden said, his cheeks rosy from the

cold. "It's even more impressive in person when I can see the slope."

She didn't know how she felt about seeing him. Mixed emotions for sure. Loving the sight of him in his dark blue ski jacket and wanting to throw herself into his arms and kiss him for days. Knowing that wasn't possible and hating the sight of him to remind her of the ache in her heart that she was trying to overcome. "What are you doing here?"

"I missed you. More than you can imagine."

Oh, she could imagine it all right.

"Seems I've been kind of moping around since you left. The guys thought I should come, so they bought me a ticket." He held out a small box. "I wanted to get you flowers, but the cold—I didn't think they'd make it."

She resisted taking the box. She wanted to see what was inside, but at the same time, she didn't want to see. She didn't want to get her hopes up. Her curiosity won out, and she took the box but considered not opening it. After all, in addition to missing him, she was hurt that he didn't want to be with her and had only taken this trip because his brothers paid for it. But her love for him won out, and she handed him her poles, took off her gloves, and opened the small box.

On a bed of cotton sat a silver ring. A plain band with two birds laser cut into it and a line connecting them.

"Since I'm a Byrd, I thought...I don't know. That if we could give this long-distance relationship a try, and if you wore this ring every day, you might think of me, and we'd have a better chance. It's kind of corny, I know." He blushed but took off his glove to reveal that he was already wearing a matching ring on his finger.

Her heart swelled with love. "It's very sweet."

"I love you, Harper, and I want to give us a try. If you'll

forgive me for not stepping up when I should have. I was an idiot, and I hope you can forgive me."

She held the box out to him.

He took it, his face crestfallen.

"Well," she said and held out her hand. "What are you waiting for? Put the ring on me. I have another race to run."

He whooped and slid the ring on her finger. She loved the feel of the cool metal as it spoke to a commitment they were both making.

She met his gaze. "I love you."

"I want to kiss you," he said, but looked down. "Um. How does a guy do that when you have skis on?"

She'd forgotten all about them. She bent down to release the bindings and stepped into his arms. His lips settled on hers. They were deliciously cold and warm at the same time. Her heart burst with love as her body tingled from his touch. He pulled her against his solid body, and she tightened her hold and deepened the kiss. This was what she'd been waiting for. Wanting. And now they were together. Forever, she hoped.

She heard people nearby clapping, and she remembered they were in public, so she pulled back only to spot a cameraman focused on them.

She looked at Aiden. "I hope you don't mind being the topic of the sports news, because the cameras are rolling."

"Nah." He pulled her close again. "It'll stop my nosy family from nagging me about what happened."

She wrinkled her nose. "I love your nosey family."

"That's good," he said. "Because when you accept one Byrd, you're likely to get a whole flock of them in your life."

ENJOY THIS BOOK?

Reviews are the most powerful tool to draw attention to my books for new readers. I wish I had the budget of a New York publisher to take out ads and commercials but that's not a reality. I do have something much more powerful and effective than that.

A committed and loyal bunch of readers like you.

If you've enjoyed *Night Fall*, I would be very grateful if you could leave an honest review on the bookseller's site. It can be as short as you like. Just a few words is all it takes. Thank you very much.

A woman on the run with no one to trust...

When a Christmas vacation at a snowy Mt. Hood cabin turns into a home invasion, Jenna Paine will do anything to protect her four-year-old daughter. Even if it means putting Jenna's own life on the line. Which she must do when the intruder threatens to kill her. She knows the invader will stop at nothing to take her out, and she can't let him get close or he might harm her daughter too.

She wants to disappear, but she can't survive on her own.

In fact, Jenna would be dead now it Brendan Byrd of Nighthawk Security hadn't come to her rescue during the invasion. Former Army Delta Force and county deputy, Brendan doesn't think twice about offering his agency's protection services for Jenna and her precious daughter.

What he does think twice about is opening his heart to Jenna only to have it broken again. But as the threats escalate, he must hone his vision where she's concerned, figure out this crafty attackers identity, and in the process, find a way to keep her alive.

Pre-order Now!

NIGHTHAWK SECURITY SERIES
Protecting others when unspeakable danger lurks.

Want to see more of the Cold Harbor and Truth Seekers characters in action? Keep reading for a sneak peek of the books in my new Nighthawk Security Series where the Cold Harbor and Truth Seekers characters work side-by-side with the Nighthawk Security characters.

A woman plagued by a stalker, children of a murderer, a woman whose mother died under suspicious circumstances. All in danger. Lives on the line. Needing protection.
Enter the brothers of Nighthawk Security. The five Byrd brothers with years of former military and law enforcement experience coming together to offer protection and investigation services. Their goal—protecting others when unspeakable danger lurks.

For More Details Visit -
www.susansleeman.com/books/nighthawk-security/

THE TRUTH SEEKERS
People are rarely who they seem

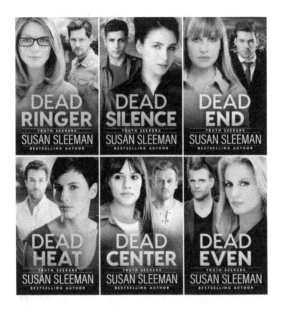

A twin who never knew her sister existed, a mother whose child is not her own, a woman whose father is anything but her father. All searching. All seeking. All needing help and hope.

Meet the unsung heroes of the Veritas Center. The Truth Seekers – a team, that includes experts in forensic anthropology, DNA, trace evidence, ballistics, cybercrimes, and toxicology. Committed to restoring hope and families by solving one mystery at a time, none of them are prepared for when the mystery comes calling close to home and threatens to destroy the only life they've known.

For More Details Visit -
www.susansleeman.com/books/truth-seekers/

BOOKS IN THE COLD HARBOR SERIES

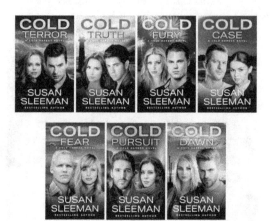

Blackwell Tactical – this law enforcement training facility and protection services agency is made up of former military and law enforcement heroes whose injuries keep them from the line of duty. When trouble strikes, there's no better team to have on your side, and they would give everything, even their lives, to protect innocents.

For More Details Visit -
www.susansleeman.com/books/cold-harbor/

ABOUT SUSAN

SUSAN SLEEMAN is a bestselling and award-winning author of more than 35 inspirational/Christian and clean read romantic suspense books. In addition to writing, Susan also hosts the website, TheSuspenseZone.com.

Susan currently lives in Oregon, but has had the pleasure of living in nine states. Her husband is a retired church music director and they have two beautiful daughters, a very special son-in-law, and an adorable grandson.

For more information visit:
www.susansleeman.com

CPSIA information can be obtained
at www.ICGtesting.com
Printed in the USA
LVHW090531301020
670157LV00004B/281